New Man in the House
Her High-School Lover

Two Novels by
Peter Rabe

Afterword by Barry N. Malzberg

Stark House Press • Eureka California

NEW MAN IN THE HOUSE / HER HIGH-SCHOOL LOVER

Published by Stark House Press
1315 H Street
Eureka, CA 95501
griffinskye3@sbcglobal.net
www.starkhousepress.com

NEW MAN IN THE HOUSE

HER HIGH-SCHOOL LOVER

ISBN-13: 978-1-944520-52-6

Book design by Mark Shepard, SHEPGRAPHICS.COM
Proofreading by Bill Kelly

PUBLISHER'S NOTE

First Stark House Press Edition: September 2019

FIRST EDITION

NEW MAN IN THE HOUSE

Roger Garland has made a career out of pleasure. He is, in fact, the perfect butler—discreet, deferential and ready to please the family, particularly the women of the house. His new employer is banker Matthew Hornaday. But Garland is much more interested in Hornaday's teenage daughter, Lorna. Lorna is just discovering sex, and Garland is certain that he can be the perfect teacher. But there is also Mrs. Hornaday to consider. She may be married to a banker, but she was once a Broadway star, and has lost none of her lust for life—or for Garland. If only Mr. Hornaday didn't distrust him so much, this could be the perfect set-up for seduction.

HER HIGH-SCHOOL LOVER

Laura Vaughn has fallen out of love with her second husband. Her first husband, Pierre, taught her all about life when they were young in France, but archaeologist Robert makes her feel like an obligation. While Laura writes letters to Pierre, her teenage son Tony seethes with rage and confusion, resentful of his mother, disdainful of his step-father, mad at the world. And Tony's friend, Tad Howard, has problems of his own— his parents hate each other, and use him as their punching bag. Each one them is seeking something and someone to make the pain go away. It is only a matter of time before Laura and Tad find each other.

PETER RABE BIBLIOGRAPHY

From Here to Maternity
  (1955; non-fiction)
Stop This Man! (1955)
Benny Muscles In (1955)
A Shroud for Jesso (1955)
A House in Naples (1956)
Kill the Boss Goodbye (1956)
Agreement to Kill (1957)
Journey Into Terror (1957)
Mission for Vengeance (1958)
Blood on the Desert (1958)
Anatomy of a Killer (1960)
My Lovely Executioner (1960)
Murder Me for Nickels (1960)
The Box (1962)
His Neighbor's Wife (1962)
Tobruk (1967)
War of the Dons (1972)
Black Mafia (1974)
The Silent Wall (2011)
The Return of Marvin Palaver
  (2011)

Daniel Port series:
Dig My Grave Deep (1956)
The Out is Death (1957)
It's My Funeral (1957)
The Cut of the Whip (1958)
Bring Me Another Corpse (1959)
Time Enough to Die (1959)

Manny deWitt series:
Girl in a Big Brass Bed (1965)
The Spy Who Was Three Feet Tall
  (1966)
Code Name Gadget (1967)

As by Marco Malaponte
New Man in the House (1963)
Her High-School Lover (1963)

As by J. T. MacCargo
Mannix #2: A Fine Day for Dying
  (1975)
Mannix #4: Round Trip to
  Nowhere (1975)

Short Stories
"Hard Case Redhead"
  (*Mystery Tales*, 1959)
"A Matter of Balance"
  (*Story*, 1961)

7

New Man in the House
By Peter Rabe

108

Afterword: The Consecration of the House
by Barry N. Malzberg

111

Her High-School Lover
by Peter Rabe

201

Afterword: Craft Ebbing
by Barry N. Malzberg

New Man in the House
By Peter Rabe

Writing as Marco Malaponte

CHAPTER ONE

She could feel his breath in her ear and she could see her parents' house through the windshield—the house was there behind the old trees. Then she could feel his hand on her body and she did not want his hand there. But she sat still next to him in the car without quite knowing why.

"Lorna?" he said.

She could tell that Ned was confused. She was younger than he and knew less about men than he knew about women but she could tell that he did not know what to do next. She thought in terms of men and women even though no grownup would have conceded she was capable of that yet. She was aware, too, that such would be the grownup's attitude.

When she did not answer, Ned moved his hand higher, ran it up her side and then around to her back—strictly a maneuver of reassurance. Lorna knew what he wanted to do, that he would much rather put his hand over her breast and hang on there until they would both want more. She knew that because they had done it before and because she really desired the same thing as he did, although maybe not now. It could be that the whole set of the day was too cool and kept her from having a slow, growing wave of heat inside her ...

Her body felt curious altogether. Sometimes she felt that her body existed and sometimes she felt that it did not. Sometimes she existed when Ned was with her like now, and sometimes she did not. Sometimes that paradox worried her.

"Listen," he said. "Come along and watch me practice this afternoon."

Football practice meant nothing to Lorna. Now she no longer felt his hand but only his fingers. They moved as if walking.

"There's a guy there from State to look over Fowler and me. So maybe this fall ..."

He kept talking and she did not listen. At one moment she felt his hand, and then again not. She wished all of him were in his hand and then again not. Then he grabbed her.

She did not even notice when he had wormed his hand under her cardigan but then she felt his hand on her breast, and she felt a pain and some pleasure.

She wanted to say, "Harder," and she wanted to say "Yes," to everything, and then again not. In the conflict nothing happened. She sat still and felt sullen.

He looked down at her very young face. She was shaped like a woman but did not altogether feel like a woman, though it was not the sort of explanation that might have occurred to him.

The girl on the other hand knew clearly about the difference between her appearance and how she felt, which of course was part of the source of her confusion. Ned was rarely confused, but she was. This worried her and she blamed it on her age. She thought being young was a sad excuse for being confused but she blamed it on her age.

"Hey, Lorna," she heard next to her ear, "come on—"

But all at once she felt disturbingly indifferent and, when she realized that, she did one of those things that startled and upset Ned.

She squirmed herself against him and bit him in the neck. She put her hand over his and pushed her breast into his palm.

Ned thought of football practice. And that he had maybe fifteen minutes to spare. And that maybe this time was it. The guy from State and maybe this time was it—those two thoughts jumped back and forth like the red lights at a railroad crossing and there was even a train roaring closer. And how come after all this time of hot fumbles and aching limbs and wild churnings under steering wheels or in back seats smelling old with damp upholstery and in dark movies and dim country lanes, how come fifteen minutes before football time and the June sun coming down white and unromantically, this stacked kid from the big house with butler and iron gate in the front and an old man who owned the bank and Ned's father's mortgage and who also had given the bell tower to the university where he, Ned, hoped to play football at the end of the summer—how come Lorna ...?

This was not the kind of train of thought to enhance passion. Too many questions in it and not enough carefree lust.

"I'm crazy about you, Lorna," he said with haste.

She said nothing. Instead she snaked her leg around and he could see her naked thigh, firm and strong and careless.

"Gee," he said.

The remark was all right for expressing an empty-headed kind of amazement but it was strictly no good for seduction. Even Ned felt this and Lorna showed it.

"Let go," she said.

"Huh?"

"You're tearing my bra."

"Honey—"

"The man from State is waiting."

She pushed the hand away from her and then she held her own breast and made it fit again inside the cup of the bra. She thought of the man from State and saw a wet cigar with a dim man behind it.

"Listen, Lorna. Tonight there's a—"

"Does he smoke a cigar?"

"Huh?"

"Let go of my leg."

He immediately let go of her leg and then she moved away, stroked herself down and looked dull and proper. She felt alone and thought of the afternoon and what was there possibly to do all afternoon in the big house that seemed empty, or what to do under the big sun that seemed empty too.

"Listen, Lorna, come along why don't you to the field and—"

"No."

"You got nothing to do. You came back from school over a week ago and you're all unpacked and nothing to do. You told me."

She disliked him for his accuracy and she disliked herself for having told him such personal things as being all unpacked and what else was there to do. Time now to hit him with something.

"We have a new man up at the house," she said. "I have to be there to meet him and so forth."

"New man?"

"Butler, for heaven's sake. You got a comb, Ned?"

He did not have a comb because he had a crew cut. On dates in the evening with her he would carry a comb, just for her, which was not so much out of consideration for her but really for his own pleasure. Escort, totally prepared with everything. Such as comb. And he liked watching her do her brown hair. He liked how her hair became full and soft and made live sounds under the comb while she closed her eyes and sat with quiet concentration...

"I haven't got a comb on me right now. Listen. Tonight—"

"I got to go now."

"I know. But tonight—"

"Give me a call," she said. "No. Don't drive up to the house. I'll walk."

He let her get out of the car and he sat a while longer, watching her round the bushes by the side of the drive and then walk up towards the house. The trees by the drive made her light up with sun and grow dark with shade, off and on, until she reached the lawn which spread pea-green all around the reach of the stone terrace. The picture was as a flat plate on which sat a wedding cake of a house.

Lorna did not see any of this. She looked down at herself, to check if she were fully arranged and innocent. Unaccountably, she felt herself again, felt herself inside of her clothes—her touching like a finger of light goading massage. She turned around quickly but there was no one to see how she felt. I wonder if the new man has come, she thought, and she slipped into the house.

Mrs. Matthew J. Hornaday, in the throes of intimacy, sat behind the window of her room where she was watching for her horse to be brought down the lane. Instead, Sheila Hornaday saw her daughter. Mrs. Hornaday smiled, which made her mouth too thin. She had a generous mouth, like her daughter, but to Sheila a smile meant compression and filtering through just so much.

How lovely Lorna has become, thought Sheila Hornaday.

Even alone in the privacy of her room with the silks on the furniture and the photographs on the walls she very fluently lied to herself about most of her feelings. I'm so happy, she thought, that Lorna has turned out to be such a lovely girl ...

In a sense Sheila's touch of surprise was hard to understand. Pose after pose in the photographs all over the wall showed Mrs. Matthew J. Hornaday apple-fresh and exciting like a first love. Or rather, not Mrs. Hornaday, but when she had been Love Apple Lindy, from chorus line to Broadway musical diva in something less than two years. And in two years more she had become Mrs. Jones-Burnham, another brevity. And so on. Finally, however, no more pictures. The banker Hornaday had made a lasting marriage with Love Apple because it had been time. The less beautiful Sheila had become, the more practical had been her intent. House, home, husband, horses—a 4H club of domesticity. And then, of course, Lorna.

What had happened for the last fifteen years, Sheila mused. Shocking the way that girl had grown up ...

Sheila Hornaday patted her hair. She did not turn to look in a mirror because there were no mirrors. The Love Apple, at this point, resembled a fairly startling wax fruit.

"Mummy?"

"Yes, dear."

Lorna opened the door and smelled lilac, a scent startling only because Sheila Hornaday was wearing a riding habit. She wore one every day, sometimes all day. The use of the riding habit had something to do with bringing out the femininity of her face while disguising the wilt of her femininity elsewhere. But Sheila did in fact also ride. She had an arrangement with the country club that kept a small stable.

"Anything special, dear?" she said. "I was just going out. I think they'll bring Roy. He needs it."

"He needs it? You had him out yesterday," said Lorna.

"He needs it every day, dear."

Sheila Hornaday sighed and picked up the crop that lay on her sewing machine. She never used the sewing machine but she used the crop every day.

"There's that difference between horses," she said and wiggled the end of the crop in the air. "Some need it every day."

"Yes," said Lorna. She felt bored and restless at the same time.

"Did you want something, dear?"

"No." The girl looked around the room and her boredom grew. "I just wondered when the new man was coming."

"Garland will be taking the same train from New York as your father. The five-twenty."

"Oh, I didn't know his name was Garland."

There was a silk scarf hanging over the sewing machine and Lorna picked up one of the strands in the fringe and then dropped it again. The scarf seemed to sink down again as if with a sigh.

"Is he English?" Lorna said after a pause.

"All good domestics are English," said her mother. "Or Irish. I forget which." And then she was on the point of leaving when she remembered something she might say to her daughter. "Walk down to the terrace with me, dear?"

Lorna shrugged and walked along with her mother. There was nothing else to do. They walked along the second-floor passage and Sheila gave a little tap with her crop to each object they passed—the bust of Voltaire that stood on a column, the Puritan hope chest farther on, and at last the five-foot bronze of a drunk holding on to a street lamp.

"What did you want, Mother?"

"Want? Oh that," and then a little laugh. "Have you seen that Ned Tyler boy since you came back from boarding school, dear?"

For a facile liar, Sheila Hornaday lacked cunning to an astounding degree. And her daughter knew this. Not only had Ned Tyler been at the house since Lorna's return but his car must have passed within easy view of Mrs. Hornaday's window no less than fifteen minutes before.

"I just saw him fifteen minutes ago, Mother."

"How nice." They went down the stairs to the hall. "And where was that?"

She wouldn't ask unless she knew where, thought Lorna.

"We parked in the bushes next to the drive and we necked."

Sheila Hornaday nearly said, "At three in the afternoon?" But that would not have sounded like a mother. Instead she said, "Lorna!"

"Yes, Mother?"

They stopped in the high-ceilinged hall and Sheila, due to the acoustics, spoke low now. The girl knew that her mother's voice would be nasty. It was therefore a surprise close to shock to Lorna when Mrs. Hornaday smiled at this point.

"Yes, Schuster," she said and looked past her daughter.

Schuster, the man from the country-club stables, stood in the open front doorway. His leather leggings and his face were the same color, though the leggings were smooth and the face was not. Schuster smelled like a horse, or at least like a horse blanket.

"I got Roy all ready for you, ma'am," he said with an old, cracked voice. "And raring to go."

"Thank you, Schuster. You're a doll."

It was the most unlikely description to think of in connection with Schuster but he liked it. He smiled. This could be surmised from the fact that his eyes were squeezed away by an excess of wrinkles.

"He's a lucky horse to have such a fine horsewoman for him, ma'am."

"Especially since he needs it every day," mumbled Lorna.

"What was that?" Sheila said.

"I said, ma'am, that there horse is mighty lucky to—"

"Never mind, Schuster. I'll be right out."

Schuster left while Sheila held her smile. And Lorna waited. She was no longer bored.

"You were going to say something, Mama."

The use of the intimacy should have warned Sheila but she had the disadvantage of being mentally distant on occasion. Nor had she gone to finishing school, where her daughter was learning the very toughest veneer against both love and hate, that is to say, polite manners.

"About that necking in the car," said Sheila Hornaday. She sounded fairly common. "How long has that been going on?"

"I don't need it every day, Mama."

"Why—"

"And it's really harmless." Lorna looked past her mother. "Ned is so clumsy about it, you know."

"What, what are you implying?" and then she added, "dear."

But the "dear" did not give the impression of a mother speaking. Sheila sounded more like somebody's landlady.

"It means," said Lorna, "that it's amusing but not really wicked. Roy is waiting." The girl walked away.

She walked down the passage leading to the kitchen. Lorna was not interested in the kitchen but the passage was dark and she wanted that. She wanted to be alone in the dark because she was not sure how she would feel in a moment.

She most certainly did not feel polite with banter, or tough. Unpredictably she had suddenly wanted to touch her mother, to ask for her arms and a hug. Unpredictably, in the dark passage, Lorna cried. Then the thought of Ned made her shudder and the feel of herself inside her clothes made her flush. She had a nervous attack of the giggles. That's like mother and the horse ...

CHAPTER TWO

Matthew Hornaday rarely took the train into New York but when he did he preferred to be called Matt. Most of the commuters, on his return from the metropolis, were strangers to him and, when surrounded by the strange he craved the familiar. Conversely, when surrounded by the familiar, as at his bank, he would crave and insist on the distant and the formal.

He had an hour-and-a-half trip back upstate and he was in the club car within the first two minutes. Matt Hornaday had a beefy body and wiry red hair and a complexion of baby hues; this permitted him, he thought, to claim less than his fifty years and gave him license for back-slapping and drink-spilling and mistakes in names—all so much jolly fun and robust camaraderie as far as Hornaday was concerned.

"Matt," said somebody and touched Matt's back.

This was not a drink-spiller-type familiarity and Hornaday instantly jerked with dignity and then looked up.

But he knew the man, so it was all right. The man was short and fat, he was real estate and City Council, and he also did not go into New York very often.

"Spike," yelled Hornaday.

Spike, the fat man in real estate, owed Hornaday's bank a great deal of money, but that was good business and they were, of course, from the same town. This meant smiles and buddy talk, and then Spike introduced Roger.

"The guy," said Spike, "who got me on the train in time, via the oyster bar and three cups of coffee."

Roger shrugged with a great deal of charm. He was a large man and rather reserved. True, he had a smile but then came quietness close to sullenness. Hornaday, who was suspicious about reserve, wondered if he could like that man.

"Don't I know you from somewhere, Roger? What's your first name, Roger? Sit down, huh?"

"Roger is the first name," he said and sat down.

"Union Club?"

"No. I'm from Miami."

Then the waiter came and there was a great deal of activity about ordering and who would pay.

All three now at the table were outsiders, in a sense, as far as the rest of the club car was concerned. The trio was not of the daily brotherhood, the regularly hounded ones from commuter kiss in the morning to pre-supper martini.

If Matthew Hornaday needed a pre-supper martini, it did not show. He had three club-car martinis before the trip was half finished and there was no reason for any of them. His day in New York had not been one of strain: he had had a chat with a schoolmate from Princeton, a rub at the club, a present for a young thing who called him Matsy, and finally an afternoon movie because he had been bored.

Spike, in real estate, was on martini number eight, counting the three before train time, occasioned by a clouded business chat he had had with his New York banker.

His friend Roger—since oyster-bar time—drank only dry vermouth, because the taste pleased him. Which seemed probable. He sipped slowly, his face quiet, the lines showing character rather than care and the gray temples not so much signs of age as of having lived through a number of things. His eyes enhanced that impression. They seemed a little tired.

Hornaday turned to him conversationally. "What's your business, Roger?"

"I'm not in business," said Roger. "I don't think I could take the pace."

Spike waved at the waiter and ordered another round. He was far enough gone to order and pay all at the same time and by himself.

"There are compensations," said Hornaday. "You know?"

"I don't know nothing of the sort," said Spike. "I get no compensations in business, I only get the business."

"Don't give me that, Spike boy. I was just talking to Childon down at the Union Club the other day and he told me he saw you at Tandy's party, the party where that bunch from the Happy Day cast was invited and you, I'm told—"

"Just a minute," said Spike.

But that did not end the conversation.

It did not become loud but it increased in intensity while Roger, uninvolved, only listened until Hornaday, struck by what might be the disinterest of Roger's silence, tried to pull him into the matter. The banker's feeling was that he, as story-teller, had to be served.

"This really happened," he said to Roger. "And the part I was telling about, I was there."

Roger felt that this probably was meant to raise interest to a fever pitch, because Matt Hornaday had been there. Roger smiled and if Hornaday had not been drunk he would have noticed that the other man was looking at him with no more than polite vacancy.

"You didn't hear the first part of the whole thing," said Hornaday, "so I'll just tell you this short."

Roger looked away and sipped vermouth.

"So the boys and me, I was telling Spike here, the boys from the Union Club I was having down at my house, we were just sitting around talking and having a few, I was telling Spike here—weekend stuff, kind of. You know?"

It seemed that Hornaday needed an answer so Roger nodded. So did Spike.

"When I say a few, I mean drinks," Hornaday said, brayed rather, and stopped abruptly to look at the two. Spike laughed shortly.

Roger smiled.

"I mean drinks and not the other, which came later." Hornaday drank with a big gulp, like a horse, and then resumed his seesawing narrative.

"Anyway, in a while we all went to the country club and picked up some boys and some girls." Matthew Hornaday smiled up at the ceiling. "I knew some but some I didn't—now, all of this happened before I was married, of course. Spike here, for example—waiter? Damn that waiter. Anyhow, we end up at this cabin Sherman has up in the hills. You know Sherman, Spike."

"I know Sherman, Matt."

"And up there, I don't need to tell you since you know Sherman, Spike, all kinds of goings on start going on. I remember that—waiter? Damn that bastard. Not the point."

"Which?"

"I'm telling you. Here was Sherman, like I said, tanked. He was here in his own cabin and not getting anywhere with any of the stuff up there at his own cabin—of course he wasn't married yet at the time—when up drives this whole passel of kids in three cars, one after the other, and there's Sherman's sister in the first car with her boy friend, some bum kid or other I forget the name. They come up, screeching and laughing I'm telling you—waiter! To hell with him. Because they wanted to see the cabin."

"Matt," said Spike. "You talking about an outhouse?"

"You drunk or something? Why don't you listen? Then we hail them all in and give them drinks. I mean, wild kids and all but here was Sherman's sister. After all. Boy, was she built hot in those days. So we give them all drinks—waiter! Hey, Roger, let me have a lick off your drink, huh?"

"Of course."

"Now you remember me mentioning Sherman, I'm sitting down next to Sherman. Hey, you remember me mention Sherman?"

"Of course."

"And he's boiled like an owl and just as blind. Pretty good that, huh? Boiled like an owl and just—"

"Very, very good, Matt," Spike said.

"And I say to him, what are you looking at, Sherman? And he says, straight across. You get the picture? Here I was sitting with Sherman on one couch and—"

"We get the picture."

"What do you want?" Hornaday said pugnaciously to the club-car attendant.

"Did you wish to order, sir?" asked the waiter.

"Beat it. I'm looking across and see trouble."

After a while somebody said, "What trouble?" and then Hornaday continued.

"There—sits—Sherman's—sister. Now get this. Sherman's sister was maybe sixteen and developed like a burlesque queen, like she was naked no matter what she had on. She's there, the skirt up with the thighs naked, she don't care or don't know, and that sweater thing she had on with the buttons and the buttons all open so the guy with her, that bum kid I forget his name, so he can get his hands on her big, ripe, pink, full, ready—waiter."

"Yes, sir."

"I been trying to get your attention so let's have a drink for everybody pronto."

It was the first round for which Hornaday was paying although he was apparently unaware of that. He went right on.

"I smell trouble when I see this. Now, there's nothing unusual about a guy feeling up all this unbuttoned—you should have seen those—thank you, waiter, never mind that now, fine. But this is the brother watching his sister. You get the picture?"

"Of course."

"Take it easy, I tell Sherman. Just hold on there and take it easy there, boy. Because Sherman, those days, he was rough and tough. But he wants to get up. He and me are struggling. Take it easy, Sherman, I keep saying to him, and I'm scared. Where's that goddamn—oh, been here. Fine. When Sherman gets hold of my arms and looks at me with those eyes of steel. Charley, he says to me, straight in the eye. Charley, don't try to stop me. I got to have that broad."

Hornaday was silent but the pause did not come off too dramatically because the train was leaning into bend, wheels whining.

"Berryville coming up in just a shake now," said Spike. He sounded anxious and he was, about the rest of the story.

"A remarkable situation," said Roger and finished his vermouth.

"There's more," said Hornaday, and he seemed anxious, too.

"Berryville," yelled the conductor. "Left side out, please ..."

"Did he?" said Spike. "Did he?"

"Wait. Now I saw right away that he didn't know who she was and then I have this idea. Why the hell not? But first I figured I better get her tight because she hadn't had any and it stands to reason she wasn't going to just get herself taken by her brother with everybody and his cousin standing around there in that cabin."

"Berryville!"

"Did he, Matt?"

"So first, me and some of the boys got her to drink some of—what's that, waiter?"

"The bill, sir."

"All right, just hold it."

"Left side, please!"

"My God, Matt, you going to tell the—"

"All right. I hate to get rushed through a thing like this, you know that, Spike?"

"Sir—"

"All right!"

The train slowed down and there was a crush of people.

"So when she was good and blind we get her and Sherman into one of the beds there and even help some with the clothes she's got left on, seeing her so blind. Then we get out of there and close the door."

"You mean you just closed—"

"Then we looked."

"Was he?"

"I don't know."

"Sir—"

"He was on the floor, drunk or exhausted, I don't know which, and she there on the bed looking ripe and ready and—"

"You mean you don't know if he did?"

"How do I know? But listen. Seeing she's there anyway, why waste it, me and some of the boys we just had us that ripe kid there, one after the other—what?"

"Your bill, sir. The train's stopping."

"This isn't my bill, feller."

People were walking out and they kept slapping Matt Hornaday on the back and saying nice, easy things to him.

"Eighty-seven dollars and ninety-three cents for chrissakes?"

"You said drinks for everybody, sir."

Whatever Matthew Hornaday wished to say or wished to do at that moment was clearly out of the question, what with the accolades from the passengers leaving the train, what with the busy air of his table companions and what with the steady stare from Roger.

"We heard you order," said Roger and he stood up. "You were most generous." Then he left.

Spike also wanted to leave but Hornaday did not want to be alone. So Spike stayed because they were buddies and because Banker Hornaday wanted it that way.

After paying for that round for the club car there was, of course, no question of going straight home. The only question for Matthew Hornaday was where to go and have one more while calming down over that club-car waiter's impertinence. He and Spike crossed the little square in front of the station and made their way to a rustic place with leaded windows, antiqued tavern sign, Toby jugs over the bar and a lot of dark wood. The place was called the Bully Bar and was fairly deserted because no real commuter dared stop there at this hour. The emptiness fitted Hornaday's mood. He and Spike sat in a booth and had drinks in silence for a while.

"I got one satisfaction," said Hornaday and kept watching the distant waiter with a dangerous eye. "I didn't tip that bastard. Eighty-odd bucks and I didn't tip that bastard."

"I thought you did, Matt."

"Like hell. I gave him two fifties and he—"

"Kept a ten out of the change."

The banker darted one hand into his pocket as if reaching for something about to slip out of a window. He dredged up less than two dollars.

"That bastard—" and he moaned, feeling weak from an assault of injustice. "And that Roger, him with his superior silence and the way he licked at his vermouth, like a cat, did you notice?"

"I think his gray hair at the side was phony. The way some actors dye the—"

"Phony bastard. Waiter!"

"I thought there was something dangerous there, you know that, Matt? That heavy look on his face. And when you told that story about Sherman's sister—listen, whatever happened to Sherman's sister?"

"We had her, I told you," Hornaday said with quiet venom. "A young broad she was, I told you, and she took on I think there was five of us and listen to this, Spike. She enjoyed every one of them."

"No."

"Yes."

"I thought they were bad in this generation," said Spike piously. "I thought—" and let the sentence drift off, thinking of Sherman's sister moaning there on the bed with one man after another.

"They're worse," said Hornaday. It was not clear if he felt gloomy or contemplative. "And that Roger telling me he doesn't like to talk about things like that. Listen, Spike. I say, out with it. Out in the open with it. Let's take a long, hard look at these goings-on. Let's not hide behind a do-nothing, know-nothing kind of a policy while those young kids go down the road towards creeping—what the hell is that word? Waiter."

"Socialism?" Spike suggested.

"No, no, that's politics. I'm talking sex."

"Of course not. I mean, yes, of course, let's talk about sex."

Which they did.

By nine o'clock they had gone up and down the road toward that creeping thing, whatever the name of it was, and several times they had looked at it with openness and a certain clarity of detail—jumbles of limbs in back seats, flash of white skin between clothes pushed into bunches, wordless sounds in the dark, squeals and gig-gles—

When they actually heard squeals and giggles, imagination blended with reality.

"Now look at this bunch of kids coming in there," said Hornaday. "Look at that black-haired one there. No, look at that stacked one there with the sort of reddish hair. She and him there with her, now don't think they're going to end up just with a coke between them. What they're going to end up with between them—"

He sounded contemptuous.

"Matt, take it easy now, take it easy."

"I can see this clearly," said Hornaday. "After they leave here, there's the movie, for a warm-up, and after—"

"Take it easy, Matt."

"Shut up a minute. I want you to take a long, hard look at that ripe, young, firm, rosy—"

"Matt, don't get excited. Lorna is a nice girl and all she's doing—"

"Lorna?"

Hornaday, as if jerked by wires, ascended from the firm, rosy fantasy of his explorations and sat up in the Bully Bar booth to stare at the group of young people in the adjoining room.

He saw twice as many as there were and some of them had two heads.

"I'm crocked," he said, the first truly objective remark he had made in hours. "Spike, help me out of here—I can't have Lorna see me—I mean, she'll misunderstand, misunderstand everything—"

They left quickly and Hornaday took a taxi home, all windows wide open.

Have to take that girl in hand, now that she's home for the summer, he mumbled. This is disgraceful, dangerous stuff ...

In front of his house he watched the taxi drive off. He looked up at the lit window behind which his wife would be reading a magazine. Still wearing those riding breeches? he wondered. He thought of his New York trip and that he would not take another in a very long time. He thought of something to hate. Spike? No, that wasn't good business. So Hornaday stood there in the dark and decided to hate Roger, and that in spite of Roger's large, physical size, because Roger had been distant and therefore like an enemy. Him and his secretive, dangerous airs ...

A Bloody Mary was the thing now. Hornaday lurched into the house and then into the library. He banged the door shut and that made such a sudden draft that the flames in the fireplace gave a leap.

Nice touch, somebody having laid a fire, he thought. He sat down in his easy chair by the fire before remembering that he first had to go after his Bloody Mary.

The fire swerved again and the door behind Hornaday's chair closed with a gentle swish.

"Allow me, sir, I thought that a nightcap might be just the thing ..."

The butler stood there with tray and Bloody Mary. He stood quietly, looking immaculate. In comparison Hornaday appeared untidy.

"Ah—Roger—good God—"

"Roger is the first name, sir. I'm Garland, the new man."

CHAPTER THREE

"Hey," said Ned, "hey, Lorna. Look."

But Lorna did not want to look the length of the Bully Bar. She wanted to listen to the chatter and guffaws at the table as if something might come up that would be really interesting.

"Lorna, wasn't that your father who just walked out?"

"Yes. That was my father who just staggered out."

"I didn't mean, I mean, when I said—"

"But you did see him stagger out, didn't you?"

"Well—"

"Well, all right."

Their conversation led nowhere but it did set the tone of their evening. Ned, defensively vague, and Lorna offensively curt. Lorna did not know whom to blame for her mood, which made it worse, and Ned wished he could talk about football, which was out of the question. Nobody at the table wanted to talk about football. A kid by the name of Jackie Sherman was at the table and almost everybody wanted to talk to him.

"But you have the key to the place, haven't you?" said Jack's girl.

"Of course I got the key to the cabin," said Jack.

"And Max has the bottle, don't you, Max?" said Jack's girl.

"Sure," said Max.

There were six of them at the table, all paired, and they had a bottle in one of the cars and there was Sherman's cabin, but there was a problem with Jack.

"You're chicken," said Max's girl.

She did not really mean it but they all knew that Jack needed pushing.

"I am not."

They sipped coke and waited for him to prove it. "Then why don't we go to the cabin?" said Ned.

"Because Jack's old man said he couldn't," said Max.

"My old man's all right and he's got nothing to do with it because how come he gave me a key to the place a long time ago?"

"Don't you want me?" said Jack's girl into his ear. She said it close to his ear not because she cared if anyone heard her at the table but because she wanted to tickle him with her breath.

"Cut it out," said Jack.

"You're chicken," said Max's girl again, "and I know of who."

"Of whom," said Lorna.

"Of Aunty Anna," said Max's girl.

They all laughed very hard, which was the right insult to sway Jack out of his indecision.

Aunty Anna was the elder Sherman's sister, a fine, strapping woman, with a snap to her voice and a fervor in her eye. She ran this league and that committee and she also ran the Sherman house because Jack's mother was dead and Aunty Anna was divorced.

"We can't go to the Sherman cabin because Aunty Anna is this very night going to use it herself," said Max, and the absurdity of the remark made them all guffaw and squeal again.

Because Aunty Anna was no gay divorcee in any sense but a stern, church-going woman with the fervor of a penitent whore. And it was true that Aunty Anna had forbidden Jack to go to the cabin after dark and it was true that

Jack was afraid of her because nobody could raise hell like his father's holier-than-thou sister.

"All right, then, let's go," said Jack.

Jack's girl gave him a hug, Max's girl squeezed her thighs together, and Lorna stood up before Ned had reacted.

When they had all piled into the one car they were using, Ned wished he were with someone else. Or even with something else. A football, he thought, would have felt friendlier in his hand than Lorna.

He touched her, thinking of a football, which did not help his artistry any.

"Stop it," she said.

"I didn't—"

"Then don't."

Max started the motor and handed the bottle back.

"Try this first," he said and Ned grabbed.

He took a pull from the neck and felt drunk before the first swallow was down. This extravagant feeling made him take three incautious swallows of raw liquor without drawing a breath.

The bottle was passed around in the car and everybody had some except Lorna. They all claimed to feel better and different now, but only Ned really showed it. He looked at Lorna and she no longer looked like the girl of two minutes ago but like the one he sometimes saw in his imaginings.

"Did I tell you what happened at practice, honey?" he said.

"You saw the man with the wet cigar."

Ned laughed and laughed. Lorna could say the funniest things.

Jack Sherman wiggled around for a better grip on his girl. Max, up front, drove with one hand. Ned grinned at Lorna and thought that she really looked like something.

She looked, in fact, almost exactly and certainly as improbable as the girl he described to his team mates when gossiping in the shower room.

"Want to know what I was practicing, honey?" said Ned, and Lorna could smell the liquor on him.

He should smell of milk, she thought inconsequentially not liquor, and she held still while he put his arm around her neck and his hand on her shoulder. Now his hand will work down, she thought, and then I must shortly feel in the mood. That's why I'm here.

"I was practicing tackle," said Ned much too loudly,

And much too violently he seized the girl to show what he meant. As far as room permitted he did in fact lay hands on her exactly the way a football tackle might a ball-carrier.

Why am I here, thought Lorna. Why ... She said nothing because Ned had knocked the breath out of her. But he let go of her immediately.

"Who's got the bottle?" yelled Ned.

Somebody gave him the bottle.

"Passion flower," he said to Lorna and held her by the neck this time. "Open up."

"What?"

"Have some of this passion juice."

"I don't need it from the bottle."

Ned did not hear her because he was drinking. Then he put the bottle to her mouth.

"Open up."

"Don't, Ned. I don't want—"

He clinked the bottle against her teeth and the girl gave a jerk.

"Don't bite it," said Ned. "It will bite back." And he laughed and laughed because nothing seemed funnier to him right that moment.

"Let go of me."

"Passion, huh! Oh boy, girl, oh boy—"

"Let go, stop that!"

"I have not yet begun to—"

"Max—" and Lorna hit Ned on the top of the head so that her hand hurt—"take me home, Max, I mean it."

Ned let go of her immediately and everybody else in the car stopped what he was doing. There was talk now and arguing but Lorna heard none of it. She could see the lights from her parents' house where the street curved up ahead and the lights shone through the trees in the friendliest way.

"I mean it," she said again. "Take me home, Max."

She heard a babble from Ned—it really was babbling—and paid no attention to it. Max slowed at the gate to the drive and turned in. The house showed beautifully now, thought Lorna. The light from the old-fashioned lamp over the door, the quiet light from the tall windows where the library was. She thought of the library and her father's chair by the fireplace. She thought of her father there, on a quiet evening, reading quietly. Ned touched her and she gave a start of disgust.

"You can stop here, Max, I'll go in through the side."

"Lorna," said Ned, "I'm sorry, honey, gee."

"Gee indeed, you drunken—drunken football player." And she clambered out of the car.

She heard the arguments behind her in the car but did not care. She ran to the house.

It was quiet and dim inside and Lorna ran through the hall to the library. She thought of her father there and that perhaps there would be a blaze in the big fireplace. She did not think of the fact that she had just seen her father drunk or that rarely was there a fire this time of year. She was still young and believed in dreams.

She opened the big door and saw the fire. She felt happy and smiled. Then she saw her father. He was holding on to the mantle with one hand and a glass of tomato juice in the other.

"Like a drunken whore," he suddenly roared. "Right there in the Bully Bar."

Then Lorna saw her mother. She wore a silk housecoat and looked wilted.

"Then why didn't you stop her and bring her home?" asked her mother.

"Because," roared her father, his glass spilling, "because I was with a business associate and damn well didn't want to embarrass the company, not to speak of my family name. And you know what she's doing now."

"Darling," said her mother. "Here she is, Matt." And Mrs. Hornaday started for Lorna who still stood in the door.

Hornaday tried to focus and saw two daughters.

"Done already?" he bellowed. "That quick?"

But where there had been two daughters he suddenly saw none. Instead he saw his wife again, double, and he quickly closed his eyes.

"You sot," he heard his wife, and that sounded in duplicate too. "Now you've hurt her feelings."

Her father had not really hurt Lorna's feelings but he had made them very hard. She ran out of the house the way she had come and all she could think of was, I hope that car is still here, I hope that car is still here and to hell with everybody.

The car was still there, where the drive curved to the house, and Ned was hunching into it.

"Ned," she called.

He straightened up and banged his head on the frame of the door. But he paid no attention to that.

"Honey—" he said. He seemed steady and sober. He was, in fact, dismally sober; "I was up by the door but then I didn't have the nerve to—"

She ran up and gave him a slap on the backside.

"That's why I'm back," she said. "I couldn't wait any longer."

"Gee—"

She ignored the gee because she did not want to feel irritated. Then she pushed him into the car.

"Everybody ready?" she said and followed Ned.

"Christ," said Max. "What did you take while you were gone?"

"Advice," said Lorna and slammed the door.

"And consent?" said Jack past his girl's ear.

"I do," and Lorna gave Ned a kiss full of vigor because she felt no passion.

By the time the car rolled up to the cabin under the dark trees her feelings had changed. Perhaps she did not feel very much passion but her vigor was gone. This was, for the time, as close as she could come to abandon. And the liquor rotated inside her head. Lorna followed them into the cabin.

Jack turned on a little table lamp and pulled all the curtains over the windows. A nice, cozy place, thought Lorna. Beamed ceiling, big couches, big fireplace.

"Let's build a fire," said Ned.

"No."

Lorna bit her lip because her voice had come out a shout. But nobody paid much attention. Max and his girl vanished into one of the bedrooms and Jack and his girl were clinking ice in the galley kitchen. Lorna flopped on the couch facing the dead fireplace.

"Another drink?" said Ned and held out the bottle.

"You have one," she said and pulled him down beside her.

He took a pull from the bottle and put one hand on her thigh at the same time. She could feel him but she could feel nothing inside of her.

"Give me the bottle," she said.

Then she put down the bottle and leaned back, eyes closed. Nausea was turning over her insides but Ned did not know this. What he saw was a languorous pose and an invitation. He put his hand back on her thigh, but on the skin this time.

If he'd only hold me a while, thought Lorna, I would be all right.

The higher his hand crept the warmer her skin felt to Ned.

If he'd hold me and stroke my hair, let me rest a while ...

She felt his fingers. She did not dare move because she thought she would throw up. And besides, besides ...

"Lorna, honey?"

She did not answer. She was tired, so tired ...

And Ned went on. With his free hand he unbuttoned the front of her dress. This relieved pressure and she felt much better. What Ned saw in her expression was pure abandon. He pulled the dress down over her shoulders, and her nausea returned.

"No," Lorna said, and moved very cautiously into a sitting position.

Jumpy about her habit of switching moods, Ned let go immediately. Then he watched with mouth open as she pulled her dress all the way off.

"Ah ..." she said, and leaned back against the cushions.

Then the door to one of the other rooms opened. Jack's girl walked by and then she stopped by the couch.

"You got her too exhausted," she said, looking down at Lorna. "How do you expect any action if you get a girl worn out all the time fumbling in the car before getting there?" Then she took a big bite out of the sandwich she was carrying and then a big gulp from the glass of milk she had in the other hand.

Providentially, Lorna did not see this. She hardly heard the conversation but lay still instead while her insides seemed to veer back and forth, awash in a brackish tide.

"Where's Jack?" said Ned.

"Exhausted," Jack's girl said.

"So why are you talking about telling me I'm doing it wrong?"

"Because I did it right, in the bedroom."

"Already?"

"I got ways," said Jack's girl. She smiled and patted her hair. Her hair was combed and she was fully dressed. "Want a bite?" and she held out the sandwich.

"Not hungry. Go away."

"I always get hungry afterwards," she said.

She put the last of the sandwich in her mouth and sat down next to Ned.

Lorna felt a great sense of comfort. She was drunk enough to feel no shame and tired enough to hear the conversation as mumbling only.

"She's built nice," said Jack's girl.

"Yeah," Ned said.

"But I bet I'm bigger."

"Yeah?"

"How come you keep saying yeah all the time? You still looped or something?"

"Lorna's bigger."

"I bet not. Here," Jack's girl said.

She put his hand on her breast and let him feel. Sounds came from the bedroom where Max was with his girl. Ned, quite suddenly, became very excited. He let go of Jack's girl and turned towards Lorna. She was no longer leaning but had slid down and was lying prone on the couch.

"Just a minute," said Jack's girl. "You have to compare it right."

Ned felt badly interrupted but was too drunk to display much will. He sat, his head lolling a little, and watched Jack's girl do the next thing. She pulled Lorna's slip down to her hips and then unhooked the bra. Then Jack's girl pulled it off.

Not yet, wait a while, Lorna thought she heard herself saying.

Ned pulled his hand back and sat up, watching. Jack's girl, it turned out, had no bra. She sat down next to Ned again, wearing only her panties.

"Now try it," she said.

Ned tried it. He no longer remembered about the contest in sizes. His concentrative ability, always limited, suffered especially now. Lorna was behind him, Jack's girl in front. With her, there was no problem of moods, there was no problem whatsoever. There was a body that stretched for him, breasts that pushed at him, a face smiling at him.

"Ah—" said the face. "Do that—do that. Take it all the way off and do that, Ned ..."

While Lorna felt luxurious comfort, nausea gone, constraint gone, except she was just a little bit cold ...

"Wait a sec," Jack's girl was saying. "Lorna's legs are in my way." Then she reared up over the edge of the backrest and called, "Jack. Jack Sherman, will you take her in back?"

Not long afterward Lorna felt warm again and for a while carried a curious weight. It was just short of unpleasant, or it was just short of pleasant, but she could not tell which. And mostly she slept.

She woke up with a start and felt the headache immediately.
"Honey," said Jack's girl. "Drink this coffee because we got to go."
Lorna sat up and felt starkly sober.
"I'm naked," she said.
"Naturally."
"Naturally," said Lorna. "Where, I mean, where—"
"Everybody is in the kitchen, drinking coffee. Here are your things."
Then Lorna dressed while Jack's girl sat on the bed. She sat and watched and smoked a cigarette.
"I didn't know you were a virgin," she said.
Lorna had her back turned and was glad that her face did not show. Then she said.
"So what if I am?"
"Were."
Lorna thought she might now start to tremble. She thought of the car and the couch and then the blank. The damn blank ...
"You used to be a virgin," said Jack's girl unnecessarily. "How was it?"
Lorna finished buttoning and then she picked up the coffee cup.
"Oh, just fine," she said to the wall. "You should know."
"I didn't like it the first time," said Jack's girl. Then she snickered. "Different now, though. You know, Ned isn't bad."
"What?"
"I said—"
"Oh, yes. Yes, I know. He isn't bad at all."
There was a pause Lorna did not understand.
"How would you know," said Jack's girl, looking puzzled. "You were a virgin when Jack had you."
First Lorna dropped the coffee cup and then she fainted.

CHAPTER FOUR

In the car they talked about how low the temperature sank at two in the morning and they kept the heater on and also the radio. This kept talk to a minimum, which was good. The painful item came up only once.
"We got too drunk," said Ned.
Lorna did not answer.

"Next time we won't, huh?" and he squeezed her hand.

"What next time?" she said and pulled her hand away. They dropped Lorna off first and she slipped into the house through the back.

The interior was dim and quiet and made Lorna feel like an intruder. She turned into the library where one lamp was on and the wood was still red in the fireplace. She sat down in the library because she felt she could not sleep. She sat on the edge of the chair and felt so alone that it frightened her. She thought of her father asleep and felt revolted. She thought of her mother asleep and, for one moment, filled with a rush of confused feelings, Lorna wanted to wake her mother and say how was it the first time for you? How should it have been, for the first time?

Lorna hunched in the chair and after a time she felt nothing but hate—for wanting to know, for wanting her mother, for sitting here dry and empty and much too awake, for having missed and lost with no gain whatsoever ...

There was a half-empty glass of tomato juice on the small table next to her. Lorna picked it up and drank with angry greed. The juice was too warm and it had a strange bite to it but she drank most of it. Five minutes later she knew she was drunk again. Not a heavy weight, as in the cabin, but this time something that lifted her. Bloody Mary, she thought. Oh, you bloody bitch, you—and she looked at herself in the black glass of the window opposite.

She also saw the decanter that stood on the sideboard next to that window. The alcohol put me to sleep the last time—the first time; so it'll put me to sleep this time—the last time.

She rose from the chair and started to skip down the length of the room. The motion made her jiggle inside her clothes. She stopped skipping immediately. She walked to the sideboard in a businesslike manner and poured herself a drink in a tall glass and added seltzer from the syphon bottle.

To the first time, and she drank.

When she put the glass down she burst out crying.

"To the last time," she said aloud, her voice cracked, and she drank again.

When she put down the glass, the tears on her face felt like something foreign, as if they did not belong to her. She wiped her face and stood by the sideboard, feeling empty. She could not bear the sense of emptiness so she took another drink from the glass. But she could not bear the standing up, either, so she returned to the chair again and sat down. Her void was filled now. She did not yet know with what. Until she suddenly said it, very loud, "Damn it, oh damn it, I've done it and wasn't even there! And I'm a virgin forever."

She took the glass and drank the rest.

She sank back into the chair. For the moment the bleariness was a helpful thing. Without any need for focus, then, or reality, she saw a man and he looked down at her with a calm, friendly eye. He wanted nothing from her she would not offer, he would give her only what she felt like asking for.

Handsome, no young snip, young snips don't have gray temples, she thought.

"Is there anything I can do for you, miss?"

"You can tell me," said Lorna, her tongue a round, rolling marble inside her mouth, "you can tell me that you'll do what I say whenever I snap my fingers."

"In a sense that's true," he said.

"And you can tell me," she slurred again, "that I'm all right."

"I'm afraid you aren't, Miss Lorna."

Whether it was the use of her name or whether it was the opposition, something had changed the anonymous man into a person. He looked the same as before but now he was a presence which was strangling her easy fantasy. She felt fright and she felt rage, a combination apt to result in the ridiculous.

"I'll scream," she said, with a voice like a mouse.

"No need, Miss Lorna. Would you like some coffee?"

"I'll throw up—"

"No need for that, either. I can give you—"

"Don't touch me. Who are you?"

"Garland, miss. I'm the new man."

She relaxed visibly but the relaxation allowed an immediate torpor to claim her. She would, if allowed, have fallen asleep in the chair. She would, if she had had the strength, struggled with Garland but he was able to help her out of the chair without interference and then he led her upstairs, to her room. Then he sat her down on her bed.

"Shall I waken the maid to help you undress?"

"No. Don't wake the maid," she said, her words slurred. Then she fell back on the bed.

Garland stood and looked at the girl for a while. Then he sighed. He touched her just enough to stretch her out on her bed and she hardly knew it. This happened to me once before, the thought slipped through her mind, and she struggled mightily to stay awake. But the only thing Garland did to her was to take off her shoes. Lorna knew this and thought it was terribly thrilling.

At three a.m. Garland felt he had put the house to bed. The phrase amused him and he smiled. He smiled only under two conditions: either alone, feeling pleased, or when the smile served a specific purpose when he was with somebody else. His smile could be electrifying.

In his room he removed jacket and vest, and sat down in the rocking chair. There was this chair, a bed and a dresser. Nothing else. Garland did not care. He had cared about his bathroom being tiled and uncramped and he had even been pleased that his dormer window looked out at the crown of a tree. The leaf-murmur pleased him. But aside from these points he was not interested in his surroundings, except for their people.

He lit a cigarillo and smoked very slowly and reflected.

Mr. Hornaday, a bully, a scared man. But therefore cagey. Despicable though he is, the man must not be underestimated.

Mrs. Hornaday, a problem. A fairly attractive female who thinks she is beautiful. And in Garland's experience such a woman was practically beyond discouragement. It was characteristic of Garland that he was annoyed as much to receive an unnecessary smile while serving table as to be asked to go to bed with someone who had wrinkled hands.

And Miss Lorna?

It was also characteristic of Garland that he should think of the girl as Miss Lorna. Actually, he did not think of her very much. He closed his eyes and saw her.

Then he considered a number of other things. Miss Lorna's age, her status as an only child, the time when she had returned home, her condition on that occasion, and of course the things she had said without knowing that he entered the room. "And now a virgin forever."

Curious thing for a girl to say.

For a moment Garland dropped it. There were two other members of the household and he pondered them quickly. Cook, a big hen of a woman and of little concern to him. And the maid, somewhat like an apple, more like a potato. Garland yawned and dropped that subject. For just the briefest moment he thought of his last place of employment, and of Mr. Chesterton Manning. He was dead now, of course. The recollection was unpleasant and Garland closed the lid on his mind as if it were a box of studs. Then he went to bed. Everyone was asleep now. Garland slept best.

The next day was Sunday, when the Hornadays breakfasted together. Lorna, however, was not at her usual place. Even though she was frequently absent from Sunday breakfast, Matthew Hornaday made a great deal of petulant conversation on the subject. He sat with coffee and watched Garland serve coddled eggs to Mrs. Hornaday. Hornaday had eaten little.

"Seen my daughter, Garland?"

"Last night, sir."

"Why isn't she here this morning?"

"She came in quite tired and asked me to apologize for her absence this morning."

"Hm," said Hornaday and, strangely enough, left it at that.

He had something else to occupy him. When Garland had left the room, Hornaday presented his new breakfast topic to his wife. "I don't like that bastard," he said.

"Dear?" said Sheila Hornaday, looking up.

"Not one bit."

"Whom, dear?"

"Last night he made the Bloody Mary too strong, you know that?"

"Yes. I know that, dear. Would you like to have—"

"Never mind," and Hornaday drank coffee.

Sheila continued eating, expecting further comment from Matthew.

"You know what he was doing this morning?" he said. She allowed him his ominous pause. "Talking to Irma," he went on. "In a corner."

"He also talked to me this morning, Matt."

"In a corner?"

"I didn't happen to be sweeping in a corner."

"And did you blush? The way Irma blushed when he was talking to her?"

"He is rather handsome," said Sheila into her coddled egg. And, in a moment, she knew she had said the wrong thing.

"Did you blush?" said Hornaday, raising his voice.

"Yes, sir?" said Garland as he came through the pantry door.

"I wasn't calling you," said Hornaday. He ducked his head, feeling an unreasonable fear that he might blush himself.

"He's gone," said Sheila quietly.

Her husband raised his head, his expression spiteful.

"Fire him," he said.

"But Matt—"

"He's no good and therefore I don't like him."

"Don't you mean you don't like him and therefore he's good?"

"Sheila—"

"If you raise your voice he'll come in again, dear."

Since this was to be avoided at all costs, Hornaday did no more than exhale noisily.

"I really find nothing wrong with him," his wife said. "What do you find wrong with him?"

"Huh," said her husband, "he creeps. And—"

"Butlers are trained to creep."

"And he—what I mean is—" Then he said it. "He's sexy."

Sometimes, thought Sheila, Matt was strangely perceptive. She said nothing, of course.

"And for example," continued her husband, "why did he leave his last job?"

"You know why, Matt. His employer died."

"That's right," said Hornaday ominously.

"Well, what's that supposed to mean?"

"Never mind. But I'm going to look into that."

She dismissed the announcement as part of her husband's usual hangover talk.

Garland, however, did not feel so cavalier about the matter. He stood at the door of the pantry and held very still. His slow, too-soft eyes became slitty and hard, although in a moment he resumed his habitual noncommittal expression. Hornaday, after all, was mainly a noisy talker, Garland thought. Or so it was to be hoped.

Unfortunately for Garland, there was a change in the conversational topic and he could not learn any more, Hornaday's ire remained but it had changed direction.

"And where, may I ask, have you been?" Garland heard Hornaday say.

A chair scraped and then Lorna with a small voice said, "Good morning."

"I asked you a question," her father said.

"I've been in bed," she said.

"Obviously," said Hornaday. "Look at you. Sleep till past ten in the morning and your face looks like a hangover."

I might, thought Garland, now help the girl.

"Or maybe," Hornaday kept at it, "you look that way from lack of sleep and not excess of sleep? When did you get in last night?"

"Didn't you hear me come in?"

That, thought Garland, was very spunky.

"I didn't hear you, daughter, because I was fast asleep in the middle of the night."

Heavily so, ah yes, thought Garland.

"When did you get in?" Hornaday insisted.

"At one."

"At one? Why, at one o'clock I was reading the—"

At which point Garland made his appearance from the pantry—frighteningly, thought Hornaday—abruptly, thought his wife—smoothly, like a dancer, thought Lorna.

"What may I bring you for breakfast, Miss Lorna?" Garland said and stood by her chair.

"Why—"

"Melba toast and coffee, to start with?"

The least offensive, the kindliest suggestion ever, thought Lorna.

"And tomato juice with a touch of lemon?"

"Yes. Please," she said.

"Mr. Hornaday, would you like some more—"

"Never mind. Lorna?"

"Yes, Daddy."

"At one o'clock, as I was saying—"

"You had already left, Mr. Hornaday," said Garland. "At that time I was serving Miss Lorna a cup of hot chocolate."

Hornaday's silence was due to shock. He had been corrected—he had been contradicted. But he had been entirely too drunk at the time in question to be clear about what had happened when. But that did not alter his hot conviction that the butler was lying and that Lorna had come home at some ungodly hour.

"Sheila," Hornaday said, "when did we go to bed, dear?"

"I don't remember, dear," said his wife.

Maybe her husband would know, she thought, that she was lying. But what could he do about it? She made her face look sweet and enjoyed his helplessness, though just for a moment. She was much more intrigued by something else. Why had Garland lied about the time when Lorna had come home? Sheila smiled at the butler and said, "It was nice of you to take care of my daughter at such a late hour."

"Thank you, madam," Garland said, and then he poured Lorna a cup of coffee. Nothing else was now happening at the table.

Garland returned to the pantry and the silence at the table beyond the door felt to him like a truce. He gave himself a cup of coffee and sipped, tasting the black liquid as if it were solid food. Then he closed his eye and thought of the three people locked in a stiff silence at the table.

The butler's assessment was automatic as to what had happened. Matthew Hornaday had been badly stung and would be a mean man to work for from now on. Sheila Hornaday had seen fit to cover for Garland's little lie and that undoubtedly to further her own advantage—which would be what? Young Lorna felt too sick this morning to demonstrate any decisive emotion, although she might well feel some slight gratitude to the butler. But that was of small consequence—she was much too disturbed altogether for clear-cut reactions. Now: why had he, Garland, covered for the girl?

The pantry door was ajar and, by leaning a little, Garland could see her back. He sipped the coffee slowly, savoring it as before, but now his eyes moved over the girl.

I've picked Lorna, he thought, although it may take a little time. Why not the maid?—she would take no time at all.

The difference between the two young women, the way Garland saw it, explained a good deal about the butler himself. His choice was, so to speak, between plain sex and intrigue, between the quick pounce and delay, between simple pleasure and something much more intricate. The nature of his behavior was based on the contradictions in his own personality. He was a large man, and strong, but doing delicate work. He had some of the instincts of the hunter but he preferred his reactions to be slow. He felt really awake only when playing pleasure and, with a touch of perversity, he sought his pleasure only in the most polite and artificial settings. That was why he had drifted into the anachronistic profession of the butler. He had been one for a long time. True, he had to change jobs periodically but he did not mind nor did he suffer repercussions. As often as not his victims were as deeply implicated as he.

He folded his arms and looked at Lorna's back again. The girl sits a little too stiffly, he said to himself. Needs softening. Then the bell rang at the front door.

When Garland opened the door he saw—as he thought of them—one of those too young men. Jacket with checks too large, crew cut with too much wax, and oaf enough to address the butler as sir.

"Is Lorna in, sir?"

"Are you expected?"

"Well, she and me, we had a date last night and I just thought I'd drop by and see how she is."

Garland wondered how a too pink person like this could in any way be responsible for last night's fiasco. Something, for certain, had been a fiasco for Lorna but, then again, thought Garland, the girl may well have been fiasco-bound no matter whom she would have spent time with. He pictured the girl's back, bare of clothes, very stiff, and his own hand moving over the naked curve, slowly.

"Is she expecting you, Mr.—"

"Ned. Just tell her Ned."

"Is she—"

"I've been expecting him," came Lorna's voice from behind Garland. "Let him in, please."

He stepped aside and watched Lorna advance through the hall.

She did not seem stiff now. She walked with a spring very nearly rapacious. And her smile was rapacious, too. But, Garland noted, if this were eagerness to see her young lover, there was no joy in it anywhere.

"Hi, Ned," said Lorna. "Had your breakfast yet?"

"Breakfast? Yeah, I had breakfast. Could I see—"

"Don't stand there. Come on in, come in," and the girl took Ned's arm and walked and small-talked through the large hall to the back, where a door led to a room with a garden view.

The explanation, thought the butler while closing the front door, is neither love nor lust. Therefore what Lorna had in mind must be an act and consequently a scheme. Garland felt so certain of his analysis that he returned to his post in the pantry without further reflection.

The proof of whether or no the butler's analysis was true was a while in coming.

Lorna had confused Ned with her unpredictability. He thought of the drunken rape and the shameful mate-mixing and, on top of that, her being a virgin. He sat on his seat on the couch as if his rump were sharply pointed. He wiped his forehead. And now maybe she wants more, he thought. Maybe she liked it.

Lorna sat next to him with no feeling of sharp points anywhere. Her hip was cocked; her knees showed their dimples, her bare arms their sheen. The way she moved her arms made her breasts squeeze up high and round where the neckline ended.

"I thought I was tired from last night," said Lorna and made an undulant, all-involving kind of a stretch. "You know, tired because of everything and it being new to me, but you know, Ned, I'm not tired at all but just lazy. Does sex make you feel lazy, Ned?"

"Lazy?"

"Yes, all loose and like open and—I don't know the word. Here, I'll show you. Touch me once, here."

"Here?"

"Here," she said, very patiently, and put his hand on her wrist and then made him run his finger up the inside of her arm. She closed her eyes and, when the finger was in her armpit, she suddenly clutched it hard and with eyes closed let out a shuddering sigh.

"Gee—did I hurt—" he started to say.

"No, no, no," she said and opened her eyes and smiled. "Just thrill, I mean, thrill. And if I were tired, I wouldn't feel that way, would I?" She leaned back and looked at the ceiling as if that too were a thrill. "Is that what sex does to you, Ned, open you up like that, all the time?"

"All the time?"

"Isn't it wonderful, Ned?"

She took his hand in hers in a prayerful gesture. Then, still holding it thus, she pressed her bosom and heaved a sigh.

The motion made Ned feel a great deal of the girl, but with his hand trapped he could do nothing about it. He did not know what he should do with his free hand. It fluttered beside him like a landed fish while Lorna went on talking as if she did not know what Ned was suffering.

"And it's only eleven o'clock in the morning, you know that? And I used to think you don't start feeling anything like this till evening, or maybe even the afternoon, but not in the morning. Do you?"

"Huh?"

She let go of his hand at that point, giving it freedom, so to speak. Ned immediately used the freedom on the girl. She closed her eyes and clenched her teeth, which Ned took to be an access of passion. In a sense he was right. It was a type of passion.

"Ned, wait—"

She stood up and stepped away from him but did not let go of his arm. He could feel her nails digging.

"Some place else," she said, and pulled him towards the door that let out to the terrace and the garden.

"But not out there, Lorna. I mean, in the open—"

"I know. Down the terrace, another room—"

But when she had the door partly open she abruptly changed her mind. Ned took another step and saw why. Mr. Hornaday was sitting in a lounge chair on the terrace and reading the paper.

"Maybe we better—" Ned started, but Lorna was turning him her way.

"We'll sneak upstairs. I know a good place upstairs. Wait. First, hold me again, no, like this, closer—"

She moved against him and she knew he was becoming excited. She kept moving against him until he felt his excitement intolerable. Then she stepped away. He did not understand the meaning of what happened next, at least not immediately.

CHAPTER FIVE

Matthew Hornaday, relaxing after the ordeal of breakfast, was reading a sentence which said in part "... will terminate their three-year engagement with a June wedding," when he heard the scream. He sat up stiff as if stretched on a torture rack, and the paper tore in his hands.

An obscenity rose up inside him like heartburn, a lust to punish this assault on his hangover delicacy. A scream again rent the air.

This time the banker was aware of more than his own anger. There was a woman screaming and he could tell she was screaming in the garden room.

"Daddy! Daddy!"

He had not been called this since Lorna had been a little thing, too many years ago. My little girl, he thought The phrase shot through his mind and Hornaday, protective and enraged, hurled himself from his inclining chair—and never mind the awful sensations this caused inside of his head.

He discovered Lorna in the garden room. Her dress was torn down the front, one bra strap was down, one breast was barely covered by no more than her own hand.

"Da-daddy, he—he—"

Not until then did Hornaday see a young lout—no, a mad dog named Ned or something.

What Garland saw when he quickly appeared in the room was the banker hauling out with one beefy arm and delivering a tree-felling clout to the side of Ned's head. The boy did not fall but staggered in a circle like a rubber-legged boxer. As Hornaday struck again, this time to the other side of the boy's head, Garland left after one look at the girl. He returned fairly soon, bringing a housecoat. By this time a violent interrogation had reached white heat.

"Don't deny what my own eyes tell me looking at my little girl here—thank you, Garland, decent of you—or I'll call the juvenile authorities quicker than you can say Jack Rubber—Jack Robberson, do you *hear* me?"

"Hornaday, sir, what I—"

"Don't lie to me."

Garland saw that the boy, who had risen and was leaning on a chair, was close to tears.

"Garland," said the banker much too loudly, "you will forget this terrible scene, of course, and bring me a tomato juice, the way you make it. While I interrogate—" menacing swing of the head towards Ned—"this mad-dog delinquent."

The butler left to prepare the Bloody Mary but forgot nothing about the scene. His interest was chiefly in Lorna's role—how her scream of virginal terror had left no residue: no sobs, no hysteria, no tears; and how she sat maidenly and demure while Ned was being raked over the coals. Why had she not left?

Garland made the Bloody Mary rather weak, because, he reasoned, this Lorna girl had wanted to watch, that's why she stayed, and that makes her a cunning little bitch. And yet she isn't, really, thought Garland, or she would have been much slicker about her theatrics in the garden room. Therefore it must have been a ghastly hurt indeed the football youth had given her. Obviously, the night before, obviously some sort of rash sex …

"… lay hands or eyes on my daughter again, you dirty—ah." Hornaday interrupted himself to watch Garland come. "By the way, where is my wife?"

"She went horseback riding, sir."

"I see. Well, let's have the Bloody—the bloody tomato juice. Thank you. Now, before I give your father a piece of my mind—Garland, this juice is not right."

The butler left, made the juice right, and came back. Somehow, in the meantime, the assault of the banker's monologue now included his daughter.

"… seems to me you could exercise better taste and discretion in the choice of the people you associate with. Thank you, Garland. Ah yes, this seems more right."

It seemed to Garland that in Hornaday's delicate chemical state it would not take long at all for the drink to make the man infinitely worse. His nasty temper would spread to embrace everything in his path.

"Well, the town is so small," Lorna was saying.

"Are you telling me there are no decent people in this town?"

"I know them, too."

"What does that mean?" Hornaday said, raising his voice again. "Just exactly what?"

"I don't know," said his daughter, who was really confused.

"Does it mean, pray tell, that you have met them and found them wanting? Such as the Fenwick boy, for example, or the Miller's, or the Sherman's, or—"

"We were with Jackie Sherman last night."

Ned winced and there was a change in Lorna, too. Her face tightened involuntarily, as if she hurt. But the banker saw nothing.

"You were in the same group with the Sherman boy," Hornaday ranted, "but your choice of companion was this, this person here. You call that discriminating?"

"All I said—"

"Don't interrupt me, girl."

For no clear reason Garland suddenly knew that things would now quickly become worse. Perhaps because the Bloody Mary was nearly gone, perhaps because Hornaday was hard-pressed for more accusations and threats. The need for inventiveness at a time like this would be a strain on the banker.

"It occurs to me," he said, "that once again I'll have to take a firm grip on the reins with you, girl, seeing you don't know which way to turn by using your own good sense."

"Yes, Daddy."

But it was too late for demureness to make a dent. On the contrary, Hornaday felt mocked and therefore doubly irritated.

"As a matter of fact," he resumed, "the best and the first thing to do is to change your environment. I think I'm going to send you to summer camp."

The butler did not know if the girl were upset by this. It would be worthwhile to find out, he thought. He himself was certainly upset by the prospect of Lorna removed for the summer.

"May I freshen that, sir?"

Another drink would help stoke the fire now, Garland reasoned—bring things to a head, clarify how he himself would spend the summer. He disliked having his plans tampered with, especially before even a smidgen of reward had come his way.

He fixed a second Bloody Mary and let Hornaday wait for it a while. This should bring out the rashness in the man, which was fine. The butler with the arrogance of the successful hunter, felt certain he could then better handle the mindless brute.

"... made that clear! Where have you been, Garland? All right, put it there. Now, I'll even give you a choice, girl, and you can pick either Miss Warbrook's School for the summer, or St. Vincenti."

"That's like asking me do I want to go to prison or to a convent."

Aha, thought Garland, in a way, little one, you and I are really of one mind.

"Are you trying to be flippant about this?" Hornaday said.

"No, Daddy," Lorna said and looked really depressed. Why was she being punished now? For what? For hating Ned because of what he had done to her?

"Then I think I'll decide where you go. There's not going to be any more traipsing around like you've been doing. No more and none of it."

"But I never—"

"Yes? Where, for example, were you last night?"

Hornaday bored his eyes into his daughter's, waiting. He knew at least one place where she had been last night.

"Just around—"

"Where?"

"At the Bully Bar," said Lorna.

"Aha, Miss Warbrook's it is."

"But we didn't do anything. We had cokes and played the juke—"

"Never mind that. Where did you go then?"

"Well, some of us—"

"You split up. You let the Sherman boy and everybody go one way and you, alone with this—this goat here, you two went off by yourselves and just exactly where—"

"That's not true, Daddy."

"Not true? What have you got to say, Ned Tyler?"

"We stayed with the others, Mr. Hornaday, sir."

"Where?"

"We went to the Sherman cabin," said Ned.

Now there was an unusual silence. No one could know, of course, what Matt Hornaday's fantasy had been while asking his daughter how she had spent the evening, but now he looked as if he had been hit in the solar plexus. And then, suddenly, he roared.

"St. Vincenti's."

His daughter seemed to shrink inside her robe. This seemed to encourage the parent.

"For certain St. Vincenti's for the summer, and maybe also for the next year of school."

"Daddy, please—"

"That's all."

"Let's ask Mommy if—"

"No need for that, none whatsoever."

"But all we did was go to the Sherman cabin and you're friends with the Shermans and Aunt Anna and I don't see—"

"No more of this."

"Sir?" said Garland from the door. It was time, he had decided, to stop listening from the corridor and to act in the room.

"What?" said the banker.

"I just heard Mrs. Hornaday returning."

"So what?"

"I wondered, in view of the situation which arose here, what I might best tell Mrs. Hornaday."

"Nothing, thank you."

Garland stayed in the room, as if not finished.

"Daddy," said Lorna again, "all we did was go to the Sherman cabin and—"

"I absolutely do not want to hear about that again."

"Sir?" said Garland.

"What, for God's sake?"

"Is that the Sherman cabin you mentioned on the train?" said Garland with frightening calm.

It was not, of course, really blackmail. It was whatever Hornaday would make of it. One thing the butler knew for sure: the banker would make war on Garland's tactic.

But Garland had the arrogance of the successful hunter.

Several days later it had been sunny and cool in the morning but during the day it had warmed up freakishly and now the night was warm, too. Garland, in his room, opened the dormer window and peered out at the dark treetop for a while. The leaves made little sounds as if in sleep.

The butler removed his jacket and vest and pulled down his tie. He did not feel like changing entirely, or like going to bed. He stepped back to the window and stood in the warm waft of night air. It was a night of slowness and torpor but it did not affect Garland in this fashion. The heavy warmth excited him.

It was time, he felt, for a real move. A move from distant manipulations, to something with touch.

He breathed deeply a few times but the act did not calm him. Not that he needed calmness, because he felt sure.

When he leaned on his window sill he could see the facade of the house where it made a right angle. There were two windows lit, one over the other. The one on the top was on his floor. The maid, Irma, had her room there. The one underneath was Lorna's.

The butler leaned on the sill and glanced from one window to the other. Then the light in the maid's room snapped off.

Garland pushed away from the sill and that simple motion washed the hesitancy out of him. He turned to his door and on the way past his bed he yanked the tie out of his collar. Then he went down the dark corridor, made the L-turn into the next angle of the house and stopped by the door of the maid.

He could hear the girl's bed, and how she tossed in the dark. He stood a while listening, and once the girl sighed.

What a simple one she is, he thought, ripe and simple, and just shy enough to make her appear much less of an animal than she probably is.

He heard the girl sigh again.

But suddenly the lazy indulgence of his imagination annoyed Garland, the taste of it all was suddenly flat, and he thought of Lorna. There was nothing lazy or indulgent in him now. There was only impatience. And greed. For what? Sex? At least that was the simplest denominator.

The butler looked at the maid's door and heard the girl turn in her bed. He smiled in the dark. It amused him to think that he was using one woman to arouse him and another to fulfill him. But none of this had actually happened as yet and he felt a new thrust of impatience. He retraced his steps down the dark corridor and turned into his room. And now he proceeded with forethought and precision.

A glance outside to make sure that Lorna's light was still on. A look in the mirror after putting his tie back on, and his vest and the jacket. A slight change of mien, a reduction of the expressiveness in his features. His face took on remoteness and he was the butler.

Garland made his way to the ground floor first, to see if anyone might still be up. All the rooms were empty. He stepped outside to stand on the terrace and raised his eyes to the front facade of the house. There was a light on in the large bathroom and there was a dim light on in Mrs. Hornaday's bedroom. The bedroom on the other side of the bath was dark. The butler wondered if Matt Hornaday was out or if he were in his wife's bedroom.

Garland mounted to the second floor and found his answer.

"Matt, please—" he heard from behind the door. "Please brush your teeth first—"

The butler did not bother to imagine the tableau behind that door. He hastened his pace, suddenly worried that Lorna might have turned off her light.

The corridor angled off into the far wing of the house. By the last door Garland stopped. There was a slit of light at the bottom. He allowed himself a lowering of the lids and a small sigh. Then he was properly noncommittal again. He next meant to go to the very end of the hall in order to close a tall window there, as pretext for his presence. He would do it noisily and would— He dropped the plan. From behind the girl's door came the unmistakable sound of crying.

The one above, Garland mused, tosses, and the one below, she cries in bed. If I had to choose on that basis alone, I might take neither.

Then he simply knocked on the door.

The crying stopped immediately, although it ended with a fairly long sniff.

"What? I'm going to bed."

She did not sound as if she wanted to see anyone.

"Miss Lorna?" said Garland.

Then there was a silence.

Politely Garland said again, "Miss Lorna."

"Is that you, Garland?" Much less surly now.

"Yes, miss."

And with unexpected promptness Lorna opened the door.

Her hair was brushed back softly and her young face looked much like a child's, her eyes swollen a little and the cheeks shinily moist. She wiped one side of her face artlessly. Only then did she think of retying her housecoat. Her nightgown underneath, Garland saw, was the very short kind that left the thighs bare. He did not look down but at the girl's face.

"I passed to close the window here," Garland said, "when I heard you crying." He paused. The girl did not bother to deny that she had been crying. "May I bring you something, Miss Lorna, something to help you sleep?"

The girl still did not talk. She shrugged. But she had opened the door, Garland reminded himself. And she would most likely have said no if it had been her father or mother.

"I'll first fix your room a little," he said, "if you'll allow me. You'll see how much cooler it'll feel with fewer things lying around. And I'll open the balcony door for you."

Lorna stepped aside and simply nodded.

Garland decided to say nothing more until she spoke. He hung up some clothes, stacked some magazines, straightened the bed and turned it down.

"Don't—don't you ever sleep?" She said it without much interest, as if she would have rather said something else.

"I need sleep less than you do, Miss Lorna. Now, then," and Garland permitted himself a rare smile.

Lorna, of course, had never seen the man smile before. Suddenly, she saw a completely different man but, before she could decide just what she had seen, what mood, what feelings, Garland had turned away.

"Now, if you'll get into bed while I go downstairs I'll bring you—"

"I don't really want anything, Garland. I just have a headache."

"And you have not had a very easy time of it recently, Miss Lorna. You can use a little extra care. A little extra attention."

When he said the last the girl turned away and Garland knew she was fighting tears again. Show her even a touch of warmth, and she is swamped with emotion, he thought.

Careful, a touch and she will sob in your arms—and regret it forever. It is still a matter of obligating her further and to make her feel safe.

Garland turned to the bed, took the two pillows there and put them on top of each other in a manner for sitting up, briefly nodded at Lorna and left the room.

When he returned with the tray she was sitting in bed, wrapped in her housecoat, the covers over her legs. Very obviously, she was waiting.

He set the bed tray across her lap and never once glanced at her. It was the girl's move again and he, Garland, would direct her from there. Concerning the art of seduction there were really no rules or it would not be called an art. And just as an artist must be born with his talent, so one may instinctively do the right thing more often than not when engaged in seduction. Garland did not think any of this out. Usually the method of his pursuit formed as naturally as breathing.

"First, take these two aspirin with a sip of water," he said.

This was more direct than, for example, "I would suggest, if you like ..."

Lorna took the pills.

"Good," he said. "And now your cup of chocolate." He smiled slightly. "The one you didn't have last night."

What is it when he smiles, thought Lorna, and she gazed at Garland over the rim of her cup. And then, as he had wanted her to, she also smiled.

"That's better," he said.

He knew she would not send him out but he wondered if he might sit down. Better not. Better stand, not too attentively, so that she does not feel scrutinized.

"Garland?" she said.

"Yes?" He left the Miss Lorna out intentionally.

"I want to thank you for everything—since earlier in the week."

"You are welcome." Then he folded his arms behind him and looked at the dark window. "Miss Lorna ..." he said.

He hesitated in order to make her wait. Then he came around to the side of the bed and put his hand on the petit-point chair that stood by the night table. "May I sit for a moment? I would like to tell you something."

"Of course, yes, Garland. I'm sorry ..."

He let her hang with the unfinished phrase and sat down. Then he contemplated her.

"It would be nicer," he said, "For the moment, I mean, if you'd let me call you Lorna."

"Please do."

He caught her hesitation. It had nothing to do with any doubts over etiquette, Garland felt, but she was simply diffident about anything personal. So he talked without emphasis but with a great deal of warmth.

"Lorna, why is it that a lovely girl like you is so surprised by even the most normal kind of attention?" She glanced away and before she had a chance to bury her reaction with some defensive remark, Garland continued. "Aren't you used to it, Lorna?"

"Attention?" she said, meeting his eyes, her face gone fairly hard. "Sure I get attention."

"What kind, Lorna, for your sake or their sake?" he said. She shrugged and looked down into her cup. "Attention, Lorna has to do with attending to and for you. Anything else can be fairly ugly."

She stared at him for a moment and then talked as if she were addressing her father, showing her dislike.

"Like a few days ago," she said, "when I attended to dear Ned?"

"Yes. That was not for, that was against."

"Well," she almost shouted, then stopped herself.

"I know, Lorna. He's done something very ugly to you." She only blinked at him. "It takes the blindness of a parent to ignore what has happened to you, Lorna. No other talent," and Garland smiled.

He smiles as if he knows everything, she thought, and perhaps he does.

She bit her lip, hoping that would keep her eyes from smarting so.

"How bad was it?" Garland said very gently.

I will not cry again, she said to herself, I am finished with that, finished.

But her voice now jumped out of her in great anguish, and full of bitter complaint. "The most terrible, like the end before I ever began."

"Sometimes that happens, Lorna. The first time."

"Not like this."

"Then it won't happen again."

"Then it won't happen again," she said, almost mumbling, and Garland saw clearly that she was not taking his remark the way he had meant it.

"You won't even have to struggle to start again, Lorna. You will simply want to be a woman."

Whatever she wanted to say, she did not say it. Instead she lay back and closed her eyes as if exhausted. He arose quietly and took the tray from her lap. He placed the tray on the bureau and then he sat down again but said nothing. He waited for her.

"Garland?" quietly.

"Yes, Lorna."

"How come we're talking like this?"

She did not open her eyes. Garland felt that what he would say next might be crucial.

"Because," he said, "it's a natural thing."

She took a deep breath, eyes still closed, as if taking his answer in with that breath, and as if needing what he had said quite as much.

"More natural," he added, "than whatever happened to you with that young man."

"Yes," said Lorna. "Yes."

Now, the butler felt, he had her. Before you walk, you must feel the ground under your feet, he thought. He was now certain that he and the girl had experienced that ground—something more than a mere sense of gratitude for favors done, something more than a night's secret accidentally shared. There was now intimacy. And now they were ready for the sure move. Garland could sense it in the air. The girl, on the bed, opened her eyes and they were those of a woman gazing at him. A slight stretch—she did not even know she was doing it and she was becoming more aware of her womanliness, Garland knew. That awareness showed in the curve of her breasts— she no longer hunched her shoulders to minimize the breasts. And then there was the fluid twist of her hip since she no longer lay stiffly. Finally, there was something like a musk in the air as Lorna saw how Garland's face seemed subtly to alter, to become something fleetly gleaming, as if there were a foretaste of gluttony ...

However and notwithstanding, Garland arose very smoothly and pulled down his vest. The gesture accompanied a slight bow from the waist.

"I'll let you retire now, Miss Lorna."

She was conscious of the change, if only because of his use of the formality. She watched him go and pick up the tray.

"Garland?" she said. He stopped to regard her from across the room. "Are you married, Garland?" she continued.

"No, Miss Lorna."

"Oh—" She seemed embarrassed, needing to explain herself. "I mean, what I meant was, you seem—you have such a—I mean you seem to know so much."

Garland inclined his head slightly and did not answer until he reached the door.

"You are not married, Miss Lorna, and so much younger than I. And you know a great deal about men."

He left then, so that she would not have to protest or say anything—for the moment.

CHAPTER SIX

Garland carried the tray down through the quiet house and he felt something like discomfort. He did not know why he felt that way until he became aware of the rapidity of his stride and its haste. His discomfort lay in his personal dissatisfaction. He could lie dormant for a long time and feel nothing. He could even delay a great deal out of politeness. But after politeness and lengthy manipulation there always came his great urgency. There would grow in him a need matched only by the force of his determination. Which was, perhaps, the reason for his attraction to women.

Everything he had left undone with Lorna he would now finish with the much simpler Irma.

He left the tray as it was in the kitchen. Another job for Irma. For later. Then he ascended to the servant quarters on the third floor.

Would she still be awake? Tossing? He did not care. He negotiated the corridor as quickly and as surely as if it had been brightly lit. At the maid's door he listened just briefly and thought the girl was asleep. He did not knock.

The room was silent except for the girl's deep, sleep-filled breathing. And her room was very warm. He passed the bed and looked at her and then drew open the window. His impatience was even greater than the directness of his actual moves. Garland had his habits.

He sat down on the edge of the bed and stared down at Irma. Her yellow hair lay loose on the pillow. There was a looseness in all of her, the relaxed face, very round and soft, the white arms that lay spread out. He ran his fingertips down the inside of her arms but she did not wake. He wanted to see the rest of her.

He pulled the light cover down to her hips, and she till slept. Her nightgown covered her thoroughly. It left the arms bare and was held over the shoulders by two little bows. Garland slipped each bow open and then peeled down the front of the chemise. She slept on. The bosom was very full and white and larger, he surmised, than Lorna's, and probably softer.

He first touched one mound, then the other, moving it with his hand. Skin heat flowed into his palm from the girl and then the heat answered in him. But the butler had his habits.

He kept his hand where it was, moving, feeling, and then with one finger rubbed and stroked. And the girl slept.

If she is as slowly responsive as this when awake, he thought, then she is more of a cow than I estimated. Or I am more of dolt than this Ned person.

It was then the girl awoke. Her eyes opened and then she responded—not with sex but with fear.

Her eyes and mouth grew wide and she suddenly clapped her hands over her face. Strange, he thought, I would have imagined her struggling to cover her breasts first of all.

Then she pressed her arms together and at the same time took a deep breath—she was preparing to scream.

"Quiet," said Garland. She held her breath. "I hope you're not cold," he said brutally, and stroked one naked breast again.

"No," she said. "Who—who are you—"

I don't know if she's more stupid or more frightened, Garland mused.

"Garland," he answered.

"Oh—Mr. Garland ..."

Under his hand he felt her relax ever so slightly. After all—Garland smiled to himself—it is now no longer a stranger uncovering her in the dead of night.

First he pulled the blanket all the way off and then he pushed up her nightgown. She lay still, tensing a little. Taking account of this, as if out of consideration, he moved his hands up very smoothly to the top of the garment to get it out of the way.

"Raise up in back a little," he said. "Or it won't move."

"Mr. Garland—"

"Raise a little."

She did and he moved the whole thing down to her hips. He would have gone further but her hips were very wide. Then he put his hands in his lap, sat up more, and looked down at her.

"Are you cold?" he said.

"No."

"Good. You look very good, very inviting." He thought of meringue and sweet custards.

She moved her hands down, to hold her breasts.

"No," he said. "Put your arms to the sides."

She did so slowly and lay very still.

"Mr. Garland, I—I'm blushing."

"I won't look at you," he said. "Would that help?"

"Yes."

He turned his head so he could not see her, and so she could see that he was doing it, and at the same time he put his hands on her again—on her shoulders, arms, and then on her breasts and belly. At last he touched her thighs.

She no longer felt stiff. She moved one thigh slightly.

"Are you still blushing?" he said.

"No," she said.

As long as I don't look at her. Ah, well, a small price to pay—

He knew her body very well before he stopped the play with his hands. And the girl was breathing very deeply now, and moving a lot. Garland listened to her and liked her for it. He liked the directness of her and the frank wanting.

"Oh, Mr. Garland—yes. Oh yes, Roger, yes—"

"Yes," he said. "But get up first."

"What?"

He helped her by holding her around the back and felt for the first time how strong and muscled her movements were, how she twisted to find her balance and how quickly she reached for his shoulders and held on.

"Why?" she said. "Why get up? And you're all dressed, Roger."

"That's why. Stand up."

She stood up in front of him and the nightgown hung from her hips.

"Wiggle," he said, "off with it."

She wiggled and kicked off the shirt. She did not wiggle like a snake, Roger Garland noted, but more like an impatient colt. When the nightgown was a heap at her feet she stood there and all her shyness was gone. She was mostly impatient.

Her greed was infectious and her excitement became his.

When she clutched him with her arms and rubbed her front into him, he toppled her over on the bed. After that, if Garland had been thinking at all, he would not have imagined a cow any more. A snake, rather.

But altogether a woman, too. They were together, and both aware of something other than the union in her own bed. Through her open window they could hear the sounds from the room above. She lay still in the dark and felt at least the same greed as the two others ...

The two in the bed on the third floor and Lorna, now alone in her bed on the second were, in fact, not the only ones still awake in the house at this late hour. There was Mrs. Hornaday, too.

To make love to her husband was, sadly, nothing new to her and nothing to stay awake about. But at one point while submitting to Matt Hornaday she had had out of boredom several fantasies involving sun-tan lotions for herself and liniment for her horse who needed to ride every day, and then, unaccountably, a fantasy about Garland.

Unexpected excitement grew in her, uncoiled and flailed—nothing unusual in her long career, but a rarity in recent years.

Her husband was finished by then and Mrs. Hornaday—Love Apple Lindy of years ago—lay awake in her bed in a high degree of irritation.

Finally she walked downstairs and then upstairs again at one point she nearly turned to the third floor. To do so, however, she thought, would have been absurd. Instead, she stayed awake and irritated for the balance of the night and was in the kitchen before her young maid came down.

"Good morning, Mrs. Hornaday," said Irma.

"Morning. And don't shout, please."

"Oh yes, ma'am," said the girl.

Mrs. Hornaday looked at her and thought the health and the sparkle in the girl's face were disgusting.

"Had your breakfast yet, ma'am, or you want me to make you some before cook comes in? Or can I eat first? I'm so hungry I could eat a—" and Irma stopped short.

"Eat a what? Why don't you finish your sentence?"

"Eat a horse. But I didn't want to say it seeing how you feel about horses."

"And what makes you think you know how I feel about horses?"

Mrs. Hornaday regretted the invitation for an answer immediately, saying something to herself about necessary distance to be kept from the servants. This idea of necessity of distance, however, logically included Garland so that she dropped the whole business.

"You may prepare your own breakfast now, Irma," she said. "I only want this cup of coffee."

"Thank you, Mrs. Hornaday," said the maid. "Didn't you have a good night, Mrs. Hornaday?"

"It was all right. I just didn't sleep very much."

"I didn't either," said Irma and she seemed to beam at the thought.

Sometimes, thought Mrs. Hornaday, that girl seems quite normal. And at other times that girl seems to be a little bit nuts.

"When Garland comes down," she said to the maid, "ask him to come to the breakfast room."

Then Mrs. Hornaday sat in the little room cheerful with prints and early sunshine. She sat there, feeling sour. She had a fine view through the bay window where she could see the flowers in the garden and she had a view in the other direction, where she had left the door to the kitchen ajar. She mostly looked that way, which is why she saw the butler as soon as he had come down.

What an immaculate man, she thought. Then the maid interrupted Mrs. Hornaday's line of vision.

"Good morning, Mr. Garland," Mrs. Hornaday heard. "Would you like some coffee? Mrs. Hornaday made the coffee this morning."

"Thank you, yes," said Garland. "Why didn't you make the coffee, Irma?"

"Because Mrs. Hornaday got down here before me. Did you have a good night, Mr. Garland?"

"From now on," he said, "you will come down half an hour earlier, please."

"Oh, yes," said Irma. "And I had a wonderful night."

She is beaming again, Mrs. Hornaday said to herself. Probably like a hussy. What is the matter with me this morning? the banker's wife thought.

When Garland came into the breakfast room, Mrs. Hornaday was glancing the other way.

"Good morning," said Garland. "Irma said you wanted to see me?"

The banker's wife turned and thought, what a wonderfully correct man he is. He is ogled by that hussy and right away puts her in her place with that order about getting down here half an hour earlier.

"Yes, Garland. Would you close the door to the kitchen, please?"

"Of course."

"Garland, I meant to ask you about Irma. Do you think she's all right?"

"She performs quite well, yes. Did you have a complaint, ma'am?"

"I don't know. I wondered how you felt about her, about the way she does her duties."

"I found her satisfactory. But if she has been amiss and it has escaped me—"

He was interrupted because Lorna slipped into the room. In contrast to several days ago, thought her mother, Lorna seems improved and certainly much more cheerful.

"Morning, Mommy," said Lorna, and then she smiled at Garland and said, "Hi," to him.

What is the matter with me this morning? Mrs. Hornaday thought, and turned to stare outside. My daughter is beaming, too. One does it like a hussy and the other does it like a conspirator.

"You were saying about Irma," Garland began again.

"Why?" said Lorna. "Is there something wrong with Irma?"

Is that child grinning? thought Mrs. Hornaday.

"No, dear. Garland thinks there's nothing wrong with her."

"I would think so," said Lorna. "Can I have some breakfast, Garland?"

"Don't interrupt, dear. Garland?"

"Yes?"

"We'll just try her out a little longer and see. Maybe you should add some duties to her schedule, just so she doesn't become sloppy, you understand."

"Garland has already added some duties to her schedule," said Lorna. "Haven't you, Garland?"

"You have?" said the banker's wife.

Garland looked at Lorna noncommittally and thought, I will have to revise my entire approach to that girl. I will first of all have to find out—but then Lorna recovered for him.

"What I meant was, the cleaning woman would do the laundry most of the time, but now Irma is doing it, isn't she?"

"Yes," said Garland, "on occasion."

"Occasional extra duties don't do a girl like her any harm, is my impression," said Lorna.

"Lorna, dear," said her mother, "will you please stay out of the conversation while I discuss domestic matters with Garland?"

"But I'm interested in what goes on in the house."

"All right, dear. But do stop talking so much. I have a fierce headache."

This was a fact, and welcome too, because now Sheila Hornaday could blame her irritation entirely upon something neutral, like a headache. She forgot about the dissatisfaction of her night and the strange imaginings of her morning and could now look at Garland again and see this most correct man, a butler, and how distinguished he really was.

"There was something else I wanted to speak to you about, Garland, but you might see to my daughter's breakfast first."

While Garland was back in the kitchen, Matt Hornaday stomped into the room, and his wife winced.

"Good morning, everybody," he said. "Did you have a good night?" He grinned at his wife.

Now he is beaming, Sheila Hornaday thought.

"I have a foul headache, dear," she said, and made a wan gesture.

"Fresh air," said her husband. "Go out there and ride that horse around in the fresh air and you'll be all right."

"Thank you, Matthew, but your medical advice is not what I need. Nor do I need a horse for my headache."

"What then, a pill?"

"Yes, Matthew, a pill will do fine. Can we drop the subject now?"

"Of course. All I wanted to know is if you had a good night—I had a good night—and that's all. Did you have a good night, Lorna?" He was a little more constrained now, talking to his daughter.

"Yes, thank you, Dad. I stayed awake a long time but it was all right."

"Stop reading in bed. What you need is sleep."

Doctor Hornaday here, thought his wife. He prescribes either a horse or sleep. All very simple.

"I wasn't reading in bed," said Lorna. "It was such a warm night and I just lay there and relaxed and listened to the sounds."

"Sounds? What sounds?"

"In the night, you know. Crickets and birds. And bees."

"There are no bees at night. Sometimes you seem perfectly all right, Lorna, but at other times you say the nuttiest things. Where's that new man?"

"Can't you say Garland, dear?"

"First I want my breakfast and then I want to talk to you about that man. I'm determined—"

Whatever Hornaday was determined about had to wait. His wife interrupted him.

"I meant to mention," she said. "I am thinking of adding some duties to his schedule."

"You are?" said Hornaday.

"Like what?" Lorna wanted to know.

Then Garland reappeared. He brought Lorna's breakfast and also the banker's usual morning fare because Garland had heard the man's loud voice and a good butler is prepared without need for constant instructions. However, Garland was not quite prepared for what came next.

"I meant to ask you," said Mrs. Hornaday, "whether would be willing to take on an extra duty, Garland."

First he finished pouring coffee.

"If I can be of assistance—" he said.

"Do you know how to drive?"

"Yes, Mrs. Hornaday."

"Then, on occasion," she said, "I would like you to drive for me, Garland, if it doesn't interfere with your other duties."

"Drive where?" the banker wanted to know.

"Well, I don't know, dear. There are any number of events going on during the summer or sometimes I would simply like to drive through the country." She saw that her answer was not satisfactory to her husband. "And this morning, for example, I have to go to the club."

"They pick you up when you want to go see the horse."

"I am not going to see the horse, dear. The tennis eliminations start this morning and you know that I'm on the committee."

"You can still ask them to—"

"I don't like to ask. And if Garland is willing to take this extra duty—"

"Of course, ma'am."

"And I'm going along too," said Lorna.

She smiled at everybody in turn and only Garland had any notion of what that smile might mean.

CHAPTER SEVEN

Garland drove mother and daughter to the country club and during the short trip nobody talked. Though if thoughts made noises there would have been quite a racket in that hushed limousine. A certain screechiness would have come from Mrs. Hornaday, perhaps a tweeting and chirping from Lorna and a constant droning from Garland.

Mrs. Hornaday, who lied most naturally to herself, had forgotten all about sex vis-à-vis her butler and had shifted her preoccupation to a righteous format, namely, how best to utilize the talents of the household staff in general and of the butler—the most expensive and also, undoubtedly, the most versatile—in particular.

Lorna did not lie that much. There was no question in her mind that she thought of Garland and sex all at the same time because she had heard the man making love to Irma in the room upstairs. But she did not think of how he had affected her when he had been in her room before Irma's. To her, Garland and sex were matters only for twitting the dignified, graying servant with sly innuendoes.

Those were daytime thoughts. Neither one of the women allowed herself any nocturnal thoughts. Garland, driving, alone had evening thoughts.

What was going on with Lorna was quite clear to him. The girl had obviously heard him in bed with the maid but he did not know yet how he might turn that fact into an advantage. For the moment, of course, the situation was untenable, because Lorna was using her knowledge for some silly game of her own that had nothing to do with his own plans for the girl. Typically, he did not feel harassed by his speculations but only by the inaction. He would, of course, have to wait until night.

In regard to Mrs. Hornaday, he suspected less of her intentions than she herself did. He felt simply annoyed by the added duties, by the prospect of silent rides with her in the car, silence dotted with small talk.

When Garland parked at the country club he still thought he would have to wait until night but, while he settled down to wait by the car, matters had started to roll again.

Lorna accompanied her mother to the courts, intending to excuse herself fairly soon. It would be more entertaining, or even vaguely exciting, Lorna thought, to go back and spend time with Garland. But then someone called to her. When she turned she saw Jackie Sherman wave to her from the pool.

Lorna wanted to turn, wanted to forget she had seen him, but he came running with the bathrobe flapping around him. She saw his fine body and the tightness of the small trunks he was wearing. She felt stiff and frightened and hurt again as she remembered what Jackie had done with her but she could not remember the act itself.

"Hi, Lorna. How have you been?"

She envied him his ease and hated it, too.

"You left your girl friend by the pool," she said.

"She'll keep."

"I won't. I have to go."

"Hey, wait," and he put his hand on her arm.

She stopped because that way he would let go of her and she would not have to feel his touch.

"Listen," he said, "Ned told me what you did to him at your house. What kind of a stunt was that?"

"Just a stunt and games. Like at your cabin."

"Huh?"

"Like at your cabin."

"Oh. Yeah, boy, but did you pass out."

"That's all there was to it?"

"Lorna, you know better." He grinned and took her arm again but this time to lead her away from the tennis courts. "Didn't have a chance to tell you, Lorna, but you're really built, you know? I mean, you can tell just so much, even with a bathing suit, but when I really got a load of you that night—"

She started to walk off.

"Wait a minute. I wanted to ask you something," he said.

"The answer is no."

"Why not? Listen. Just you and me alone. And we do it all different. What we'll do—"

He stopped because Lorna slapped him hard across the side of his face. Then she walked away not caring what he might think or who might have seen the slap.

She was sensitive to others' opinions but was much more disturbed by something else. She had stopped Jackie from telling her more because she was suddenly shocked by her own imaginings when he had said he would tell her just exactly what he and she would do.

She ran through the main building from the back to the front but could not shake her fantasy. Everything they could have done—everything she had missed...

It was this incident that now started to play into Garland's hand although he did not know it. Nevertheless he took full advantage of it.

The first thing he noticed when Lorna approached him was the change in her mood. She was not flip anymore and she was not teasing. She sat down next to the driver's seat and said, "Garland, please take me home."

"Is your mother—"

"You can pick her up in an hour."

"Very well, Lorna."

He had used her first name calculatedly. Her mood was similar now to the one she had been in last night in her room, and he sensed the need in her to return to their brief intimacy and—to go a step further.

At first he drove without speaking. He drove slowly because he thought he might need the time.

"Don't worry too much, Lorna."

She folded her arms and looked away.

"What do you know?" she said under her breath.

But he heard it well enough.

"I'm not much for games with words, Lorna. But I do know things. And some are the same as you would like to know." Had he gone too far? Her silence was heavy. "We needn't talk of them," he said quietly.

"If I—" she said, hesitating, but then she went on. "I wish I didn't just have to talk of them."

"I know, Lorna."

He knew she was not finished and he gave her the time to come out with it. He picked a street that would make the trip to the house longer.

"Garland?"

"Yes, Lorna."

"I heard you last night."

A little bit of the prankish child characterized her manner, just a touch, as if she were teasing. But she was not teasing. The butler knew she regarded what had happened over her room much more seriously. As he had intended.

"I should have been more discreet," he said.

"Oh, no—" She stopped, then quickly caught herself.

"What I meant was, it didn't disturb me. I mean, it's natural."

"Yes."

"And I mean, what I mean is, I can understand it. I mean, after all."

"Oh, yes," said Garland with a straight face. Then he waited again.

"You mind talking about it, Garland? I mean, if it embarrasses you—"

"I'm not embarrassed. As you said, it's a natural thing, and we both understand it."

"I know." Then she said, "Is— I mean, was Irma a virgin?"

"No. She's a little dumb sometimes, you know, but she is a very straightforward and therefore an honest person, with others and therefore with herself—ah, it seems I'm making a speech," and he laughed a little. "Anyway, judging by that I would say she hasn't been a virgin for some time. Besides, she told me."

"Yes? When— I mean, what did she tell you?"

"She had her first lover when she was fifteen."

"Oh."

"Yes," said Garland and pulled the car through a curve.

"Garland?"

"Yes."

"Does she, I mean, does she enjoy it?"

"She wouldn't do it if she didn't. Yes, I think she joys it very much."

"Hm," said Lorna and stared outside. Oh the one hand she felt wonderfully adult to be talking like this to older man, but on the other hand, when she thought of Irma, especially, Lorna felt badly left out and like a child.

"Perhaps," he said, "you might like to talk with her. I don't think she'd mind."

"Oh, I couldn't do that. I mean, if she were a girl friend perhaps— Well, maybe—"

"There's a much better way, of course," said Garland.

This time Lorna's silence was not a waiting silence but an absolute standing still. She could talk about this and could treat it in her imagination, but the real act was something else.

"And some time, you know," Garland kept on, "You'll feel good about it too."

"I don't know anymore—"

"Yes, you do. Even now you can think about it without any trouble."

"I think about it all the time. Sometimes I think there's something wrong with me for thinking about it all the time, you know that, Garland?"

"It's the other way around, Lorna. What's wrong is that you have to think about it."

The butler was getting bored with the talking. He felt that any more theorizing would not do a thing.

"Are you going to see her again?" she said.

"Am I going to make love to her again, do you mean?"

"I meant that, yes."

"I rather think so. But not in her room," he added.

Lorna, giving the statement thought, said nothing now.

"I want to thank you, by the way," he said, "for being discreet and for not making trouble."

"Oh, of course. I mean, that would be very narrow-minded."

"But I'd still better be more discreet," he went on, "so as not to involve you, too, by some mischance. Instead of the house," he said, "I'll take the girl into the garden."

Where in the garden, he mused, Lorna will have to figure out for herself.

They had nothing else to discuss. Garland drove straight for the house.

When Mrs. Hornaday came home much later—she had after all decided to spend some time on her horse—she found her husband waiting for her. He had already changed out of his office clothes and sat on the front terrace with a glass of beer.

"Sheila, I want to talk to you," he said.

"Ah," she said. "It's good to sit down." She sat down on a sun chair next to her husband and stretched.

"I went into the kitchen before," he said, "and what do you think I saw there?"

"The stove."

Mrs. Hornaday was feeling much better after her horse. Her husband ignored the remark.

"The maid and the butler," he said.

"Oh, yes," she said. "I asked him to bring me my riding clothes to the club and then sent him home because I was going to stay too long for him to wait there for me, and then I had one of the bar people drive me home with the car they have at the club. You must have seen it in the drive."

He had not thought about Garland's chauffeuring chore that morning and did not know what his wife was talking about or what anything she said had to do with anything.

"Let me finish," her husband said. "I told you about him and the maid and that she was blushing."

"That was a few days ago, dear."

"Today she wasn't blushing."

"When did you get back from the office, dear?"

"Will you listen, please? Today she wasn't blushing and you know what that means?"

"She has lost her shyness."

"Right."

"Oh, good. May I have a sip of your beer, dear? Oh my, it rhymed." Mrs. Hornaday noted that her husband was blushing at this point though not from shyness but because he was close to having an apoplectic fit. "Do go on, dear," she resumed. "What were you saying?" She gave him back the beer.

He took a violent swallow, coughed some of it up again, regained his normal coloration, and took a deep breath.

"I am trying to suggest to you," he said in measured tones, "that when a young, innocent girl like our Irma blushes in the presence of a lecher one day and in the presence of that same lecher does not blush another day—that something has happened to that girl during the time in between."

"You lost me, dear."

"I am trying to say that this innocent girl isn't perhaps so innocent anymore."

Mrs. Hornaday thought that was the funniest thing she had ever heard and indicated this with a prolonged peal of laughter.

"I've got grounds," said her husband as the laughter subsided.

"Pass me the beer, dear?"

"I have grounds for my suspicions."

"That's all they are, dear, I'm sure."

"Don't interrupt, because I've been checking around."

"In the kitchen?"

"With the agency. I've always disliked that man and you know it, and I know that when I have strong feelings like that right from the start that means there must be something to it. Feelings don't lie, I always say."

"You mean suspicions don't lie?"

"Listen to me. Do you know that man has changed jobs seven times in five years?"

"Of course. I've seen his references. They're all dated."

"You have only six references. And he's had seven jobs."

"Maybe he just wasn't on the seventh job long enough for some good, legitimate reason and—"

"Precisely. That job was with a seventy-year-old dowager on Long Island and she let him go after one week."

"Maybe she made advances to him and he left, dear."

"Maybe he made advances to her and she fired him."

"Garland? A seventy-year-old woman? Matthew," said Mrs. Hornaday with total conviction, "don't be absurd." She leaned back and patted her hair. "Garland doesn't have to do that, I'm sure."

This was the very worst thing to say to Matt Hornaday.

He suddenly had the insane notion that maybe his wife could vouch for the fact that Garland slept only with women up to the age of forty-eight, Sheila's age. This thought so rattled him that he quickly switched to something else.

"I'm going to investigate him."

"Why don't you do that, dear. Why don't you call up that old lady on Long Island."

The banker had already done so but the old lady on Long Island had been so polite as to say nothing.

"I'm going to check into that last job of his, the one with Chesterton Manning down there in Miami. Seven months he was there, and that's all."

"Mr. Manning died, wasn't that the reason?"

"The reason I'm checking is that the Manning reference was the deadest, the most impersonal and noncommittal reference of them all."

"Garland explained that to me. It was written by the secretary who didn't know much about Garland and his work."

"And why, I ask, was that?"

"Because Mr. Manning was dead, dear."

That ended the conversation, but it did not end the banker's dislike for Garland. Nor did it curtail the several ingenious steps that Hornaday proposed to take.

That night it required no important amount of ingenuity for Lorna to determine when the butler would have his tryst. It would have to be after everybody else had really or ostensibly retired. And as for the place, its location was not much of a mystery, either. There was the garage, there was the gardener's shed, and there was the summer house, as it was called, a little gingerbread thing close to the back wall and under the trees. But that place was locked because of the furniture in it. Lorna could not imagine Garland bedding down in the moist grass.

In the evening, first the maid left for her room. Then Lorna retired to her room half an hour later. She sat quietly before her dressing table. There were no sounds of movement in the bed above her. Just the soft squeak of a woman's footsteps.

Next, Lorna heard her mother go upstairs. After the playing of the original cast recording of a Broadway musical, there was a click, then silence, then Lorna heard her mother tossing and turning.

Hornaday took much longer. He stayed in his study behind a closed door and made several telephone calls. Once she heard him shout, "I said Bar Harbor, Maine. Not Bar Harbor, Michigan." She did not wonder what he was up to.

And last, Lorna heard Garland. In the darkness where she sat she could tell when he turned on his light. It stayed on a long time. She sat rigidly still and imagined what he might be doing, but the light stayed on so long that all her guesses had to be wrong.

Then she gave a sudden start and saw that the butler's light was out. She had been asleep.

She felt stiff and unrested and jumped up so rapidly that she became dizzy.

Had his light been extinguished when he had gone into the garden or had the light been turned off after he had returned to his room? She felt an unreasonable haste and could not think straight. She took another deep breath and felt dizzy again and had to sit down. She thought of Garland and Irma and what they might be doing now and Lorna jumped up again. Now it was easier to move than to think, and she went quickly downstairs. But how foolish she would feel, creeping around out there in the garden, while those two might well be back in the house. Lorna almost turned around again, but she could not go back. She stepped outside.

The grass in the back garden was indeed moist, she observed. Was it the morning dew already?

I am taking a walk, she said to herself. I can't sleep and happen to be taking a walk. I don't feel like a thief in the night. I live here. I will think of absolutely nothing and just stroll.

In the garage were two cars and a rat. Lorna trembled at the sound and left quickly.

In the gardener's shed were tools and a rake leaning on the outside wall. Lorna blundered into the rake which made a fearful racket. This time she ran away. She felt humiliated and was afraid she might cry. She only wanted to go back to the house now, to her room, and to bed. But if, on the way, she should run into Garland or Irma, as they came back into the house—another humiliation.

She stayed in the garden. She collected herself there in the dark, shivering a little because the damp grass was starting to soak through her slippers. And I'll take my walk, she thought, simply because I can't sleep.

The self-deception was easy. She could, in truth, discover no further interest in Garland and the maid. At that point, after rounding a hedge, she saw the small summer house by the back wall, and the dim light inside. I'm taking a walk—that way, for just a moment ...

Actually she heard before she saw anything. She heard the girl, a low sound like moaning, but not like pain.

There was a glass door, with a curtain, and there was a window on the side wall. The girl moaning and stopping and making her sound again seemed to reach inside Lorna and turn and pluck. Then Lorna stood by the window and saw.

They did not have the lights on but only a candle. They were on the couch and the couch did not face in Lorna's direction. She could see Garland leaning towards Irma, and then Lorna could see Irma's head that lay on the rounded arm of the couch. Each time the maid moaned she rolled her head back and forth. Once she threw it back.

But it was the sound that held Lorna and caused her to tense with growing excitement. She clenched her hands, not feeling how moist her palms had become.

"Why?" she heard. "But why, Roger?" Irma was saying.

"Because it is more exciting," said Garland.

"But I—" She stopped because she gasped.

"Was I right?"

"Yes, yes, but I can't wait any longer, I can't—"

Irma reached for Garland so that Lorna, behind the dark window, could see the girl's naked arms. For a moment both arms disappeared below the rim of the back rest and there was the sound of Irma breathing hoarsely.

Lorna stood in the dark and felt the sweat itch on her skin.

"No," the butler was saying. "Not yet."

"Please—"

"Stand up."

"Now?"

"Come on, stand up."

Irma arose quite slowly. Lorna saw the girl's face in profile, then her bare shoulders. Finally, Irma stood up in front of the couch and Lorna saw that the maid was completely unclad. Her belly trembled, and then she moved her hands up to hold her breasts. She clutched at them hard.

"Touch me," she said, "touch me."

Garland touched her. He stood in front of her and touched her somewhere. But Lorna could not see what he did. She only heard again: now Irma made a gasp and a long sound—and suddenly her bare arms circled Garland's back, clutching him.

Is this it? But they are standing—and he is still dressed—and I can't see— I don't know if I want to see...

Then Lorna stepped away from the window and without thought or planning she ran around the small house in order to reach the opposite window. Once she snagged her foot in a vine and she fell. She bruised her hand, felt pain, felt excitement, and scrambled up again, not caring if she had made a sound. She started licking her lips, which were very dry, and she tasted the salt where the sweat stood on her skin. Then she could not go any farther. Between the garden wall and the back of the house was only a narrow space, but it was blocked by a great stack of cordwood.

"They'll finish—and I'll know nothing, like before—too late—run—

She did run. She ran back and around the house in the opposite direction. She did not dare glance in at the first window where she had been standing for fear she might see nothing, for fear she might see them sitting there, all finished …

When she reached the second window from the other side she would have been hard put to tell if her breathing were fast and heavy because she had been running or because she was excited. She was so stirred up now that at first she saw nothing from her new post, or perhaps she saw but it did not register. In a moment, though, matters were clear.

Irma was on the rug. She lay on her back, arching now and then, covering her face with one arm. Was she biting into her arm, Lorna wondered. Irma's sounds were muffled. Garland was next to her. He was chewing at his lip and his eyes were closed. He lay raised on one arm.

His free hand ran up the side of the girl, down again, making the girl squirm.

Lorna shivered—and suddenly she was frightened. Because she saw Garland, then, pounce.

Lorna ducked. She folded at the knees and sank down and bit into her fist, cowering there. The sounds from the girl in the summer house reached like a long-fingered hand deep into Lorna and stirred and stirred ....

She had to peer in once more. What she saw this time was the man's wide back, a pebbly sheen of moisture on the skin, and the girl's hands on his back. Sex like a red wind rushed through Lorna.

But she stood still and did nothing because she was alone.

CHAPTER EIGHT

Garland sat on the couch, slipped his feet into his shoes and buttoned the cuffs of his shirt. Then he took a cigarillo and smoked while watching Irma. She was not finished dressing because she had kept lying on the rug, afterwards, relaxed and recovering. Garland had been faster. He sat on the couch now, very still and controlled, because he had left the girl without finishing. He avoided looking at the dark windows but he felt it would soon be worthwhile that he had not tired himself on Irma. But she was not bad. She was really not bad, loving the act the way she did.

"Can't you dress a little faster?"

"I'm so tired, Roger," she said.

"You can call me Garland again, hm?"

"Yes, Mr. Garland."

He saw the girl's face change, not relaxed now but held in, as when speaking to an employer. She feels like a prostitute now, thought Garland. I needn't have done that to her.

"Only for practice," he said to her. "So we don't make a mistake in the daytime, you know?"

Her face relaxed and she smiled at him.

"I know," she said. "You're not a mean man." Then she finished dressing.

I'm worse, thought Garland. I've used her without any meanness at all, but with indifference. He didn't like the thought, so he shrugged and dropped it.

"Go to bed now," he said, getting up. "And forget about the extra half-hour in the morning. Won't be necessary, I'm sure."

"Thank you, Mr. Garland." She hesitated a moment, smoothing her dress down. "Aren't you coming, too?"

"I'm going to sit a while. Good night, Irma."

"Good night." She stopped at the door. "You want me—I mean, tomorrow night, do you want to see me?"

"Not tomorrow," he said.

"Oh? Well, good night."

"Sleep well, Irma."

She left and thought how nice it would be if she could sleep with him all night and he holding her and that's how they would wake up. But she was too tired to think about it for long and was asleep a few minutes after she had lain down in her bed.

There was no question of sleep for Garland. His wakefulness was close to irritation. And it was a mistake, perhaps, he thought to himself, to have handled it this way—I'm apt to rush the Hornaday girl, apt just to drive at her. He stopped the thought, feeling a most uncommon greed.

He was sure she had watched. He thought he had heard her at one point although that was not the reason why he was sure. He simply knew because he knew Lorna and her mind by now, and because of the intimacy they had already established. He had not bothered to think what might happen once a real touch and sexual intimacy was added to their rapport.

He was also sure she would enter the house last, the best way for her to avoid running into him or Irma. Lorna would watch from the dark, watch Irma and Garland walk away, watch the windows light up and go dark— or, Lorna might now come into the summer house ...

He waited long enough to be sure that Lorna was not going to appear. Her feet must be damp, he thought, standing out there in the dark. Not to speak of what this wait is doing to me. I'll relieve both of us. He arose, blew out the candle and left, crossing the garden without looking back.

Lorna stood in the dark and watched the butler disappear. If he had left sooner, she argued with herself, then it would have been easy for me to stop him to call him—and not from courage, but from simple, open excitement. I wouldn't have cared about anything, but now I've lost out again. I've waited too long and lost out, and I'll probably never again, probably never— She did not want to finish the thought because she did not like where it would lead. She shut her mind, clamped down on it, the same way she clamped her teeth together now and her lips. Then she crossed the damp lawn to the house.

She could feel herself move inside her clothes, the soft rubbing, the skirt on her thighs stroking her. And she tightened her mouth again. I could have gone to him, I might not have lost out ... Something like anger grew in her, balled up, stiffened her body.

Inside the house she turned off on the second landing. The thought of her room stiffened her even more. She could therefore hardly move when the shock came. Garland stood there. Without a word, he put his hand on her arm and turned her back to the stairs.

He has combed his hair since, she thought inconsequentially. And I hope he says nothing. I hope there is no need for talk anymore. I hope, I hope ...

They made for his room in silence, both knowing the same thing, and there was therefore no need for talk. He kept his hand on her bare arm and felt her skin, firmer than the other's, he thought, firm like an apple, everywhere, which I will soon know, and he felt the heat grow in him, much too soon, he thought, much too soon.

Lorna felt something reach her from the man next to her, something that melted away her stiffness little by little. And there was the same red wind she had felt passing through her at the window before.

He closed the door and did not turn on the light. What do I say now, she wondered, what—

But there was no talk. He stopped her with his hand, turned her by the arms, and then she felt his hands on the front of her dress, where the buttons ran down. She felt the hands tremble and suddenly loved him for it, wanted him for it. His breath on her face, she thought, was the color red.

Then she was nude and stood there in the dark and heard the sound of his clothes. I must touch him—I can't see and must know everything by touch now ...

"Now," he said, and one hand ran up her back and the other held her side. "Now you will really know."

She started to tremble when he pushed her down. She felt her breath fly in and out of her, beyond control.

"I saw you," she said, "I saw you. How you waited, and everything. Please don't wait now."

To her surprise, Sheila Hornaday found her daughter at the breakfast table before her. The girl was downing an enormous portion of scrambled eggs and chicken livers. She seemed bright-eyed and alert but, curiously, also tired.

As Mrs. Hornaday sat down, Garland appeared. He also seemed tired. It must be the heat, she explained to herself, this early-morning heat. She herself felt uncomfortably restless.

"Good morning, Lorna, Garland. I'll have my usual, Garland," she said. "Did you sleep well?"

"I had a very good night, ma'am. Thank you for inquiring."

"Then it must be the heat, everyone looking so tired."

"Yes, it must be the heat." Garland returned to the pantry.

"And you, dear, do you have any plans for the day?"

"Yes, I'm going to rest," said Lorna.

"What on earth from, dear? You never do anything."

Lorna finished her mouthful and then she corrected her mother.

"It's not what I'm resting from, but what I'm resting for."

"How clever you can be." Mrs. Hornaday smiled.

Then Garland brought in her breakfast and she now paid attention to him.

"Do you think, Garland, you have time to drive me this morning?"

"Yes, ma'am. I can postpone a number of things I have to do till the afternoon. I'll leave instructions with Irma and then I will be free."

"You and that Irma, Garland. I meant to tell you that you certainly have a way with her."

"I beg your pardon?"

Lorna's head was averted over her plate and she did not see Garland's face. But there had been a most untired alertness in his remark.

"Well," Mrs. Hornaday said, "after you spoke to her about tardiness, and so forth, she certainly recovered in the shortest possible time."

"Yes. She has that facility."

"I stopped in Lorna's bedroom before coming down just now and Irma had already made the bed. I must commend you on that, Garland. Please compliment Irma about it, too.”

"I most certainly will, ma'am."

Garland did not find a chance to note Lorna's reaction because she kept her head down, and he had only a few minutes to say something to her before attending to Mrs. Hornaday. However, when he descended from the third floor after having changed his jacket, Lorna was waiting for him at the second-floor landing.

"Garland," she said, making him stop close to the wall. "You mind if I keep calling you Garland?"

"Please don't stand so close. We can practically be seen from your mother's—"

"How long are you going to be with her?"

"She said about noon. Now as regards your oversight with that bed you didn't sleep in—"

"Garland, this noon—"

"Put your hands down, please," he whispered.

"Garland, you know what I want this noon? Garland, I never thought this could be so—so much."

The disturbing thing to the butler was the fact that the girl could arouse him at will. Her will, not his. He felt like a green adolescent sneaking a rendezvous on some deserted stairs, snatching at a moment, rushing a sensation—none of which was his way, or his wish. But Lorna had that effect on him. Like a flower suddenly burst open, she exuded an air of desire, a strong female desire for touching, for giving, for taking. It seemed, almost, that she had changed physically. There was a freshness to her skin, an electric thrust in her motions, and something like insolence in her female curves. Each aspect of her body called to him. Her every movement said, here, this is what I am, this is what I want.

"Garland, just touch me once," she said and took his hand, lifted it and pushed it against her breast.

"Lorna, you must—"

"Again."

"Lorna, you're going to ruin this for us. Now I want you—"

"The other one, this till later."

Garland worked his hand free from her grip and discovered to his consternation that his forehead was moist with a light sweat. Oh yes, and how, later, and how—but for the moment—

"There you are."

He could see Mrs. Hornaday step out of her room, and therefore she could see him. And Lorna.

"What are you doing, dear?"

"I am trying to rub this spot out of Garland's lapel and he won't let me."

A nice, a most adroit recovery, thought Garland, except that the girl's nipples show strong through her dress, the way she stands there, and Mrs. Hornaday stands there with a suddenly melting softness, and safe with age.

"Oh, never mind the spot," said Mrs. Hornaday and she turned back to her door. "Would you come inside for a moment, Garland?"

That finished, of course, the tableau on the stairs, for which Garland was fiercely grateful, but an entirely different emotion, also fierce, took hold of Lorna.

The emotion was unexpected to her but none the less real. Aside from her lust for Garland, she was unaccountably jealous of her mother.

The girl watched Garland go down the corridor and her desire for him gained edge from the competitive hate she felt toward her mother. As is not uncommon in cases of mixed emotions, Lorna simplified the whole thing by calling the experience a stab of love, made increasingly more intense by the fact that Garland did not emerge from her mother's room for about an hour.

When leaving the girl behind and going to Mrs. Hornaday the butler experienced an unmistakable sense of relief. Where the daughter had been aggressive, the mother relaxed Garland with her passivity. Where the daughter had been tense with emotion, the mother soothed Garland by being positively flaccid. Not that tension and the demands of a female were unbearable to Garland, but he was not used to being literally pushed against the wall at nine in the morning on an open staircase. Therefore the aspect of Mrs. Hornaday reclining wan and weak on her divan was a positive relief.

She had been dressed at the table but now she seemed largely undressed again. A diaphanous house robe and a posture of suffering gave her rather a dying-swan type of expression. She smiled bravely.

"Would you close the door, Garland?"

He closed the door and stood by it.

"I'm not able to leave just yet, Garland. I have such a ghastly tension headache all of a sudden."

"I'm sorry to hear it, ma'am."

"I wonder, could you suggest something to relieve such tension?"

He could think of something to relieve it but instead he said, "Perhaps if you simply breathe deeply, ma'am, perhaps ten times in a row—"

"I'll try it, Garland. Would you come here and see if I do it correctly?"

He stepped closer and Sheila Hornaday sat up. Ten times in succession she rather gave the effect of pumping herself up and then deflating again, though each time there did seem some slight gain in strength. She was, after all, not really a sickly woman but one who exercised on a horse daily.

She breathed in and out. Each time she inhaled she pressed her hands on her stomach and her rising bosom showed solid enough under the diaphanous stuff. She alternately opened and closed her eyes. Each time she opened them she gazed at the butler. A progressively stronger tint of vitality colored her skin.

"Is this—good—Garland?"

"It depends on how it feels, ma'am."

"How does—it—look?"

"It looks rather good, Mrs. Hornaday."

"Yes?"

"Well, it does feel much better now. You are quite marvelous, Garland." The butler inclined his head.

"But I'm not yet entirely relieved, Garland."

"Perhaps a brisk—"

"No, no. Not the horse, today."

"Yes," said Garland.

She reclined again, doing it rather prettily.

"There is this marvelous masseur at the club, Garland. I was wondering—"

"You would like me to fetch him for you?"

"He is a she, actually."

"Ah."

"No. I think I can get over this without her. It's pretty much confined to here now, the tension." She gestured vaguely.

He felt she was including everything between her feet and her head.

"If I were to lie on my stomach, Garland, do you think you could lightly rub my back for a moment?"

"Certainly, ma'am."

He felt unmistakably now that he was not so much dealing with an employer as with a woman. But the humor of the situation kept him relaxed.

"You have done massage before, Garland?"

"Yes, ma'am."

"On whom?" She was turning on the divan now, to lie on her stomach.

"During my last employment."

"Oh. You mean old Mr. Chesterton Manning?"

"Yes. He was bedridden and towards the end enjoyed an occasional rub."

"It can be enjoyable." She finished turning and settled down prone. "An occasional rub. Now, Garland, let me show you."

He stepped up and looked down at her. The way she had herself belted gave rather a charming emphasis to her small waist and the once-famous hips.

"The tension is mostly here, Garland." She gestured definitely at the muscles of her shoulders. "And here." She precisely indicated her lower spine.

"Where would you like me to—"

"Here," she said, indicating the shoulders, "first."

Massage, with an accurate though completely gentle touch, came naturally to Garland. He discovered immediately that Sheila Hornaday was wearing nothing under the robe. He did find the muscles in question rather tense, but the feel of her in general was mostly soft. Not Irma's softness, which was rather like baby fat, but a softness of body that comes with experience. If given a chance, thought Garland, Mrs. Hornaday might relax totally and quite at will.

He kneaded away with a motion somewhat like munching. His thoughts munched too.

If she did not have a daughter named Lorna, if there were not the spring-time excitement of a young one like Lorna now, yes, he thought, this one would be an entertainment. And most likely appreciative of entertainment. But now, let there be merely massage. Perhaps all she wants is massage.

"Garland?"

"Yes, ma'am."

"Since your arrival you seem to have taken rather an interest in my daughter."

The massage slowed. The munching motions turned into something like a gag in his throat.

"I find the way in which you take," she continued, "an almost personal interest in the members of this household very commendable. Beyond the call of duty, so to speak?" Mrs. Hornaday said with a pretty laugh.

"I am not uninterested, or else I could not perform adequate service, ma'am."

"Well, I'm grateful. We are all grateful, Garland. The way you took care of Lorna that night she came home late, apparently, is the sort of thing one expects from only the best of servants."

"You are not relaxing, Mrs. Hornaday."

"Oh, you felt that, didn't you, Garland?"

"Yes, ma'am."

"You are most sensitive. And your part in that unfortunate affair on Sunday morning, the way you helped soothe my husband—"

"Could you untense a little more, ma'am?"

"—and took care of Lorna again at that time, I just want you to know I appreciate such personal interest, Garland."

"Thank you, ma'am. You are kind."

"Oh, no. But I'm grateful."

She was relaxing beautifully now. Garland could feel it with his hands.

"And now," she said, "if you'll just move down a little."

She showed him with her hand where she experienced the remaining tension and Garland moved down there.

"Yes—ah, yes," she said. "You do it so gently. I will tell my husband how competent you really are, Garland. It might relax him a little, too."

"I hardly think—"

"Did you know he suffers from nagging backaches?"

"I am really not that qualified, Mrs. Hornaday."

"Do that again."

"I beg your pardon?"

"Very good," she mumbled into the crook of her arm but did not explain any further. "About Lorna now," she resumed. "You being a man of the world, Garland ..." Out of both prudence and puzzlement, Garland said nothing, and she continued. "A girl of her age, you know, is apt to present a problem to her parents. What I mean to ask—you met her young man, of course?"

"This Ned?"

"Yes. What do you think of him?"

"I have hardly thought of him, ma'am."

"I hope neither has Lorna. Do you think she has, since that unfortunate affair?"

He felt certain she used the term affair in its general sense.

"I don't think she has concerned herself any more with that affair, Mrs. Hornaday."

"I'm very glad to hear you say so, Garland. I have always thought that servants often know so much more than they care to reveal, and I'm most grateful. I find it so helpful when you share your knowledge with me."

"I can only share my opinion with you, Mrs. Hornaday, that your daughter seems well in hand, so to speak."

"Good. You might move a little lower, Garland."

"Yes, ma'am."

Her hips, he noticed, were softly padded. Now and then they gave a soft little nudge of a motion, but neither he nor the woman seemed to pay too much attention to that. Mrs. Hornaday's attention, in fact, appeared solidly riveted on something else. She pursued the subject.

"As a man of the world, Garland, would you say my daughter would gain by associating with someone older than this Ned person?"

"If older in experience, yes, ma'am."

"I meant that, yes, Garland."

"Yes, Mrs. Hornaday."

"You can stop now, Garland."

"What?" he said, feeling distracted by the weave of their many-leveled conversation.

"I'm wonderfully relaxed now and I think I'll just rest a while, on my back."

The butler stepped back immediately. He watched her turn over on her back, recline in the standard pose of a female on her private divan, and close her eyes.

"She is such a pretty little thing," Mrs. Hornaday said as if musing, "and almost ready to step out into the world, so to speak. I'm very anxious for her to take the right steps."

"Naturally, ma'am."

"The way you took a hand with Irma, maybe you can do something of the same sort with Lorna, Garland."

He merely cleared his throat.

"I mean, you seem so effective, Garland, that it would be foolish not to avail myself of your aid."

The advantage in this conversation, he realized, lay entirely with Sheila Hornaday. Where he suffered from certain complexities of the talk, she did not. Where he was uncertain of meanings, she was sure. And, most surprisingly, she had not displayed once the sort of vapidity she affected most of the time.

Perhaps, he thought, this has to do with the fact that she suddenly knows what she wants.

When she dismissed him from her room she was most definitely certain of what she wanted.

The truth about Sheila Hornaday, the once-celebrated Love Apple Lindy, was that under the studied mannerisms and the layers of faking, she was as direct and simple as Irma, and as eager as Lorna. And in spite of the deceptions that accompanied her station in life, she was most certainly not a prude. Or else she could not have made it as Love Apple Lindy, and from there—over a rocky road strewn with many beds—as Mrs. Matthew Hornaday. She was as insensitive about her daughter's violation of mores as she had always been about her own. That is, as long as appearances were satisfied. This was, also, not prudery but calculation. The reason Sheila Hornaday had fixed on Garland was only partly because she felt he might be very good in bed. He was in addition a man of uncompromising decorum and at least as interested in preserving appearances as she had to be. She lied to herself about many things, all unpleasant. She never lied to herself about the pleasant things. She had married Matt Hornaday in the full knowledge that he was both rich and stupid. She had also learned that a servant is the best lover because he is both dependent and sly.

Of course, she thought, Garland had slept with the maid. The placid aura of satisfaction in the girl had been unmistakable. And, as far as the former Love Apple Lindy was concerned, the Irma arrangement was a very good sign of the man's capabilities. That he had seduced Lorna—or she, being her mother's daughter, had seduced him—was also probable.

And that, the thought ran in Mrs. Hornaday's mind, could become a most happy advantage ...

CHAPTER NINE

Garland, while sharpened by necessity, was given no inkling of the crisis to come.

Matthew Hornaday, for example, had ceased all hostility and largely ignored Garland. This was in part due, as the butler surmised, to the soothing influence of Sheila Hornaday. But there was also another reason for Hornaday's new mood that Garland knew nothing about.

And Mrs. Hornaday, for another example, refrained from making any further and extra demands on her butler, giving him approximately two weeks of tranquility.

And Irma made no demands. But not trusting such selflessness, Garland spaced three visits strategically, the kind of visits that allowed the girl to call him Roger. One was a fifteen-minute affair at six in the morning that left the girl limp for much of the forenoon because she was not allowed any rest afterwards but was sent down at once to start on the day's chores.

Another time he had her simply on the rumpus-room table. She seemed impatient because of a four-day delay, and Garland became impatient of ceremony and simply took her in the afternoon, clothes and all.

The third time was the one that Irma liked best. Garland came to her at eleven at night, slipped into bed with no lengthy tricks and stratagems to drive her frantic and then, best of all, let her sleep on his arm the rest of the night.

That was the night Lorna stayed over at friends'. For the rest, she seemed to be there all the time, starting right after Garland emerged from Mrs. Hornaday's room following the massaging session.

He was wondering, then, as a matter of fact, who, in that instance, had been given the massage. He had not time to think this thing through because, as he set foot on the first floor, Lorna was standing in the kitchen passage. She wore a terry-cloth bathrobe and her hair was gathered up to make a short ponytail. She seemed altogether gathered up in a rather ominous mood that showed in the way she had her arms crossed, and the way she said nothing at first. A silence, that made Garland think of marriage.

"You look tired, Garland," she said when he was close.

"We know why," he said and smiled at her briefly.

But she did not let his smile affect her.

"I mean," she said, "more tired now than when you disappeared into my mother's room."

"That's simply because it's later. No other reason."

"Oh?"

"Well," he said, trying for lightness, "you don't seem tired. You look well, Lorna, and wide awake."

"I am wide awake. I am wide awake to the fact that you treated me like a—like a child or something."

"Dear Lorna," said Garland, and his murmur was full of appeal. "Hardly as a child. You know that."

She liked hearing that. She did not right away want to show him how much she liked it, but his manner and his words had dissolved the anger in her. Her arms were still folded but now the posture was more like a hug. She squeezed herself a little.

"I guess you're not driving her to the club?" Lorna said.

"No."

"Why not? Is she lying down?"

"She had a headache, to begin with, and we discussed domestic matters, to end up with. Your mother is now writing letters."

But Lorna was not really interested in the explanations. She was, in a most single-minded way, interested only in Garland. And she felt the greed of the hungry and the honesty of the fully awake.

"Garland—"

"Yes, Lorna."

"Please tell me this can happen again."

"Yes, Lorna, it can. It's your wanting that makes it so."

He had sounded a little bit too paternal and that brought the anxious edge back into her voice.

"You said you're not driving Mother?"

"That's right."

"Then drive me, please."

"We're talking too much on stairways and in dark passages, Lorna. You must learn—"

"I have. With all due regard to decorum," she said, "we are neither going to talk too much nor are we going to do it in the house." A short silence and then she clutched his arm impulsively. "It. I don't mean it. I mean you, Garland. I want to know that last night was true."

He liked her demand because it was made so frankly.

He very briefly put his hand over hers and smiled. "I made an honest woman out of you, eh, Lorna?"

"Both. Woman and honest."

The intimacy was back between them and they did not talk anymore in the dark passage. He headed for the kitchen and gave instructions to the cook and the maid. He would be gone for a few hours, to drive Miss Lorna. Then Lorna called from the breakfast room that she was ready and then walked into the kitchen. Her bathrobe hung open, showing much body skin and just a little bit of bathing suit.

"I'm going swimming," she said unnecessarily.

Then Garland drove her to the club.

Parked at the entrance, Garland watched the girl mount the steps, swinging a polka-dot canvas bag. A few minutes later Garland walked away, too.

With simple precision Lorna had explained to him where to walk, where to meet her. It took him twenty minutes to make an appearance in the club cafeteria, drink coffee, leave and circle the club property till he reached a lane by a meadow. The lane followed a rise and meandered into the woods on the other side of the golf links. Where a brook ran through the culvert, he turned off the land and angled into the underbrush. Another five minutes and he was at the sun-hot clearing the girl had described to him. Lorna was already there.

This time they were slow. She wanted to lie with him in the sun but he pointed out to her that it would never do for him to return to the house with even a hint of a tan on face or back. He spread her robe under a tree and made her lie down. During the first fifteen minutes he took off the bra of her bathing suit and during the next fifteen minutes the pants.

The heat lay on them like a heavy sleep and they took so much time that they could pay attention to all the cricket sounds. For the fulfillment of a ripe, sensuous mood, all this and the girl were enough for Garland. But Lorna found a thrill in something else. From where they were she could see—down the drop of the rise—the country club in the distance. She stretched, slow and naked, while Garland slowly worked slippery sun-tan lotion into her skin. She felt like purring with each stroke. And every so often she gazed at the distant pool down below, at the tiny people whom she could see but who could not see her, saw the groups making chit-chat and carrying on mannered flirtations, while she, naked, turned herself under Garland's hands.

Then she could not simply lie there and contemplate. She closed her eyes and made little sounds. For a moment this reminded her of Irma and how the girl's moaning had excited her, and then Lorna did not think of anything anymore. She simply felt, and her want grew like a storm. When the man took her, she felt for the first time that she really sequestered him and that he was not simply using her ephemerally. This was another newness for her. And when she collapsed from a great height of desire rearing in her and fell into the finished blackness like a sleep, she felt, without any concern, that she might never desire again.

Half an hour later they made love once more.

Without question, Garland was a very good lover.

But now Lorna was too.

There was no problem, of course, in having Garland around. He was the butler. The problem was in being with him. He had his work to do and he had his rules about conduct.

"For example," he said, "You don't look at me that way when I'm serving dinner."

"Like what?" Lorna said.

"As if you were about to eat me instead of the dinner."

"I was. I was thinking it would be another three hours before you were done and I didn't want to have to wait three hours before I could have you."

"You have me, as you put it, almost every night."

"But sometimes I want you right then and there and as often as not it's daytime."

"Don't be childish, Lorna."

The following day Garland was seated at his small desk that stood at one end of the pantry. He was going over bills and readying the checks for signing when Lorna appeared.

"Look," she said. "I've been lying in the sun for hours."

And she showed him. She opened her terry-cloth robe for him and let him see the fine bronze color of her naked body.

"Close that up immediately," said Garland. "The maid is right behind that swinging door in the kitchen. And your mother—"

"Is out. And I've seen Irma naked, you recall, and if she'd like to watch me this time, it's all right with me."

She let the robe fall around her again but did not tie it in front. She stepped close to Garland's chair and leaned her bare stomach against his arm. He could smell the warm sun odor of her skin.

"Come to think of it," she said in a low voice, "I just got very excited thinking about Irma watching me. You think that's bad?"

"It's extremely bad timing. Now will you please—"

"No. Touch me."

"No."

But they had their addiction. They both knew this about each other. Lorna did not leave and Garland did not send her away. She did not press him for the moment and he pretended to concentrate on the checks again. But that was not easy. To feel her stand there, just inches away, and not to touch her, was exquisite in itself. Perhaps Lorna was aware of this as she stood idly near his chair while the feeling built in Garland.

"Just touch me once," she said. "Any place."

He touched her hip, tracing it with his finger. He wanted to tell her then to cover up and go, but he did not. Instead he moved his palm on her so that her skin felt like warm silk.

"Go upstairs," he said. "I'll follow in a few moments."

"No."

Her refusal excited him with such a suddenness that it showed in his face. And she was pleased.

"No," she said again. "I don't want to go upstairs. I want it here. On the desk."

"You're out of your mind." He rose abruptly and pushed his chair back.

"And you, too," she said and leaned against him. "I won't make a sound," she whispered.

She leaned back on her arms and closed her eyes. Garland could see a pulse beat in her neck.

At one point, toward the end, Garland thought she was going to fall down from sheer exhaustion. But then she took a deep breath, smiled at him and slid off the desk. She tied her robe and walked into the kitchen. Later he could hear Lorna and Irma talking there, giggling occasionally.

This incident convinced Garland to take particular pains not to be drawn into anything similar again. Matters were going too well for him to jeopardize his intricate pleasures.

But on the other hand Lorna discovered one boring afternoon that she was faintly dissatisfied. While puzzling about this in the deck chair on the back lawn she fell asleep.

When she awoke she felt hot and irritable and twice as bored as before. She stepped into the house and stopped first in the kitchen. Only Irma was there.

"Where's Garland?" Lorna asked the maid.

"It's his hour off, miss."

"I asked where he is."

"I don't know. He went out."

"And you?" Lorna scrutinized the girl up and down, noticing for the first time that Irma was not wearing her uniform.

"I'm just going out, too. I got the afternoon off."

"You have the afternoon off, too, huh? With Garland?"

"Why, no, Miss Lorna."

Lorna ran a glass of water from the tap and watched Irma, who was eating a sandwich.

"What do you do on your day off?" Lorna asked her.

"I got a date."

"In the afternoon?"

"Sure. And then the evening, too."

"How come you're eating before you go out?"

"He doesn't have very much money. We don't go to dinner or anything like that."

"Some fun," said Lorna, feeling ill-tempered.

"Oh, it is. We go swimming and then later the show— I'm paying for the show this time—and then, you know, spend the evening together."

"Yeah, I know," said Lorna and left the kitchen.

She was hoping that the date Irma had was really with Garland. That would give Lorna something to blame the butler for. It would be worth a distracting scene—not really, she thought, not with the maid. Irma had a date, Irma was going out, Irma wasn't sitting around full of boredom, Lorna thought sullenly.

She took a shower, dressed, but felt only slightly better. Downstairs she saw Garland approach out of the kitchen passage. They simply nodded at each other.

"You had a call while you were upstairs," Garland said.

"Who?"

"This young person called Ned."

"To hell with him," she said.

At that moment her mother came downstairs. Sheila Hornaday was not wearing a riding habit but something fluffy and flowered that spelled garden party.

"Lorna, dear?"

Lorna stopped in the hall and waited for her mother. The girl had nowhere to go, anyway.

"Dear, you had a telephone call while you—"

"Garland already told me."

"Oh. Are you still seeing Ned?"

"What do you think?"

"Well, I don't know what to think. Are you seeing anyone at all these days?"

"I know only bores," said Lorna and in a sense she meant it.

The fun and games of the crowd she had gone with had lost their flavor since the advent of Garland and the incident in the Sherman cabin. She had something better now, didn't she? Lorna thought. Then why was she so angry?

"Garland is driving me to the Carters', Lorna. Why don't you come along?"

"And drink tea?"

"What else? You're too young for whiskey."

"No, thank you. They're too old for me."

"Well, we could drop you in town, if you have any errands."

The girl had no errands but she let herself be dropped off in town. She watched the car drive off, she watched shoppers walking and then she watched herself in a big plate-glass window. But that did not really interest her. She knew how she appeared and she had no quarrel on that score. In back of her a car pulled up to the curb.

"Lorna—"

She knew who it was before turning and did not quite know how to handle this. Then she faced him and said, "Hi, Ned," but she kept her expression indifferent because that was how she felt. But one wrong word out of him, she thought, and the whole mess might come alive again.

Across the street Irma walked by. She was swinging a big polka-dot bag from one hand and holding a young man's arm with the other. They were both laughing and Irma seemed very happy.

"Lorna?" said Ned as he walked over to her.

"Yes?"

"I've tried to call you a few times. I've wanted—"

"I know."

"Oh. How have you been, Lorna?"

"Quite good, thank you."

"Are you still, I mean—"

"I've recovered, thank you. If that's what you meant."

"Yes. Sort of."

Lorna watched Irma stop by the refreshment stand in the square where she bought a bag of peanuts.

"Lorna, I don't want to bother you. If you'd rather I leave—"

"No. That's all right."

Irma and the young man had sat down by the lawn in the square and were throwing peanuts to the pigeons. Now and then they had a peanut themselves.

"Would you like to buy me an ice-cream cone, Ned? I forgot my money."

"Would I like—why, sure, Lorna."

They sat in a booth in the drugstore and Lorna could see Irma through the window. Then Lorna contemplated Ned. She felt good to be able to look at him and to feel no more dislike, but no particular liking, either.

"Been lying around at the pool a lot?" said Lorna.

"No. I got a summer job."

"Oh? Doing what?"

Then he looked up, his expression fairly serious. Or at any rate, thought Lorna, he doesn't look so silly anymore.

"Never mind the job. Not important," he said. "Reason I've tried to reach you was for only one thing."

"Like what, for instance."

He ignored her hostility. He dripped ice cream on his hand but that did not distract him, either. He simply wiped his hand.

"Just to tell you, Lorna, I've never been so sorry about anything in my life— about that lousy deal up at the cabin. That's really all. I wanted you to know that."

"Thank you," she said.

"And so help me," he said down at the table, "it feels—I don't know. Like it changed me."

He did seem changed. He did not talk when he had nothing to say nor did he grin when he felt awkward.

"It's changed me, too," said Lorna. And if he knew how, she thought, that would be very funny.

"I can tell," said Ned.

He smiled at her for the first time but did not tell her how he thought she had changed. Lorna stared past him, beyond the window. Irma and her date were clambering up from the grass. They brushed each other off and then ambled away as if they had no place special to go but that that did not matter.

"Have you been around much lately?" asked Lorna.

"No. I've been working, mostly. You been out much?"

"Not at all, actually. Much too lazy, for one reason or other."

"It seems to become you," he said and then he worried lest she take the remark as an advance.

"How?" she wanted to know.

"Well, I don't know. Sort of content, maybe."

"Contented cow, eh?"

And speaking of cow, Lorna thought, here comes Irma.

The maid and her date stepped into the drugstore and had one coke between them at the counter. To her surprise, Lorna suddenly found herself wave at the girl and call her name.

"Why, Miss Lorna," said Irma and came to the booth.

"Hello, Irma. Are you still going to the movie?"

First Irma said, "Hello, Ned," and then she said, "Yes, right after the coke. You going, too?"

There was just the briefest pause and then Lorna said yes.

"Like a double date, huh?" said Irma.

"We don't have a date," Ned told her. "But I'd be glad to take you," he said as he turned to Lorna.

Irma introduced her date, whose name was John. Then Lorna and Ned slid out of their seats. As they walked across the square Lorna thought that she was not so much going because of Ned but more because of Irma. There was an intimacy between her and the girl—one-sided though it probably was—but based on the fact that they had both had Garland. And, by a strange quirk of fantasy, for Lorna to sit now in the dark movie next to the maid was a lot like having Garland along. That was a strange image for Lorna to have because she could think of Garland in two roles only, serving table, or in bed with her.

Ned, all this while, did not intrude at all. He had not touched her, he said very little to her. He was either tired, or constrained, or he was embarrassed by her company.

"Ned," she whispered.

"Yes, Lorna."

"What's this work you're doing?"

"Just a summer job."

On the screen a man, with a mountain for a background, was taming a horse.

"Doing what?"

"I work at the creamery. Washing the cans out in the yard."

"Oh," she said.

On the screen a woman, with a bed for a background, was trying to find her other stocking.

"And nights I mostly work at home," Ned was saying.

"What?"

"Math. I'm taking a summer course. I must brush up on my math."

"You do?"

On the screen a horse, with a hay bin for background, was chewing through a rope.

"I got that scholarship I once mentioned, you remember? The football thing. So I'm going to State to study engineering. But I got to catch up on math."

"Oh." On the screen the rope was chewed through. A great cascade of hay landed on the horse. He bolted. "Congratulations," continued Lorna who had not seen a thing that was happening on the screen.

"Thank you."

On the screen in rapid succession the woman found her stocking, the man caught the horse, the barn was on fire.

"I mean I'm really glad for you," said Lorna. "I mean it."

"Thank you, Lorna."

"What happened?"

"The horse set the barn on fire."

"Really?"

But it is strange, she thought, that none of this feels silly to me, or awkward with Irma here, or tense with Ned. Perhaps I've changed, too.

When the two couples left the theater, night had fallen and the air felt warm.

"Ned can give you a lift back, if you like," said Lorna to the maid.

"No. Go on ahead. I'm going with John first," said Irma, and she took her date's arm.

I'm sure, thought Lorna, that John isn't as good as Garland, but Irma seems happy with him.

Lorna watched the couple walk away and then accompanied Ned to his car. The ride was short. Ned drove while Lorna made small talk. Such as that the movie was nice, what she saw of it, and that she hoped Ned wouldn't have to study his math yet tonight. Then Ned pulled up in front of the Hornaday house and opened the car door for her.

At the front door he watched her put the key in the lock.

"Ned?"

"Yes?"

"That trick I pulled on you that morning, I wish you could forget that, too. I'm sorry about it."

"I had it coming. We'll forget it."

"Thanks."

"Good night, Lorna."

"Good night."

He drove away when she stepped inside the house.

He had not touched her once but he had said one or two nice things to her, she thought. Perhaps he had been afraid to touch her, but then it might simply have been the new way between them.

In her room she undressed in the dark. Wearing her robe, she mounted the stairs.

Garland was awake in bed and moved over for her. "Had a good evening, Lorna?"

"Pretty fair."

"I've been waiting for you. Full of mad fantasies."

"You don't need them. I'm here."

"Are you tired, after your evening out?"

"Not at all," she said and stretched. "But stop talking so much."

"I just wondered—"

"Just make love to me. Slow and long."

The butler made love to her, slow and long, but sporadically he had the feeling that some of the time Lorna seemed to be lying there thinking of other things. She enjoyed the love-making but she seemed to enjoy the thinking, too.

CHAPTER TEN

A true animal, living alone, can now and then be seen to lift up its head and sniff the air. Its nose points this way, then that, off and on. Garland, while most of his instincts were intact, was not quite so much of the true animal. Since events ran smoothly, as if with compliance with his will, he felt no need to sniff the air for strange odors. There was even a bonus event at this time, something to remove further friction. Matthew Hornaday made the announcement at dinner.

"Lorna girl," he said, "take advantage. You've been pestering me to go shopping in New York."

"What advantage?" said Lorna.

"Take advantage of my generous mood. Ask me about going to New York."

"Can I?"

"Yes, you may."

She turned suddenly into a very happy child, Garland noted.

"When can I go and how much can I spend?" she said.

"I'm going on the nine-ten and you can come with me."

"You mean you're going to go shopping with me?"

"No," said Hornaday, chewing roast beef. "Maybe your mother wants to go with you."

Mrs. Hornaday reflected a while before she answered.

"And come back when, Matthew?"

"There's the seven-twenty out of Grand Central."

"Making that train cuts right into the late shopping," said Lorna.

"Next train doesn't go until ten thirty-one," Hornaday said. "To get you in here by midnight."

"That's awfully late," said Mrs. Hornaday. "Perhaps," she said to Lorna, "you'd like to stay over with Harriet's parents."

This time Lorna pondered a moment. Then she said, "I'd rather come back the same night and sleep here. I don't care if it's at midnight."

Garland, discreet as ever, left the room at that point.

Mrs. Hornaday with a kind of hot mist fuming inside of her, had a most penetrating thought, why, that girl is positively addicted to the man. Then she thought of something else much more subterranean.

So it seemed that Lorna would have her cake and eat it, too, both the day in New York, which was not frequent or usual, and the night with Garland, which did seem frequent and usual. And who knows, Mrs. Hornaday pursued the train of thought, who knows about the daytime, or the forenoon, or the afternoon.

She was vastly overestimating Garland's inclination and ability, but her preoccupation had surpassed reason.

"And will you come back at midnight too?" she asked her husband.

"No. Garland?"

Garland stepped in to appraise the moods of the two females and the man and, incidentally to take Hornaday's order.

"Some more of that juicy part in the middle. Is there more of it?"

"Yes, sir. Of course."

"Don't of course me, Garland." The edge was there, although too sharp a one since Hornaday felt expansive that evening. "That juicy part in the middle never lasts, eh? That's life, I always say, just like life."

"I beg your pardon?"

"I'm just generalizing about life. You have to grab it when you can and wherever you find it. That's my motto."

The butler felt slightly worried by so much expansiveness in the man. And perhaps, like a true animal living alone, it was at this moment that Garland raised his head, so to speak, and tested the air. But smelled nothing he could identify.

"That's my motto, as I was saying, thank you, Garland, and some more beer. What's your motto?"

The butler poured beer.

"I have nothing which could really be called a philosophy of life, sir."

"That so? Not so much of a head on it, please. Then how do you go through life without a head on? How do you go through life without a motto? Just drift and blunder? It doesn't sound like you."

"In Garland's station," Mrs. Hornaday suggested, "mottoes may not be needed. Might that be true, Garland? Simply go along with the rules you find—that sort of thing?"

"Perhaps it might be put that way."

"What a life," said Hornaday to his roast beef. "Well, maybe that works for the man who has his whole twenty-four hours regulated for him. Guess that's you."

"Yes," said Garland. "I am most content when my twenty-four hours are predictably regulated."

"Sounds like a bore, Garland. No excitement, no challenge of the unexpected to put a tingle in your spine."

"Is it a bore, Garland?" Mrs. Hornaday wanted to know.

"I don't think Garland is leading a boring life at all," said Lorna with noteworthy sureness. "Isn't that right, Garland?"

"You are quite right, Miss Lorna."

"But no tingle in the spine," Hornaday said again.

"I can think of better tingles than spine tingles," said Lorna.

There was general silence after that, except from Hornaday. He waited just long enough to finish his beer. Then he burped.

"You don't know what a good tingle is, young one," he said to his daughter. "Wait till you grab a hold of life. And start living. Well, there's time for that. What's for dessert?"

Dessert was something like a custard with chocolate marbling running through the gook and the banker attacked this concoction as if it were life in the raw, and he had three helpings.

"Dear?" said Mrs. Hornaday when her husband slowed down. And then, "If you're not coming back with Lorna by midnight, will you take the seven something or other?"

"Oh. That. No, I'm not coming back. Business trip came up and I'm taking the plane out of New York for Miami."

"Miami?"

"Be gone just a few days. Business, you know."

"Oh? Can you say what business?"

"Well, I don't want to discuss it in front of servants."

Garland withdrew immediately but listened with keen suspicion for the rest.

"I'll just say it's to clean up a mess, you know," Matthew Hornaday finished.

"No, I don't know," said Mrs. Hornaday. "Are you a banker or a garbage collector, dear?"

The banker, because of his mood, took no offense but laughed very hard.

"Neither," he said. "Has to do with a life-policy type of thing and I'm going down for consultation."

That was double talk, thought Garland, if I ever heard any. But at the next comment he relaxed.

"Financier is involved," Hornaday said. "Has to do with a radical business reorganization. That's all. Nothing for you to worry about."

"I wasn't worried, really," said Mrs. Hornaday. "I just wondered when to expect you back."

"Anxious, huh?" He laughed again.

Sheila Hornaday thought his expansiveness was really becoming disgusting. And by such signs, she could always tell at the dinner table what her husband would then want at night. Anyway, during a little part of the early night ...

My father's spine is tingling, thought Lorna disrespectfully.

"It helps to know," said Mrs. Hornaday with measured patience, "in the running of the affairs of the house."

"Oh, that. Well. Now I don't want to be tied down to a schedule but I'm going to combine several things—I'll even take off an extra day and go to the beach—you can figure on no less than five days. All right?"

"It's not all right with me, dear. But if you must go away on business, there's nothing I can do, I suppose."

"Well, now you know. Want to know something else? What time is it?"

"Seven," said Lorna. It was Garland's evening off and he had, of course, planned something with her. She prepared to rise from the table.

"Seven. Hm. Want to know something else?"

"What, dear?" asked Mrs. Hornaday.

"Let's you and me go upstairs and watch television in the bedroom. Get real comfortable and watch television."

Hornaday himself did not realize it, but this was invariably the code for conjugal intercourse. He would, in fact, watch television from the bed in his room and then at one point, about one hour later—Mrs. Hornaday had no idea of what went on during the interim—he would charge into her room and propose sex as if he had just thought of it—had, in fact, just invented it.

And so spun out that predictable evening.

Mrs. Hornaday ending up a restless insomniac ...

Lorna, later, dead on her feet ...

Garland, alone, at last, in his dark room, his head lightly lifted—as if sniffing the air ...

Somewhat to his own surprise Garland was acutely aware of Lorna's absence during her day in New York. But then, he thought, why be surprised? And then his emotion changed to one of appreciation. The girl's absence had the advantage of giving him something like contemplative quiet. Not that he was tired of the girl—far from it—but then a man, after all, does not live by woman alone.

Her absence altogether allowed the butler a restful gathering of the senses, and a calm appraisal of just how delicately or how securely he, Garland, had made his position.

Except for a totally irrational worry about Matthew Hornaday's chronic dislike, there was truly no need for concern about anything, the butler judged.

Irma was submissive enough to content herself with no more than occasional service. Garland might give it to her, and he might not. He might instead give her a bonus afternoon off, so she could go elsewhere, an act that appeared generous of Garland.

Lorna, of course, was no problem but an established pleasure. And this might last for some time. Termination, by Garland's lights, would be up to him.

Mrs. Hornaday, happily, had turned out to be a reticent woman. Perhaps she had a secret vice, or perhaps she had simply a vast, generous soul, as a mother content simply to protect her young daughter. Although Garland tended to doubt the latter. Her secret vice, it occurred to him, was patently that, made sexless by cruel blows of fate—her husband, for example—she derived a vicarious and unadmitted thrill from the knowledge that her nubile daughter was having an affair. And that thrill made more palpable by the fact of the girl's physical presence, and her lover's, in the house itself. Garland had run into far more bizarre forms of satisfaction, so that Mrs. Hornaday's seemed highly probable.

And so Garland's day was good. He was even given time off because Mrs. Hornaday would be gone all of the evening, and he took a quiet walk through the darkening country. He passed two places in particular—though without premeditation—where he had been with Lorna, but no matter his memories he felt content. Only around eight at night did he persistently return to the thought of Lorna—her sounds, her feel, her motion, her smell—and he wondered if she might not have decided to return on the early train. And if she did she would look for him, and if she did he would want her.

He returned to the house by nine, driven now by a perceptible urgency to be with the girl and to have her. I'm addicted to her, it occurred to him, and therefore can never have enough of her.

The house was quiet and had the feeling of emptiness. Only the hall light was on. But as if drawn by subliminal cues, Garland headed straight for his room. The closer he got, the more certain was his uncanny knowledge that a woman was waiting there. He trusted his senses and he simply knew. He opened the door to his dark room and was certain. The female presence was palpable in the air.

He smiled. He closed the door, unbuttoning the front of his shirt.

"I'm here," she whispered.

"I know," he said and smiled again in the dark.

When he was undressed he sat down on the bed and she threw back the covers. He reached out and felt the warm skin, felt her body motion, and he lay down wanting to feel the rest of her with all of him.

Whether it was his hesitation first, or hers, was not clear but there was the touch of unfamiliarity in their motion which made both of them tentative.

His hand was on her neck and he felt too much skin. His hand slid to one breast and there was a most confusing give under his grip. And the hip was too softly padded ...

"Yes," she said, feeling the question in his touch.

"You—"

"I surprised you?"

He sat up and felt his face click into its official lines.

"Of course, Mrs. Hornaday," he said.

The next interval was a little confusing because Sheila Hornaday became fairly frantic and because Garland found his situation totally new.

The thing was, he thought, that he must get out of bed. This was his firm resolve. The thing was, she thought, that she must keep him in bed. This was her firm resolve.

This was an unseemly struggle, Garland felt, and his keen sense of decorum finally defeated him. He relaxed and lay down again. This calmed Sheila Hornaday.

"You lie so still," she said, only touching his arm. "We don't have much time, you know. I mean, not this evening."

"Mrs. Hornaday."

"It's a ridiculous name in bed, you know that, Garland?"

"I don't know what to say."

"There is nothing to say. Make love to me."

But Garland, as an aesthete, despised the command performance. This was evident to Mrs. Hornaday soon enough, who was touching Garland here and there with considerable, remembered skill. And since she was chronically close to a state of irritation she suddenly became wildly angry. She jumped out of bed and Garland could hear her rustling a robe. He arose, too. When he was putting his bathrobe on she flipped on the light.

Mrs. Hornaday, livid now, was not without attraction.

"It's like this, Garland," she said. "I want you."

"Mrs. Hornaday—"

"Discreetly, serviceably, and at decent intervals as long as you are here."

"You are treating me like—like something at stud."

"You chose the wrong word, Garland. This is not question of making offspring but solely and preeminently of making a great deal of pleasure and satisfaction."

Her directness made her much more attractive, thought the butler.

Also he remembered the skill of her hands. But then he collected himself. The situation would be impossible.

"And for that matter, I would much rather we did this because you want to and not because I forced you," she added.

"Madam," he said, "a man cannot be ravished."

"Then you will simply have to change your attitude towards this—what shall I say—relationship, so that the idea of rape is superfluous."

"Out of the question. I will, of course, be totally discreet about this."

"Too late. You have not been discreet enough as it is."

"I beg your pardon?"

"I'm coming to the part where I force you, or, if you will, where I make a bargain."

Something incredible dawned on him. And then she said it.

"I will allow you to continue having an affair with my underage daughter in return for this." Her gesture was vague, but it ended up towards the bed. "You seem pleased with her," she finished.

He could not find his voice.

"Is the bargain a bargain?" she said.

"Madam, I find it distressing that you stand there having to, so to speak, buy—"

"Garland," she said. "I'm confident that I can buy you with no more than— my knowledge, shall we say?"

Her stance was suddenly fabulously attractive. It was not really sex heat that emanated from her, but something like the glitter of skill. He frowned and she saw it.

"You could always leave, of course." She ran a hand down her side, effectively. "And I could always have you charged. For—what is that complicated long phrase?"

He did not answer.

"Contributing to the delinquency of a minor," she found the phrase herself. "Ugly, isn't it?"

"Yes."

"And it needn't be ugly at all."

"If give me a moment to recover, to think clearly."

"While you do that I'll tell you something else, Garland, to show you how nice I am."

She stood close enough so that some part of her lightly touched him. But she was not actively trying to be seductive.

"Once over this shock—" she shrugged. "I don't know what came over me, playing a trick like that," she said, nodding at the bed. "Anyway, once you've recovered," she said, shrugging again, this time rather prettily, "come to bed with me. I don't mean as part of a bargain." She smiled. "As I said, it might not require any bargain, after this, to come back again. I can be rather nice. I remember I was even better than that."

"I don't doubt—"

"Let me finish. You see, after that one time, even, any legal step I might take will have so much less force, don't you see, because then I'm tarred very much like you. Isn't that nice of me?"

"In fact, yes," said Garland, feeling rather surprised.

She smiled up hopefully. She slowly rubbed her hands up and down his chest.

"Yes?" she said.

"I rather—admire you for this," he said. He felt her hands and they seemed to him remarkably knowledgeable even through the bathrobe. It was as if two strangers were gradually recognizing each other, strangers with similar interests, similar skills. "Yes," said Garland.

For a moment, without any faking, Mrs. Hornaday let her head sink on Garland's chest and he felt her sigh.

"These years, with that—that banker, and he is still like a customer. Garland, you have no idea what I've been going through."

"I can imagine it," he said. He had just gone through something similar himself.

And so they spent the next hour in revealing their mutual skills without further argument. They were both professionals. In the end Garland could say to himself without any self-deception that Sheila Hornaday was an enticing success.

In evidence of which, the butler was fast asleep when Lorna opened his door after midnight.

CHAPTER ELEVEN

Mr. Hornaday extended his Miami stay from five days to eight days, and then to fourteen. For the first time Garland began to wish fervently for the banker's return.

The decent intervals of which the banker's wife had spoken turned out to consist only of twenty-four or so hours. And Mrs. Hornaday had exhausting skills.

Lorna, with whom a routine was by now based on precedent, turned out to be totally uncomprehending, especially since Garland did not want to give the pat explanation for his altered performance.

Naturally he gave Irma that extra afternoon off, but of course this maneuver made hardly a dent in his output.

He thought of leaving but he was not quite ready to give up everything. He thought of taking a firm stand and making rules, but he was not rigid enough to maintain such a course. Both Sheila Hornaday and Lorna each had her real appeal to the man—one, like the pleasure derived from a very complicated perfume, and the other like the pleasure derived from sun smell on a healthy skin. But the simultaneity of the two females was proving to be something less than a lark.

Garland's growing distraction served to demonstrate that the aesthete, when subjected to excess, tires.

And when Mr. Hornaday returned to introduce his own crisis, Garland would not have said lightly that he despised the banker for it.

He arrived just before dinner, an aggressive exuberance, akin to cruelty, shining out of his face. He was tanned, he showed his teeth, he laughed like a horse and once, in the very beginning, he slapped Garland on the back so that the butler thought he might collapse.

"In the library, everybody," said Hornaday loudly, "and you too, Garland. Yes. You, too."

Wife and daughter and Garland gathered there and waited for the banker to begin.

"Well," the banker launched, "I must say you ran the house well, whoever ran it, and that you're all looking fine. Irma looked happy when I saw her in the kitchen. Lorna girl, you look healthy as hell, and you, my dear," he said to his wife, "have a real glow about you. That's a fact, I mean it. Garland?"

"Yes, sir."

"You look lousy."

There was no point in answering.

Then the mood changed. Hornaday lowered his lids, his jaw, his voice. He looked and he sounded ugly. "And you're going to look even lousier once I'm through with you," he added.

"Dear," said Mrs. Hornaday but got no further.

"You keep quiet and you listen to this," he said, dropping his voice again. "I've never liked that butler and I was right in my feeling."

"Maybe that's simply—" Lorna started but got no further.

"And you keep quiet too. It's because this man here is a pervert and I've sensed that all the time, being normal myself."

"Matthew, what are you saying?"

"That I've always known he was fishy and now I've found out. And after I tell you this, he gets out of the house."

Garland felt dull. But he still gave a start when Hornaday yelled again, although it was not at the butler.

"Lorna, you leave the room now while I must speak of acts of my life you should know nothing about."

She threw an anxious look at Garland and then hid behind the door in the hall.

"Now," said Hornaday, "I went to see some people in Chesterton Manning's household and dug up the facts. I got no satisfaction phoning them down there, so I went myself." He cleared his throat to make a pause. He liked the fact that his wife sat very still, huddled there like a cold bird. And he liked the sight of Garland standing there thin and cold.

"I obtained information from the secretary Manning had, and from one of the nurses. And also from what you might call a cheap showgirl. Know what I'm talking about, Garland?"

"I do. Though I don't see the relevance."

"You don't? Morals are the relevance. And you're out of a job is the relevance. And having a minor in this very house is the relevance that will get you a criminal suit."

"What did you say?" Mrs. Hornaday managed, and then her mouth hung open.

Hornaday turned, very patient.

"I said morals are—"

"Never mind that," she said. "The other."

"I'm firing—"

"The other."

"He's been having Irma, hasn't he? And she's just short of consent age in this state."

In the midst of doom and damnation there was now a breath of relief. Hornaday passed right over it.

"I asked Irma just before, in the kitchen. Didn't take much of a pinch to get it out of that dumb cluck. I asked her because of the type of sex ghoul this bastard is."

"He is not a—"

"All right, listen. Old Manning, dead now, used to be quite a blade. Eighty and all, he was a heller. And this Garland here, calls himself a butler, brought the whores in for Manning almost all of the time. Is that right, you pimp?"

"A change in vocabulary and you are almost correct, Mr. Hornaday. Though nothing as questionable as your experiences at Sherman's cabin."

That did not work anymore. Hornaday yelled right through it. "That was before I was married and besides I can hurt you and you can do nothing to me. Listen to this, Sheila. With this life Manning was leading—he's eighty or so—one day he gets this stroke. Any more excitement says the doctor, and the next stroke kills you. Well, at first Manning lays off. What can he do? He's near dead from top to bottom. And then this creepy butler here makes a suggestion."

"Not my suggestion, Mr. Hornaday, though it hardly matters."

"It matters to me who's got the filthy mind around here—you. Him there," said Hornaday to his wife, "he does it for Manning. Props him up in the bed with the blinds drawn, gets in that room there with some young whore, that's right, and goes through hours and hours, I hear it told, of the most violent love-making—just for Manning to watch. I think Manning didn't even want to watch. I think Garland just wanted Manning to have that next stroke. And that, Garland, is how you killed Chesterton Manning."

The butler did not bother to answer.

"You got ten thousand dollars in Manning's will, didn't you, Garland?"

"Yes."

"So that proves it."

"Can you use any of this in a court?" asked Sheila Hornaday.

"I wouldn't bother," he said, sounding exhausted. "I got the satisfaction of knowing he's a dirty bastard and he's leaving this house."

Which ignored totally Mrs. Hornaday's problem, how to keep Garland on. However, she started quite gently.

"All this happened a long time ago and not in this house," she said. "In this house Garland has been an excellent—"

"You out of your mind, defending him?"

"I want him to stay."

"You out of your mind?"

"Now you've had your fun, Matthew, blackening this man, and now you can see straight again, I should hope, and listen when I tell you there have been no objections to Garland from anyone here."

"You crazy? What's behind this?"

"All I'm saying is that this man—"

"Man? He's a monster."

"He's a better man than you, Matthew Hornaday, and that for twenty-four hours a day."

Hornaday stared at his wife. "What are you saying—"

"I'm pointing out to you that a flab and a gutful of wind like you can't get away with pushing everybody around forever."

"Are you telling me you've been sleeping with him?"

"I didn't say that. I say that if you force Garland out against my wish with a charge about his sleeping with Irma, I say that in that case I might spread it around just lightly that the real cause was that you're such a dud in bed your wife had to go elsewhere."

The banker, his most sacred illusion ruptured—about what a man he was—turned into a pitiful heap on his chair.

"What's it going to be, Matthew, dear?"

"Let me think—just let me—"

"I'll tell you what it's going to be, mastermind. Garland stays, and you take it, and you keep your mouth shut. Or I won't keep mine shut, tiger."

It might work for a while, Garland thought, it might work forever. But this excitement and tension was not the sort he craved.

"Shiela—" the banker began.

"Well?"

"I'll say yes, Sheila, if you tell me one thing. You—you've been sleeping with him?"

She was clever. "No," she said.

Hornaday relaxed so much that for a moment it appeared as if he might slide off his chair. "Well," he mumbled, and "Well—"

For Mrs. Hornaday, all was saved and concluded. Garland had reached his conclusion, too.

"Are you offering me the job back, Mr. Hornaday?" the butler said.

"Sure," said the banker. "Sure."

"That is heartening though unimportant. I am leaving today."

Both Hornadays stared at him. He turned to the wife.

"Please understand how impossible it would be," Garland said. "And that I am grateful to you."

Garland meant to bow then, when suddenly Hornaday recovered. He built up to a violent roar very fast.

"He isn't taking the job. And he never slept with you, girlie! So now what's going to stop me from suing the bastard from here to hell? I'll do it, I'll do it, to keep his kind from coming into a decent house, and I run a decent house. I'm going to make an example—"

Garland thought Hornaday had stopped shouting because he, Garland, had turned and was leaving the room. What had stopped Hornaday cold, however, was his wife who was saying very quietly, "Under your eagle eye, looking through a whiskey glass most of the time, in this house you run so well with your total neglect—this happened: Garland seduced Irma, yes. But then your daughter Lorna was his mistress and would still like to be, and then I was his mistress and would still like to be. Do you hear that, Matthew Hornaday? And all this in your own house, which you can't even see through that stink of your self-importance." She took a deep breath and then she said, "You flop, you," and she walked out of the room.

Two more things happened, and the first one right away. Garland turned to look at Hornaday and caught the man's hasty dash for the nearby desk. The butler did not care to move. He stood still and watched the banker's hand pull a gun out of the drawer. Hornaday pointed the gun at Garland.

"You will still be the same after you kill me," said Garland.

But it was his eyes that conveyed the whole significance. Garland gazed with no hate but with a sure knowledge. Then Hornaday's eyes wavered like something flapping in the wind. His true weakness suffused him and he sat down in the chair. He sat down so as not to hurt himself and that was all the strength he could muster. He sat and looked faded. Then Garland left.

The second thing that happened was a few hours later when Garland stood in the station to wait amid his luggage for his train. The episode was brief and quiet.

"Garland," she said, and touched his arm.

"Lorna."

"I'll never say Garland again. Now you're Roger."

"Thank you," he said and looked away.

"And I'm going with you."

He peered down at her and saw the coat over her arm and the small suitcase.

"Sit down, Lorna. Next to me."

They hardly touched but there was the intimacy.

"You cannot lead my life, Lorna, and I won't—"

"Do you know that I love you?"

"Yes, I do."

"Don't say puppy love, Roger."

"No. It isn't puppy love. It's more real."

"Therefore you—"

"Let me say it," he gently interrupted. "Therefore you can't be with me. I can find pleasure, Lorna, but you can find meaning. I can make an orgy, but you can make love."

"Roger ..." She felt sad for him for knowing so much, and for not doing enough. "Roger that's no reason for which I'd let you go. You understand that?"

"Yes. You've grown up in several ways."

"And you did that for me."

"Then think of me as something good that passes by but not something good that stays." He rose and touched her wrist briefly. "But you are, Lorna."

But she could not accept his reasons.

"You remember what we had between us, don't you, Roger?"

"You cannot come with me, Lorna."

"And I can't let go either."

The train was coming. He took her hand. "I've tried to tell you, but—listen, Lorna. This takes waiting. I'll write to you from New York. Once I've taken my next position—"

"But when, Roger?"

"Not long. I can usually find a position quickly."

She thought that was a fairly grim thing for him to say but she was not interested in double meanings now.

The train pulled in and he talked faster.

"As soon as I'm settled in I'll write. From New York, white envelope— Roger Kent."

"Kent—"

"It's a name I've—I made up. Watch for it."

He waved and jumped on the train and the train left.

While Lorna walked back to the house she had the uneasy feeling that all of this was like a delay, and not a solution.

CHAPTER TWELVE

The only obvious change in the house—other than Garland's absence—was that Mr. Matthew Hornaday, the banker, could not look any of the women straight in the face. He disguised the handicap by soaking himself in beer in the morning and hard liquor in the afternoon. For this period of time, of course, he did not go to work. Eventually he did go back to work and gave everyone a difficult time. But not those in his own house. His family had seen his flaw naked and no manner of cover-up was ever going to be good enough again. But they left him alone, and he left them alone.

As for Mrs. Hornaday, her brief interlude with Garland had left no mark on her at all. She mostly rode her horse again. Between horses she might sit in the club and ponder or speculate on the men. But she did not do any more than that and perhaps she never would.

Between Lorna and herself there had grown up a certain closeness, based perhaps on the fact that they had shared the same lover, but also on the mother's daring defense of Garland. But Lorna was mainly preoccupied with thoughts of Garland vis-à-vis herself. First she missed him. Then she loved him. And then she doubted that he had ever loved her. And every day at ten in the morning she turned into the hall to look on the silver tray for a letter from Robert Kent. There was none.

She started going out again, now and then, but it was a poor distraction. Then Ned called.

Her father picked up the phone and mustered up some of his old bluster. After all, Ned was not a member of his household.

"And don't make me tell you again, you lout, that your presence and your voice are not welcome in this house."

And then he banged down the phone, which was what attracted Lorna's attention.

"Who was that?" she asked from across the room.

"That young rapist friend of yours, that's who. And I told him in no un-certain—"

"I heard you."

"Good. Then I don't have to repeat what I said to him."

"I wanted to speak to him myself," said Lorna.

"You what?"

But Lorna had the good sense not to expose her father to any more overt opposition and her father had the good sense not to call her back. She made her call from an extension.

"Mr. Tyler, this is Lorna Hornaday calling. Could I speak to Ned?"

"Why, yes, Lorna. How have you been?"

"Fine, Mr. Tyler. Could I—"

"Hear about Ned's scholarship, Lorna? I guess you did, being an old friend of his. Don't you think that was a fine break for the boy?"

"Yes, I really do. I—"

"Not just a break, mind you, though you need the breaks. But like I always say, you have to give a break a chance to come your way and when it comes your way, I always say, you have to be smart enough and on your toes—"

For a moment the phone was dead, except for some faint hissing in the background that could have been angry whispers. Then Ned came on.

"Lorna, are you still there?"

"Yes. I was just going to hang up."

"Lorna, please don't. I'm sorry, I mean—listen, can I come and talk to you?"

"Why don't you tell me on the phone?"

"I can't. Now."

"All right. I'll be out front. At the gate."

Ned drove up to the front gate about ten minutes later and jumped out of his car. They both said, "I'm sorry—" at the same time. Next, a short silence, because neither dared laugh although it could have been funny.

"What I wanted to say, Ned, I'm sorry the way my father—"

"And that's what I wanted to say."

They didn't laugh this time, either, but they smiled at each other. Then they were serious again.

"Look, Lorna, I don't mean for you to stand out here chatting or anything, I only called to ask you if you'd like to go to New York with me."

"What?"

"I mean—let me finish. I have two tickets for a show from an uncle of mine. And if you'd like to drive in with me for dinner and then that show—well, I'd like that."

And somewhere in New York there is Garland, thought the girl, doing something, not writing.

"I'd like that," said Lorna.

They made the date and Ned drove off.

Curiously enough the arrangements for being allowed to go to New York for the evening presented no problem at all in the case of Lorna's father— Lorna was going for the day only, to be back around midnight—but there was some trouble with her mother who asked Lorna to join her.

The room was the same as always, Lorna found, but there seemed something different about her mother. For one thing, she had lost weight. And she seemed older. The aging, oddly enough, became her because the show of some age took out the faking.

"Sit down, Lorna. Why are you going to New York?"

"Well, I didn't want to say at the table, with Daddy there, but I'll tell you easily enough. Ned asked me to go in with him, to see a show."

"What show?"

"*The Deft and the Dumb.*"

"Go on."

"There's nothing to go on about, Mother. You know how Daddy feels about Ned, and all we—"

"Does Daddy know how you feel about Garland?"

"What?" Loma's surprise was genuine at her mother's perspicacity.

Mrs. Hornaday turned her back, took a cigarette for herself and lit it before saying anything else. Since she did not inhale, her sentence was accompanied by smoke signals.

"Lorna, dear, try to grasp for a moment that your mother has been as young as you." She sat down and stretched. "Younger, in fact."

"Mother, I don't know what you're talking about."

"I'm talking about the fact that you had a good thing, and your first good thing, at the age of sixteen. At that age I had been at it for three years."

"Now Mother, I'm going to New York in order to see a comedy by the name of—"

"Go ahead and lie to me if you want. I'll just ignore it."

Lorna quite prudently, said nothing.

"Look, dear," Sheila Hornaday then continued, "all you know about men and love I've forgotten. Unfortunately," she added and laughed. But then she became serious again, which in her case sounded casual. "You are going to see a show and you are going with Ned. And you are thinking of Garland who is in New York."

"I don't even know for sure he's in New York."

"Well, he is. He told me so."

"Oh, he did?"

"Naturally. He needed a reference for his new employer and that's how I got the information."

"Sure."

"I'm not seeing him, dear. It wouldn't be convenient for me. Though I'd undoubtedly get more out of it than you, Lorna." Mrs. Hornaday saw her daughter bridle and then clamp her lips shut with a vicious expression. "I say that, dear, because I would use him for what he is best—which does not happen to be romantic love." Is she going to cry? thought Mrs. Hornaday. I'll go easy now.

"Lorna, honey, you had the good luck right from the beginning to have it very good with a man. Now I wish you'd have the good sense to go on to the next one, for the next thing, and not hang on to an impossible situation."

"Like you? The way you went from one to the other?"

"No, dear. Not like me. I went from one to the other because none of them was satisfactory. And then I went from one to the other because I knew of nothing else to do."

There was a pause and this time Lorna did cry a little, a shining in the eyes and one tear rolling down, and that was not for herself but for her mother.

"All I'm trying to tell you, Lorna, is that what's good enough or even the best in one case is not good enough in another."

The girl sat in silence, as if letting things sink in, but she was too confused to know what they were.

"I'm going to New York with Ned," she said.

"Of course, dear," Mrs. Hornaday said and stubbed out her cigarette. "But try not to forget everything I've said."

Lorna nodded and stood up.

"If you don't forget, it may save you from having to hang so many pictures on the wall," Mrs. Hornaday finished, as if to herself, and the gesture with which she waved at all the framed photographs was tired and a little bit like a goodbye.

One obvious consequence of Mrs. Hornaday's talk was that Lorna, in New York, thought of Garland much more than she might have done otherwise.

On the day Ned and Lorna drove to the city the morning mail was late and when the couple left at eleven o'clock in the morning no letter from Garland had yet arrived.

In New York Lorna and Ned took a ride on the ferry, a walk in Central Park and, since they had time, they rode the elevator to the top of the Empire State Building.

The girl forgot herself now and then and had fun. Every so often she noticed that Ned would not even take her arm.

Before the show they went to a good Italian restaurant and ate so much that they both felt very tired. This took a lot of the subterfuge out of their conversation.

"It almost feels like the day is already over," said Ned, "and we haven't even gone to the show yet."

"Did you have fun?"

"Yes," he said.

And she felt that he was not lying. And he had not touched her once.

"Why did you ask me, Ned?"

"Huh?"

For a moment she felt the old resentment at his unnecessary slowness.

"Why did you ask me to go with you?" she said.

He glanced at her and obviously did not know how to say what he wanted well.

"Because I've thought of you often," he said, as if it explained something. "And because I've always felt," he went on, "that I missed with you."

She misunderstood him and said, "I know you have. Funny—" and her laugh was rather brittle—"all the sex situations we've been in, you and I never made love. Did you ever think of that?"

"Yes," he said and he lowered his eyes. Then he raised them again to her. "But that's not what I was thinking of when I said I'd missed with you."

"Oh? what then?"

"I don't know—I missed you. Something like that."

"Maybe I wasn't there," she said and looked away.

She had thought hers would be a good, flip remark to make at a fairly awkward moment, but what she had said had not come out flip. Nor had Ned been awkward. He was changing, she felt. He was changing a lot. But, what of herself? To hell with changing when you don't have to change and have Garland—the absurdity of that struck her only for the briefest moment and then she dismissed it. There was certainly nothing absurd about the way Garland had reacted at the station, how his face had changed and how his hand would not let go ...

"You thinking about something?" said Ned.

"No, not really. I'm sorry. You look so lost suddenly." She smiled politely.

"I did feel lost."

Her polite smile vanished and she stared at him and saw that he really did look lost. She felt a dinner partner's obligation to come to his rescue, but Ned recovered all by himself.

"We'll just talk about something else. Where I won't get lost," he said, smiling. "I have no business talking to you this way anyhow."

"Oh, but no," she said and felt lost herself.

Because she did not want to lose touch with him she did the quickest thing that came to her mind and asked him about his plans and career.

"Hell, Lorna," he answered, "I haven't got a career yet. Just the plans."

"Tell me about them."

He smiled and said, "Ask my father. He knows all about it."

"I doubt that," she said. "He talks more, and all the time about himself, but I think you know more." To her own surprise Lorna now felt interested and the talk was not just to fill time.

"I'm going to State," he said, "where I'll have to play football and—"

"What do you mean, have to? You like playing football."

"Sure I like it. But the big thing is that I want to go to study engineering." The difference made sense and she waited for more and he resumed. "I don't know which engineering yet but it's going to be the kind I understand best. Naturally." And he laughed.

"And then?"

"Leave town."

"That's important?"

"Christ, yes."

"And go where?"

"How do I know, Lorna? It's just going to be where my work is, and where—well, I don't know."

"Could be our town, too, you know," she said. With all of Ned's lack of concrete plan she still envied him his direction. "We have the power plant there, for example. That plant does use some kind of engineer, doesn't it?"

He shook his head and said, "Wouldn't do. The town, to me anyway, is like a kid place, you know? I grew up there." He bit his lip a few times and then said, "Where I'm going to live is going to be any place but it's going to be a grown-up place. I don't even know what that means but I'm going there."

She no longer envied him but felt something like admiration. And would she herself ever change? She wanted to hear more from him and listen more so that she could learn how he had accomplished the change ...

When they looked at the clock they discovered that the show had been on for more than an hour.

"I don't know when intermission is," Ned said with some haste, "but if we rush right over there we have more than half to go yet, I think."

"You feel like rushing over there?"

They looked at each other and knew that they could not care less.

"After that big meal ..." said Lorna.

"After all that big talk ..." said Ned.

The drive back to town seemed very short to Lorna, although Ned did not drive very fast and they hardly talked. She looked at him now and then and once she almost fell asleep. She did not think of Garland at all.

When Ned opened the gate for her in front of the house he held his hand out and she took it. She thought it was perhaps the first time he had touched her in any way since—when? That Sunday, that Saturday night?

Something happened in Lorna, a feeling of softness stole over her, the softness of receiving.

When he walked her to the front door of the house she took his arm and it was almost like a leisurely stroll. At the door he stopped, moved his arm out of her hand and turned her way.

"Good night, Lorna. I'm glad you came."

"Thank you, Ned. I liked it," But that said too little and sounded too stiff and then he started to leave. "Ned?"

"Yes, Lorna."

"Would you like to kiss me good night?"

They had just the one kiss, but it was warm and very long. Then Lorna stepped inside.

On the hall table, in the silver tray, lay a white envelope with a letter inside from Robert Kent.

By the time Lorna had reached the second landing she became aware of the light sweat on her forehead. As she ran down the long hall the insides of her hands prickled and she was sure the outside writing on the envelope would be smudged.

"Lorna, dear, is that you?"

The girl stopped by her mother's door and of course had to answer.

"Yes, it's me. Good night."

"Come in a moment, dear."

Lorna opened the door to her mother's room but did not go in. She looked into the large room that seemed larger only because a small lamp was lit by the bed. Her mother, Lorna noted, was wearing very baggy pajamas.

"I wanted to tell you there is a letter for you downstairs," Sheila Hornaday said.

"Thank you. I found it. Good."

"Who's Robert Kent?"

Who's Robert Kent: Garland, the girl thought. Who's Garland: I'll know once I open the letter.

"Somebody I met at the pool, at the club. Just somebody who came up from New York."

It never occurred to Lorna that her mother might have recognized the return address.

"How was it in New York? Have a good time?"

"Quite a good time. And we didn't even go to the show; we got to talking so much at the restaurant."

"Really," said Mrs. Hornaday and laughed. "I hope we'll be seeing more of Ned."

Lorna hardly heard that. She said good night, closed the door and ran to her room.

There she did a curious thing. She first started to rip open the letter and then she stopped. She put it down on her dresser with studied slowness, practically with languor. And then she undressed. She did this slowly, too, in front of the mirror. She did not watch where she dropped her clothes but only watched how she bared her body. She ran her hands over herself a few times, up and down, and felt the strong heat and the open wanting she had learned not too long ago. Then she picked up the letter and lay down on the bed.

The letter was long and handwritten with soft curves in black ink.

Dearest Lorna,

How much better it would be to tell you all this in person, even with-out language. Still, I'm writing you so that we can be together again soon—

But in the typical Garland manner he did not tell her what she wanted to know at once. She was tempted to flip to the end of the letter but he had taught her well. She read only in sequence:

I would tell you immediately, dearest, how we will arrange this but then you might not read the rest of the letter. Though I want you to know how I live now, what I do, what I think and feel.

I think and feel of you and cannot stop the feeling. I work hard and with much preoccupation, to fill out the time. You must have noted by the return address, dear Lorna, that I work on the East Side of Manhattan, taking care of a rather large, very beautiful apartment and of a rather large, very beautiful family. The Pear-sons are a young couple with four wonderful children. Since Mrs. Pearson supervises her own children and since a maid cleans the place, and since Mr. Pearson lives frugally—spending almost all day in his study, which has five telephones—you might won-der why they need a butler. They are a close-knit family requiring no outside assistance, but Mr. Pearson's business—he is a producer, fabulously successful—requires a great deal of entertaining. I pre-pare for and serve at those gatherings. It has also developed that I take two of the young children for a daily walk in the park or a drive to the zoo. This is only because I so much like the children and it allows Mrs. Pearson time with her infant.

It seems strange at this stage in my life that I have discovered a new and surprising satisfaction in completely platonic relation-ships. I have, as you know, been rarely in such a work situation—and yet, you know, such pleasures go only as far as they can. And so I write to you to come to me again. My day off is Thursday. I know a discreet place where we can meet—the address is below—and I know that, with the added freedom we can have here in con-trast to that of your house and your town, we might learn to know each other more truly.

If you cannot meet me next Thursday at one o'clock, write to me. If I do not hear from you I will assume you are saying yes.

Say yes, Lorna. Please, dearest.

There were five days between Lorna's first reading of the letter and the pro-posed meeting on Thursday. By then she had read the letter several more times and of course did not write to Garland. That meant yes, as he had said. And each time she read the letter she saw new things, or saw old things in a new light. She became happier and increasingly expectant. There were, in fact, five most significant points raised by Garland and once she would see him again she would ask him about each of them.

Summer rain threatened in New York and the first thick drops fell when Lorna reached the lobby of the hotel. It became suddenly very dark and the rain slammed down with a heavy prattle. The dark lobby was empty.

The little lamps, attached to columns, brightened up and the lobby resembled something British and Nineteenth Century.

The address was right, Lorna knew, and the name of the hotel was right, but everything was wrong. Was this Thursday?

I have his letter, she thought, and that's all I will ever have now, because he isn't coming—he never meant to come—or he never thought I would come ...

All possibilities of mistake and mischance occurred to her then.

But her spirits revived as a taxi came around the corner, speeded up in her direction, slowed down. Then it stopped under the canopy of the hotel. The door behind Lorna swung open and someone wrapped in a raincoat dashed for the cab. While the car pulled away Lorna thought anxiously of peering into the cab to see if Garland were inside. She ran out. She felt despairing and foolish and angry all at the same time and then she felt like crying.

"No, no. It wasn't me—"

And when she turned to the voice she saw Garland.

He came striding through the rain, long steps, warm smile—and when he touches me now, she thought, I'll melt or faint ...

She did neither. When he touched her she clung to him with a sensation of everything inside her being made of wire and the wire wanting to wrap itself all around him.

"Now, now—of course I was going to come. Lorna, don't you hear me?"

She wanted to kiss him but she feared he would not allow it here on the street. She let him lead her into the hotel, past the desk where an older man nodded at Garland, and then into the elevator. She held on to his arm all this time.

He did not kiss her in the elevator either. How he waits, she thought. While I'm dying ...

They turned down a very dark corridor and then into a little room that seemed to be under the roof. The small window was blind with rain and she could hear the rain rattling overhead.

Garland first took off her wet coat and his own. Then he kissed her.

He kissed her well and long and held her with appreciation. When he let her go she was glad because she felt she might faint. He laid her down on the bed. He took off her shoes, rolled down her stockings and dried her feet with a towel.

I don't care what he does as long as he does it, she thought, and with that she relaxed so much that she very nearly fell asleep. But she was conscious enough to know that he was undressing her. He opened buttons and hooks, he lingered, he peeled things away and he touched her to make her shiver. Then she waited patiently. She waited, eyes closed.

This waiting is Garland, she thought. I only and ever will wait like this for Garland. When he touched her again she gasped. She heard the rain overhead and thought it was a beautiful sound. But my sound is better …

He tuned the whole length of her now, with his hands, then with his mouth. She could feel him, so it seemed, in many places at once and the confusion was a delight now, and then an ecstasy that seemed to scream all around her. She did not know or care how long all of this was taking, and then she collapsed into a dark, sleep-filled place. When she woke up, she knew only that she had slept.

Garland was leaning up in bed, next to her, gazing outside. It was still raining and the room was full of a cozy dimness.

"Hi," she said, looking up at him.

He smiled down at her and then he leaned over and embraced her. Then he sat up again. He looked at her and she felt very beautiful.

"How your eyes shine," he said to her.

She wiggled in bed, feeling very good. "So good," was all she could think of saying.

"Yes," he said.

"You know, dearest, we've spent all this time and have hardly said a word to each other?"

"Maybe that's why it was so good."

Later, she was to remember this, and that he had been right. "Still raining, isn't it?" she said without glancing at the window.

"You can hear it on the roof."

"And here I thought we'd do all kinds of things together. I mean like going out and things in public we haven't been able to do before."

"And?"

"And now I would just as soon stay here," she said.

She reached for one of his hands and put it on herself under the covers. But mostly she wanted to look at him and she wanted to talk in the warm bed and she told him how much she had loved his letter. "It was full of wonderful things and I've memorized all of them."

"You must tell me, so I know them, too."

"There were five."

"How pedantic of you. I thought there would be untold numbers of them. Or at least a thousand and one."

"Oh, yes. Those too. But I tidied the whole list up a bit and I just think of five. I don't need to think of the untold one thousand and one, you know."

"I know," he said. "They're the ones for when we don't talk. Anyhow, tell me about the selected five."

"Well, they all came out like this. I'm just telling you now about the new things about you, the new things I saw in your letter I didn't know about because of the way we had to live before."

Garland's hand held entirely still.

"All this," she said and folded her arms behind her head. "You talk about all the many more things we can do now. And about the very new kind of thing that has happened to you in your new job. You know, platonic you called it. And how you plan on staying in that job a very long time. And then it was in there, Roger, dear, how you love those children. That's something I never knew about you."

He shrugged and looked away. "That's only four things, I believe," he said.

"Yes. The other one was— I mean, it was just something that gave me a tremendous feeling about you, when you said you were taking care of that family. And how you enjoyed the family." She glanced away and gave a small laugh. "It's just something that gave me a tremendous new feeling. About you."

He was silent for a moment but then he was fairly direct.

"Did you mean *us*, instead of *me?*"

"Well, I don't really know about you. Just about me. I know how I feel."

I can be brutal to her, Garland thought, and tell her that all I find here with her is sex. And then I lose her. Or I can lie to her and keep her. Is there nothing between brutality and the lie?

"Lorna," he said, "don't you remember anything I told you at the railroad station?"

"Sure I do. And how you looked at me and that you would write."

A most unusual impatience took hold of Garland, impatience with the girl's easy forgetting and with her facility to remember only what fit her wishes. But he did not want to lose her. He said, "What I said about children is true. If I had any children I might well feel as I said."

She was a little puzzled by his indirection but took what she understood and liked it. "I'm glad you never had any before, Roger. Have I asked you before if you've ever been married?"

"Twice no."

"Hm."

"But I have told you before," he said with a real wish to be straight with her, straight in the important things anyway, "that I've not considered marrying."

"I know you never did before," she said blithely.

She and I are not the same kind, he thought. And if I really showed her, I would lose her.

And Garland also knew for a fact that the only way he was capable of holding the young girl was by making her want him, making her desire him with the kind of exclusive, physical passion that few men besides Garland had a talent for arousing. And everything else was interference.

Directly he applied himself to the task of changing the subject his way.

He soon had Lorna purring like a cat and stretching herself under his hands.

He did all this slowly and gently but not cleverly because he did it gradually enough to leave her room for thinking.

"Roger," she said.

"Hm?" he said with his mouth on her neck.

"You haven't told me yet how much you want me."

"Do I have to tell you?" And he intensified his physical response to her question.

She was altogether willing. Only for a fleeting moment did it strike her that he had not really answered her question by making her more excited. She became more excited and then wanted him with a passion. But since the passion had no solid footing in the bed of all her unanswered questions, her unresolved doubts, her desire was erratic and she could steady it only by forcing her passion. She forced it into a dry heat that seemed to sear her without consuming. She screamed once, in the end, and the sound could have been lust, or anger, or simply a petition for release …

The rest of the evening was vague and besides there was not much of it. Garland put Lorna on the train without much conversation between times. It helped that the girl was quite tired, while Garland was disturbed.

He was not sure how he should proceed. It would be such a shame to lose her …

CHAPTER THIRTEEN

In the middle of the night Lorna suddenly woke in her own bed and no more than two seconds later she knew why she had—Garland had not made the next definite date with her.

But he had not said that they were finished. Ah, just the Garland method, this slowness and delay, she thought. He would write again.

But was she to wait for days, perhaps, for a firm answer? Not only would that be unbearable but it would be totally unnecessary. There was no need to set date, place, and intent. She knew his day off, she knew the hotel and she knew how he wanted her.

She squeezed herself in her bed, thinking of how Garland had wanted her, how he had shown it and how good it had been.

And then she thought again, besides, I have no fixed date with Ned, but does that mean I won't see him?

The hour was late and Lorna fell asleep with that thought.

Between Thursday and Thursday no new letter arrived from New York. But Lorna looked at the good side of this. A letter could mean no, and no letter each day strengthened the conviction she had found alone in her bed after leaving Garland.

Twice in the interim she saw Ned. The first time was by chance, although important. In the middle of small talk on the street, where she had met him, Ned suddenly said, "I've decided, Lorna, that I want to see you again."

"Oh?" And she laughed. She was not sure why, but she thought it might be because she did not want to feel flattered—or glad. "Have you asked the other party in the case?" she said.

"No. That's part of the deciding. The deciding isn't finished with a word, I think. It takes seeing each other. I think, with you and me, it takes time."

They said other things but that was the part that stayed with Lorna in the midst of her sureness about Garland, or because of it.

The second time she and Ned met was not by chance but because she had called him.

There was in the downstairs library and for no good reason a book with the title, *Basic Engineering Mathematics*, and Lorna one day spotted the book. She then called up Ned to tell him she wanted to meet him in town for coffee and that she had a present for him.

In the drugstore she made him a present of the book, the first gift she had ever given him: "If my wishes can help you succeed—you will." And she signed it.

"I want to say the same thing to you," said Ned.

Lorna was happy that day because the next was Thursday.

When she left the train in New York the sun was shining and she felt even happier. The next time, she thought, I'll come in the morning and Roger and I will have all day.

She reached the hotel fifteen minutes early. She did not mind sitting in the lobby. The old man behind the desk did not bother her. Once a young couple walked by, and once an old lady. The old man at the desk nodded at all of them the same way.

She did not look at the clock in the lobby until it was one-fifteen. This gave her a start but she was in a good humor.

At one-thirty and after increasingly frequent glances at the clock, she finally arose from her chair and walked to the desk. She did not feel shy because she felt sure. But she felt slightly angry.

"I'm waiting for Mr. Garland," she said to the old man.

"Yes?"

"I said I'm waiting for—"

"I understood you, miss. If you wish to wait ..." and the old man, indifferently, waved at the quiet lobby.

"The reason I said I'm waiting is that he's late. Do you know where he is?"

"No, miss."

"You know Mr. Garland. He and I were here."

"I know Mr. Garland."

"Well, I've been waiting for half an hour. I'm—"

"I only know Mr. Garland, miss."

"And what's that supposed to mean? We came in last week and you nodded at him."

"Which is perhaps why I did not see you, miss."

It was not until that point in the conversation that Lorna felt humiliated. She felt like shrinking away and like hiding.

"Did he—did he call, maybe?"

"No message on the switchboard, miss."

She left, looking as if she were afraid to make a sound. But out in the street she found her anger again.

This was not her fault, this humiliation, it was Garland's. He had mixed up the appointment.

More in an excess of rage than from a deep sense of longing she prowled the street until she could hail a taxi. Once inside, she gave the driver Garland's address on the East Side.

The building towered and the gold-liveried doorman was impressive. I'll go straight up, she fumed to herself, and ask for the damn butler. I will ask for him by name, Garland, and say that I'm his daughter, by God.

Nothing could have stopped Lorna, except the doorman. He looked authoritative and was also very polite.

"May I ask whom you wish to see?" he said.

For a moment she was taken aback in her interrupted rage. It suddenly seemed awkward to ask this grand doorman for the whereabouts of a butler. For that matter, by what name—Kent or Garland?

But she recovered in a moment when she remembered the name of the family for which Garland worked. "The Pearsons, please."

"The Pearsons?"

"Yes. They have four children."

"Four children," said the doorman and put one gloved hand to his impressive chin. "You must be mistaken, miss," he said, and he smiled. Lorna was blank for a moment. The doorman continued. "They have three children, miss, and their name isn't Pearson. It's Kincade."

"Oh, well yes. Kincade. I don't know what I might have been thinking of. The producer."

"Mr. Kincade is a scrap-iron dealer, miss."

Lorna could no longer control gloomy suspicions. "And besides," the doorman was saying, "the Kincades are in Bermuda for the summer."

"Oh," she said, and it was barely audible. "What mistakes—what mistakes—"

"There is, of course, a Pearson living here," said the doorman with a touch of compassion. "But it's not a family. Miss Emily Pearson."

"Just Miss—Emily—"

"Yes. She has lived here for years, longer than I have been here."

"But—the family—"

"Then she can't be the one you would want to see. Miss Emily Pearson is quite an elderly lady."

Then Lorna felt that she would give up. She nodded, walked away slowly. She meandered most of the afternoon, she sat quietly in the park and once she cried for a long time. When it was dark she felt calmer, and not so confused.

But everything was still in her head and she would make one more try, for the certainty.

The same doorman was still at the building and he recognized her. He even smiled.

"Does Miss Pearson have a butler, please?"

"Oh, yes. There are several butlers in the building and—"

"Is his name Garland?"

"Why, yes. You know Garland? Very nice man."

"Yes."

"He and Miss Pearson went to dinner about three hours ago."

"He went with her—"

"Always does. They should be back around now. Well, now! Excuse me—" And the doorman ran to the curb. The big car had rolled up very silently.

First the chauffeur jumped out and came around to the curb side of the car. He was nobody Lorna had ever seen. He swung the rear door open and helped out an old woman who tried to make up for lost sparkle with a great deal of jewelry. She was not bad-looking but she looked more like a statue somehow coming apart than a live woman.

And then Garland left the car. By way of gesture the chauffeur helped him, too.

Miss Pearson took Garland's arm and by the time they had reached the large door the doorman had swung it open.

Lorna could not think of running, or shrinking, or sinking away. She thought of nothing that had to do with motion and simply stood still. Garland did not see her at one side of the door until he was quite close.

He stopped. Curiously enough he did not seem startled. He turned to Lorna as if to offer a total view.

"What is it, dear?" said Miss Pearson.

"A young friend," said Garland quietly, gazing at Lorna. "A former friend."

"Why, how nice," said Miss Pearson. "Perhaps your young—"

"Allow me, Emily," said Garland, and he patted the old hand on his arm. Then he turned back to Lorna. "Can you still remember what I told you at the station?"

The young girl closed her eyes and remembered. She took a very deep breath and then, rapidly, she walked away.

"Would you have liked to ask her up, dear?" said Miss Pearson.

"No. She has grown since I knew her last, and changed."

That comment, for her own purposes, gave great satisfaction to Miss Pearson. She turned her back to Garland and said, "Do unhook me, Roger."

He did so in silence.

"And you, Roger, have you changed, dear?"

"No. I don't change, ever," he said to her but his thoughts were some place else.

He thought of Lorna alone on the train out of town and he thought of his own helplessness.

Lorna sat very still in her seat and somehow the loneliness was going away. She recalled the butler's words: "Think of me as something good that passes by, but I am not something good that stays. But you are," he had said.

And if Ned helps, she thought, if his wishes can help me, then I think Garland will be right.

THE END

The Consecration of the House
By Barry N. Malzberg

The hastiness and perhaps desperation which can be inferred from this pseudonymous late novel are evident; Rabe, whose compressed, prolific career was already crumbling and who probably took commissions for this novel and the other reissued between these covers commits a number of amateurish mistakes. They are mistakes to be less ascribed to lack of professionalism than to haste and despair; the novels were probably written very quickly for a bottom-market publisher. Rabe himself was fading, a string of intermittently ambitious novels had attracted little attention and he was probably writing at speed and without looking back. Some very good Cornell Woolrich novels were written this way and I have committed a few myself, some of them even interesting, but it is no prescription for a novelist, particularly one as aspirant as Rabe was at the outset of a spasmodic career.

Rabe switches viewpoint within a scene, often several times; there is no law against a multiple-viewpoint work of fiction but switching viewpoint en passant is very rarely done and not recommended. The product is disjunctive, muddled, often confusing and the failure of consistency can disorient even a sophisticated reader. This is problematic enough in "serious" literature (whatever that might be) but for the pulp, the paperback audience it is almost inevitably a mistake. It is a mistake not because the audience is stupid, it is in the main as cognizant as any, but because the genre paperback original novel was created to be a highly successful and simply situated work; anything which shakes credulity or consistency of narration tends to get between the reader and text to an unhappy result. There is a scene in *New Man in the House* early in the novel in which Rabe uses three viewpoints throughout (Lorna and Sheila Hornaday, Garland) and intermittently the lurking maid, Irma. Sometimes he switches viewpoint within a paragraph. The inferred lack of patience or control has to affect the text and the reader; identification is ruptured, the scene lurches rather than proceeds. Procession does not have to be graceful in a paperback original (or anywhere else) but it must be consistent and that is a quality against which Rabe's narrative attack works.

Part of this difficulty may have come from the author's contempt for the market itself. Softcover Library was an imprint of Beacon Books, a bottom line paperback publisher which achieved some modest distribution in the 60's and faded as did the category of softcore pornography by the end of the decade. "Softcore" pornography (i. e., no actual description of genitals or actual intercourse, no penetration, no unusual sex practices, nothing of the mechanics) became in the wake of the famous Lady Chatterley decision in the early 60's, briefly a successful category, taken over quickly enough by more explicit pornography and publishers literary or category who by the late sixties had virtually abolished taboos. Perhaps the best precis of the category is Donald Westlake's 1968 *Adios Scheherazade*, an autobiographical novel based upon his experience with soft and hard core during the decades. Mockingly accurate, accurately contemptuous, *Scheherazade* is regarded by unhappy alumni of that market as a kind of demented Bible or perhaps Confessions of St. Augustine. The constantly shifting taboos, the primness at the core of salaciousness, the careful and sometimes frantic balancing of the softcore sex scenes with what veterans of the trade called "tweenies"—that is, all the non-sexual material deliberately placed to make the novel "socially redeeming"—all of this is laid out by Westlake like a patient etherized upon a table and the novel makes clear why almost every author self-trapped into the category regarded himself (and often herself) as a victim, an appropriator and servant of taboo rather than passion. It was for a writer like Westlake the first station on the train or sleigh ride; it was for another kind of writer like Peter Rabe the last stop or close to it. Often one could not tell the difference. The sex scenes by standards only a decade later were laughably innocent; the guilt, abstemiousness, ambivalence of the characters read closer to *Fanny Hill* than anything Kozy Books was publishing as early as 1963.

I had my own experience with the market. (My first published novel, *Love Doll* was in fact a Beacon Book published in December 1967 and is mercilessly now lost even to the all-seeing eyes of eBay or ABE.) It was a first station on what I feared at the time was going to be a very short ride, *please exit at the next station, please,* and by 1968, barely half a decade later than *New Man in the House* I was writing for Maurice Girodias and his doomed Olympia Press America producing sex scenes which would have made Ejler Jakobsson, my editor and Rabe's at Beacon Books, blush like a surprised rodent. My first Station of the Cross however turned out to be that and I was able like contemporary writers for Beacon or Midwood or Beeline to flee. This was not true of Rabe, however. Rabe was as irreparably approaching the end of his career as I was (not so irreparably) scrambling for the initiation of mine and it is a palpable resentment along with that cited despair which seems to come from every anguished page of this novel.

And "anguished" is the correct adjective; every chatacter in this novel is in a well-fitted hell. Mother and daughter Hornaday are trapped in an unhappy marriage and a sexual desert, Father Hornaday is an impotent, stupid, rage-filled banker, Garland, "the Butler" who as the periptery of the plot has Adamic knowledge of both mother and daughter is desperately conflicted, daughter Hornaday's boyfriend Ned is sexually naive and emotionally paralyzed and it is his inability to sexually perform with daughter Hornaday which drives her into the bed of the household's new employee, Roger Garland, "the Butler." Garland suffers from satyriasis and guilt, a very bad parlay but neither or both prevent him from congress with mother and daughter. Sexuality for him is as entrapping as it is frightening to boyfriend Ned. All ends well for these characters but it does so only because Peter Rabe has reached 40,000 words, an acceptable minimum for a Beacon Book and a slam-bang resolution ends the characters' agony in equivocating ambivalence. It is an ambivalence which probably motivated Rabe to undertake the assignment and which accompanied him throughout commission and the rapid resolution—as clumsy, as forced, as truncated and desperate as the resolution of any Gil Brewer novel approaching its 40,000 word limit with 90,000 words of scheduled plot never to be written—resembles the never-described orgasms of the character. Wham bam slam *nothing*.

Rabe might have judged his career in those terms: Wham bam slam—*nothing*—although projecting motive or attitude upon a writer, particularly one as intelligent, damaged, luckless and angry as Peter Rabe is certainly a mug's game. A similar mug's game might be trying to recreate for contemporary readers the sense of the time and the market for which Rabe was writing. Well over half a century ago, the world of Beacon Books is as distant to us in time as were the publisher McClure's Syndicate novels of Booth Tarkington or Gissing's Grub Street to me in the Spring of 1967 when I was struggling over a kitchen table and an open window to finish *Love Doll*. I had as little grasp on that novel as the unfortunate Sheila or shapely Lorna had on the industrious Roger Garland and it was only a series of assumptions (most of them financial) which got me through. Rabe must have had assumptions too. I cannot speak for them but this novel is as contemptuous, desperate and serious as the sexual desires and frustrations of its readership might have been and what comes through it perhaps more than anything else is some sense of the period.

It was a period of possibility, a period of repression, the best of times, the worst of times for the writer of sex books and her publisher and Rabe might have had some grim pleasure in thinking that what he had reached was the cusp of his career if not the pinnacle. He was very smart, he had a doctorate, he was a practicing psychiatrist, he knew more than he dared express but somewhere in the abyss of this novel lies a sense of the period and the country for which it was written. In and out, hail and farewell, call the keeper but even in the flame of the Cuban Missile Crisis and the greater horror of the JFK assassination beat the heart of the keeper and his creations: No. Yes. Yes. No. Yes Yes Yes. No Dealey Square and the Grassy Knoll shuddered in the distance.

April 2019: New Jersey

Her High-School Lover
By Peter Rabe

Writing as Marco Malaponte

CHAPTER ONE

The woman dropped the pen and looked out of the window. She saw a tree on the abortive lawn, a sapling, actually, with a stick to support it, and then the quiet street. To the left, the street led to the campus; right, to the supermarket. And this for six years, she thought, and nothing changed in the view except for the transplanted tree, there only two months ...

She sat at a little toy of a desk, delicate, old, and since she rarely wrote letters the desk was coated with a thin layer of dust. She looked into the pigeon-holes and found her cigarettes. She lit one and blew out a trail of smoke. She looked all around the front room—many more lovely old things and all in genteel order—and once more at the view from the window. Then she retrieved the pen and bent over her letter.

Cher Pierre, she read, and the rest was in French, too. She had not written or thought or spoken in French for six years but she wrote now as if there had been no interruption. *Cher Pierre*—

> I do not know why I thought of you today, Pierre, after all these years. Six, it is, I think, to be exact. Perhaps one would say, "idle curiosity," but if I am to be honest with myself, and with you, I must admit that there is more to it than just that.
>
> Have you remarried, Pierre? I sweep away all delicacy with this question, but it has preyed on my mind. If you feel you cannot answer, I will understand.
>
> Write to me because you are well.

She signed Laura, and under that in parentheses, Mrs. R. Vaughn.

She looked at the name and felt suddenly and unaccountably old. Vaughn, an old-sounding name, she thought. I am thirty-seven and how I feel should be up to me, but this name weighs me down. The name seems old, because it is, but I ... She stopped, for she saw the mailman come into the street, from the left where the college was. Robert walks the same way, she thought, when he comes back from his classes. An old man burdened by artifacts.

She dropped that thought too, stuck the letter into an envelope, sealed and addressed it—has Pierre moved, she wondered—and went outside to wait for the mailman.

The mailman did not much like this street. He delivered on this route at three in the afternoon, at which time the men were still at work and the women all seemed to be at some club meeting or other. He rarely found anyone home. And there were no children on the street, which had to do with the age of the habitants, and no dogs, which had to do with the regard the habitants had for their furniture.

It was a boring route. And then he saw Mrs. Vaughn. This, he thought, is an unusual woman. He could not tell her age. It was enough for him to consider a woman unusual when he could not tell her age—just as an envelope plastered with stamps from an indeterminate country would have struck him as exotic. No foreign stamps, of course, ever came to this street ...

He dropped something in a brown envelope into the slot of Miss Lettie Ambru, something flat from a certain League for Spiritual Transmutation. There was another package, too, in a brown wrapping which would not fit into Miss Ambru's slot. This brown thing was not marked and he left it by the door. Then he glanced toward the lawn where Mrs. Vaughn stood as if waiting for him.

Now if this one were really waiting for me, he thought, at which point the woman turned her head and no longer gazed at the postman. She no longer looked as if she were waiting for him though this did not stop the postman's train of thought. On the contrary, he wallowed in lasciviousness.

He ignored her profile, which was beautiful in definition, and the female curve of her neck, which carried the head with a sense of restfulness. He looked, in fact, at the woman as if she were dismembered. Breasts here, butt there. Both obvious. He could not see her legs. He imagined her in slacks and then he imagined her without slacks. His greed for perfection came close to the reality, though he could not have known that. When he drew nearer to her, he became confused and thought of brown envelopes, foreign stamps, and Miss Ambru, who was a totally sexless fifty. Then Laura Vaughn looked at him.

"I got a letter for you," he said quickly.

"I have one for you, too." she said. "I don't know what postage it needs. Would you take it and let me know tomorrow?"

She held out the airmail envelope to him and he accepted it without touching her fingers. He was conscious of not touching her fingers.

"France," he said, and inspected both sides of the envelope. "Fifteen cents, I guess. Doesn't seem overweight, Mrs. Vaughn." He grinned at her. "Ain't you French, like I hear tell?"

"No," she said. "I've lived in France but I come from Idaho."

"Izzatso?" he said and nodded his head because he had to do something to interrupt staring at the woman. "I thought you was French. You look sort of French."

"I do?"

She had no idea what he meant by a woman looking French.

"Yeah," he said. "Like not from here. You know?"

She smiled and said that he was right, she was not from here, which was nothing new to either of them. Her husband, Robert Vaughn, associate professor of archaeology, had at one time gone to dig amid subterranean stones in a dank, damp section of Bretagne, and the speculation had been that here might be the lost site of the Holy Grail. He had not exhumed the Cup. He had found, instead, Laura, a young divorcee, and he was still fond—after six years—of the observation that he had not discovered the Chalice, but a wife—and to hell with mythology. Robert Vaughn's professional joke had that kind of longevity.

"You said you had a letter for me," Laura reminded the postman.

"Uh—yeah. Here." And he handed it over.

She took the missive and looked at the name of the sender and then she went back into the house. When she closed the door it struck her that she had forgotten to thank or to say goodbye to the postman. She sat down at the desk that she so rarely used and read the letter. Next she went to the hall in which one of the two phones was located, and dialed her husband. There was no one else she could call.

"And when only stone is available," Professor Vaughn said with a touch of crescendo, "then you make do with that."

He looked at his class and the silence was the silence of a deep pond. Then he resumed. As soon as his attention was diverted, the plumpish co-eds resumed their whispered conversations.

"He talks like he's got a pipe in his mouth."

"He usually does."

"I know. I bet he makes love with that pipe in his mouth."

"Can you imagine him making love?"

"Not to me," said the blonde in the third row, and the brunette answered, "But have you seen his wife?"

"No."

"You should see his wife!"

"I can imagine."

"No you can't. She's chi-chi."

"What's that?"

"The end. You know."

Then they took notes on the Cro-Magnon man's brain capacity.

"Move your hand! I can't see your scribbles!"

"He's repeated himself six times, stupid."

"I know. What's so important about brain capacity, anyway?"

"If you gotta bring something up and all you got is brain capacity …"

"You oughta see his wife."

"You said that."

"Wow! What a dish she is."

"Wonder what he did to deserve that?"

"He must have something."

"Bread. Did you know he's got bread?"

"College professors don't have bread."

"This one has bread. I know that because Daddy's bank handles the trust which pays ..."

"Did you get that brain capacity just now?"

"Whose?"

"The Neanderthal."

"No. He'll bring it up again—don't you worry."

"He is kinda cute, you know?"

"Because he's fragile and has all that black hair, you mean. I know your type, sweetie."

"What do you mean, you know my type?"

After that the conversation deteriorated as Professor Vaughn prepared another crescendo.

"... so that one look at the fertile female shape of their woman-depicting artifacts convinces us that we here deal with that kind of abstraction which ..."

Vaughn stopped abruptly, dropping soundlessly from abstraction into practicality.

"Yes?" he said and brushed his thick hair away from his forehead.

An old colored man wearing rimless glasses had come into the classroom and now he was plodding toward Vaughn's glazed desk. Upon passing the blackboard, the old man's instincts prevailed and he wiped at a chalk mark with a chamois. Then he leaned over and gazed into the professor's eyes. Vaughan could smell chewing tobacco and cleaning compound.

"Phone call for you, Doctor."

"Tell whoever it is that I'm in class—and to call back in ten minutes.

"It's your wife, Doctor."

"All right," said Vaughn. "I'll speak to her."

He said nothing else as the janitor left the room and then he told the class to read the chapter on Pre-Cambrian glacial formations for the next meeting.

"I'm sorry but I have been forced to dismiss you early."

The co-eds murmured *sotto voce*.

Vaughn went immediately to his compact office. The custodian had placed the handset on Vaughn's desk. The black receiver, lying on its side, looked like a small animal shot through the head and dead. For this reason, Robert Vaughn was overcome with fear and he quickly estimated his past actions in order to determine which might have made him responsible for disaster. None were hazardous in any way whatsoever, so by the time he had picked up the instrument he felt totally irritated.

"Laura?"

"Robert, I'm so glad you ..."

"In case it has escaped you, Laura, you called me in the middle of freshman class. You know how feel about the importance ..."

"Dear, I'm sorry I interrupted you, but I felt so upset that time never entered my thoughts and just dialed you, Robert."

"And speaking of time," he went on, "my feeling about classes at the end of a semester ..."

"Robert—"

"Yes?"

She could not tell just what his yes meant. She wished she could see his face and, also, that she did not feel so alone. She was sitting in the dark hall of the house and one arm was resting on the table near the phone. This posture placed her breast in contact with her hand and she stroked herself unconsciously.

"It's about Tony," she said quietly. "The school wrote. Again," she added.

"What have they got to say about our dear boy this time?"

"Robert, I don't think we should have sent him there. I wish ..."

"We didn't send him. I sent him. I went to military school myself and, I might say, to my best advantage."

"I feel like such a failure. To send the boy there is an admission that I—that we—can't handle the boy."

"Let's not discuss it now."

"But we never discuss it!"

Her fingers dug into her breast and she wished again that she could see Robert. He was still standing by his desk, his thin face full of annoyance, and with an affectation of boredom, he fluttered through the leaves of a book. The text was filled with photos and drawings of archaeological treasures.

"I am rather busy," Robert said into the phone. "So I cannot concern myself with your son's problems at the moment. I know very little about his upbringing or his father, but I think that I have tried to furnish him with a code of values."

Robert Vaughn wanted, right now, to wash his hands of responsibility.

"And Tony is seventeen," he went on. "High time to straighten out."

"I know we shouldn't discuss it on the phone but ..."

"Then don't, dear. I'll be home in a couple of hours."

"The letter ..."

"What letter?" He stopped on a page with a photo of a small clay figure whose protuberances bespoke femininity.

"The commandant himself wrote this one," said Laura. "He is sending Tony home."

"Ah?"

Laura could hear the turning of pages.

"He's been thrown out of school!" she said sharply.

There was silence at the other end, then the flick of a page.

"Disgraceful," she heard, and then, "I'll be home in two hours."

After the click Laura slowly cradled the receiver. She wished she had not made the call because she felt more alone and more useless now than before. She felt that her son needed her, but she did not know how to help.

CHAPTER TWO

Tony lay on the bed with his arms behind his head and—because the woman was out of the room momentarily—allowed himself a few private thoughts. He watched the sun leaking into the window to illuminate the brown stain on the flowery wallpaper. Cheap tenements had always made Tony feel good. They meant, I don't belong here. I'm just passing through. Without progressing to the next thought in logical sequence (and where to from here?), the boy turned over.

His glance swung around the room to the uniform hanging over a chair. He grinned. He had taken it off for the last time. He would change into the clothes he had kept in the closet and leave the uniform here in the whore's room. This is where that goddamn uniform belongs, he thought bitterly. I'll leave later and won't tell her that I'm not coming back. The premeditated deception gave Tony a sense of power and the sense of power excited him.

"Hey, Maggie," he called.

"Yeah, wait a minute." Then there exploded the unmistakable fizz from the opening of a beer bottle. "You want one?"

"No, sweetness," he said, barely able to keep from blurting, your beery breath will do, sweetness.

The thought excited him the more. He lay still, exulting in his rise of heat. He was fully aware that the beer on the breath of the woman revolted him, that he therefore disliked the woman, and that this dislike was as necessary for him and his excitement as love might be to somebody else ...

She sauntered into the room, the beer bottle in one hand. With the other hand she held her kimono together. The kimono was thin and the woman was naked underneath. The intended effect, allure, was obliterated. She looked just plain sloppy. Tony watched her walk and he stretched his body under the sheet.

"Look at you," she said, and gave a professional nod at the boy where the sheet covered his length.

Tony grinned at her. He had mistaken her boredom for surprise and admiration.

"Sit down over here and earn your living, Maggie."

"Tony, the way you talk."

But she sat down on the edge of the bed her hands sliding up and down the bottle of beer. When she noticed his eyes on her, she said, "What nice eyes you got, Tony. You know that?"

"Thanks."

Tony had inherited his mother's large, dark eyes, and he knew that they were capable of expressing a feminine softness. He watched as Maggie raised the bottle and observed how the gesture opened her kimono. One breast was revealed, large and pink and without any sexual meaning for him.

"You're lovely," he said.

She did not catch the sarcasm in his voice, an incongruity with the sudden movement of his body. She swallowed some beer.

"You really go for me, don't you, Tony?" she asked.

Maggie rarely permitted herself any feelings. She even more rarely allowed herself to reach out for approval for fear of receiving an insult. The indifference which saved her from one also saved her from the other, but sometimes—and it wasn't the beer—she did reach out. And she did this with Tony. She did it because he was young and because she did not believe his callousness. She knew that since he had begun seeing her, two or three months before, he had been with no other woman. She knew also, on purely professional grounds, that she was his first woman—and that despite his detailed accounts of dozens of other affairs since the age of thirteen.

"Don't you, Tony?" and she leaned over a little, smiling at him.

He did not say anything. He hesitated as if he could not make up his mind what mood he should allow to show and then suddenly shot out a hand to her breast.

She closed her eyes and said, "My God." Tony read this to mean passion. He did not catch the disappointment in her voice.

"Come here," he ordered.

"Let me finish the beer, Tony."

"All right. But don't stop what you're doing."

She knew what he liked her to do because he had told her many times. His hand on her breast relaxed its grip and he made a sound in his throat.

"Tony?"

"Huh?"

"When school's over, you'll take me to the lake for the weekend, before going home?"

"Sure."

"Will you, Tony?"

"I said sure."

She looked at him to see if he had really meant it but she was unable to decipher his expression. His eyes were closed and his face was rigid. His cheekbones, which were rather high, seemed to stretch his skin, making it look shiny. She set down the beer bottle and touched his face.

"Sometimes you look like a Chinaman."

"My old man was a Chinaman."

"The professor? Don't kid me," she said and laughed.

"My old man was French and not a professor."

"Ah, that's why," she said. "I figured that about your old man. Do you like him better than the professor?"

"Who needs him?" asked Tony without making clear to the woman about whom he was talking.

He hardly remembered his father; after all, Tony had not seen him for twelve years. Tony remembered only his stubbled chin, his deep voice and the odor of his cigarettes. Ages ago.

His hand slid from her breast to her back and he forced the woman against his chest. He arched against her and when the woman gasped, he mistakenly thought it passion, although he had actually hurt her by twisting her hair. He started to thrash on the bed because the lady, professionally speaking, was good.

"Hold it," he said.

"What?" and she raised her head. "But you haven't—"

"Shut up. The table," he said breathlessly. "Come on—"

She arose and he pushed her and then she started to take off her kimono on the way to the table. "Leave it on." He talked fast. "Leave it on, I said."

And then he had her lean on the table. She leaned as if she were resting on a balustrade and admiring a fertile valley far below. He was nearly overcome by the sight, but he took her, took the heat and odor of her, and he reached and reached until he burst into flame ...

Then he realized for the first time how utterly bored she was with him.

"Oh, baby," she said flatly, raising herself on her arms, "that was so good."

He looked at his wristwatch and saw that one hour and twenty-three minutes would have to be killed before train time.

The whore, Maggie, let the kimono fall down and around her again and gathered it up in front. She looked much the same as before when she had come out of the kitchen with the beer bottle in one hand. Now she circled to the side of the bed, picked up the bottle, said, "Excuse me," and took the bottle into the kitchen on her way to the bathroom beyond.

Tony heard the water running and then the voice of the woman humming a pop tune. He rubbed first his nose and then his neck. He felt deflated.

"Honey?" she called from the bathroom. "You want to lie down and sleep some, or would you rather get dressed and go to the Emporium? They got this kooky film about two goofs on a vacation who meet a girl, the daughter of their boss, and—"

"Oh, yes," he said, feeling suddenly wretched.

"Yes, what, honey? You want to sleep?"

"No." He stood up and went to the chair where his underwear lay in a heap. He put on his shorts, ignoring the uniform.

"No," he yelled. "I prefer to see that kooky film."

"You're a doll. Let me take a shower and we'll go to the film."

By the time he had said, "Yes, of course," the shower was making a rushing sound and Tony thought briefly of the slap of hot water on Maggie's rump, the skin color changing, her not unpretty face turned up to catch the stinging rush.

He took a fresh shirt from her closet and put it on. Pierre, he thought, once patted me on the head and said, "till we meet again," and his laugh was like sand scratching. Mother had run into the bathroom and had not come out until after Pierre had gone for good. So why in hell should I call him my father, Tony thought savagely. Why did Maggie bring up the subject?

He had buttoned his shirt wrong but did not notice. Then he hurried into his slacks and shrugged into the jacket which he had kept in Maggie's closet. As he dressed, his eyes fell on her clothes hanging there. For some inexplicable reason they offended him. With a single motion he tore out the hanger bar. Dresses, coats, skirts slid down one side of the bar into a shapeless heap of fabric.

"Till we meet again," he said softly as he walked out of Maggie's life.

CHAPTER THREE

"Perhaps," remarked Laura to her husband, "Tony's money was gone and he had been forced to hitchhike home." She stood by the bedroom window and looked down at the street, dark save for two widely spaced street lights.

"Nonsense," said Vaughn. "His allowance isn't large, but it is adequate and any right-thinking lad would have saved enough to last till the end of term." Robert sat on the bed and pulled off his socks.

And next he will say, Laura thought dully, that hitchhiking home will teach Tony a damn good lesson and so cast the whole thing off like one of his socks.

"Laura?"

"Yes?"

She looked at him from where she stood, hoping that he would say something nice to her.

"Please don't stand at the window like that, Laura. What if somebody should see you?"

Laura read warmth and concern into his comment. And next, she hoped, perhaps he'll say, come sit with me on the bed instead of standing there all by your lonesome.

"I don't mean to correct you so frequently," Robert went on, "but you know the kind of neighbors we have, dear."

She was grateful for the "dear" and ignored the rest, only foolishness to her. She was wearing a housecoat and her hair was combed and foremost among the neighbors to whom her husband was referring was Miss Ambru. There was nothing anyone could do about Miss Ambru. To that old bag, open-toed shoes meant indecent exposure.

Laura pulled the curtain and turned to her spouse. To her surprise, the bed was empty. Then the shower started up in the bathroom. Robert Vaughn did not take a shower every night. He was a hot-tub man, often lying in water up his neck and reading a book. This would exhaust him most pleasantly and then he would sleep soundly. But at other times he would take a cold shower at night, for stimulation and wide-awake vitality.

Is it Wednesday? she wondered. Of course, it's Wednesday and I had forgotten. Robert takes a shower only before making love and he makes love only on Wednesday. After making love he takes a shower again. Before he smells of something called The Queen's Escort and after he rushes away for a dose of manly, coniferous-smelling talcum.

How does Robert in essence smell? She sat down in front of the mirror and could not remember the odors of which her husband was composed.

When she had met him in Bretagne that summer he had smelled of earth and wet leaves. He had worn a corduroy jacket and boots covered with clay and had tenderly guided her through the graveyards, pointing out this famous tomb, and that well-known cross.

Robert had been happy to discover a fellow American and he had talked a lot about the land and the excavations and his future as an archaeologist. He had been altogether happy that summer, and so had she.

He had not made love to her for weeks after their first date, although she had been willing to stay with him from the start. Why? He had known that she was not a virgin.

Looking back over her first marriage—the one which had produced Antoine—and the intervening years, none of which had been entirely loveless, she wondered why on earth she had chosen to share her life with Robert Vaughn.

She decided that it was because Robert had not wanted to be alone and she had craved that. When they had first made love, she had ignored everything which had not been fulfilling because when a man is good in his heart, she felt, he will soon become good with his body. And she had wanted the warmth and the shelter he offered.

Laura closed her eyes.

That first time his shyness had been a goad. Their union had not occurred in his room but in hers and young Tony had been sleeping in the next room, his breathing unending and sure.

"Is he quite asleep?" Robert had asked softly from the door.

"For the whole night," she had assured him, beckoning to him from the quaint bedroom with the view of the woods.

"Good," said Robert. He had run his hand through her shaggy hair. His walk was gangly and she had thought all his mannerisms terribly charming. "Laura," he had said, backing off toward the window, "May I stay with you for a little while longer?"

"That would be wonderful," she had gushed. "We'll have to be very quiet. I wouldn't want the boy to wake up."

And Robert had done the safe thing, gone to the window sill on which the wine bottle had been sitting and poured another glass. A drop of the dark red liquid had splashed on to his trembling hand. She had walked over to him and leaned against him.

"I can smell the dark woods outside," she had said, "and the warmth of your hair. They fit together."

But the reference to his hair had made him feel shy. She had been able to tell by the feel of his arm that he was afraid.

"And the wine," she had gone on, "that's a slow, green smell."

He had set down the glass, carefully keeping his mouth closed—this last, perhaps, from shyness, too.

"And I like it," she had said, bending down to kiss him on the mouth.

She had kept her mouth there, quite calmly, until she had felt him relax. His arm had gone around her. The tail of her blouse had come out of the skirt and his hand had touched her bare skin. He had moved his fingers in a slow circle.

"Let me sit," she had murmured.

"The bottle—"

"Throw it out of the window."

He had obliged and then they had moved to the bed.

He had quickly moved his hand away from her hip, where she had placed it.

"Darling, have I ever told you about the Upper Jurassic period of Europe?"

"Oh, Robert," she had said, "please ..."

"Yes?" he said. "What, dear?"

Then it had struck her how to seduce him. She had ducked down her head so that he could not see her face and mumbled into his shirt. The shirt had smelled warm and of wool.

"Please, Robert," she had mumbled.

"What, dear? What is it?"

"I—I feel shy, Robert. I don't know why."

"But darling," he said, his voice becoming sure, caressing, "you needn't be shy with me, really. Come here," and he had tried to lift her chin.

"But I do. This is the first time in my life I've felt completely helpless."

"Now, now," he had said, trying to reach her mouth. "Why shyness?" With her help, he had managed to kiss her.

Then he had been bold enough to say, "What we are doing is pleasant and natural, is it not? It is in the very nature of closeness and mutual regard that one should—"

"Robert, don't talk. Just kiss me again."

"Ah?"

"Yes, show me, Robert."

She had become soft and limp in his arms and he had felt like showing her Everything, which included more than he himself had known. But soon their loving had become no longer a matter of awkward fumbling. She had felt the demand in his hands; and he, the heat in her skin. When he had struggled with her first button, she had stretched out beside him, reached with one hand and turned off the bed lamp with wonderful timing. The click of the switch had seemed to do something for him. He had pulled down her blouse, pinning her arms to her side.

Feeling her in that position, he had gone wild. He had torn at her bra and fumbled out her breasts. Then he had enclosed them with his hands, his mouth. She had encouraged him, making soft, kittenish sounds in the dark. He had suddenly felt a great sureness and had touched her more slowly, her lips, her nipples, her belly. But then the woman's impatience and rapid breathing had goaded Robert, and he had clutched and pressed as if possessed.

She had wanted all of him and that was how it had been. He had been twisted as if in a great tornado, and her excitement had met him like a rushing wave. Rather suddenly then, lying beside her, he had gone to sleep. She had held him and listened to him in the dark and had felt loving and tender toward him. She had thought briefly of her son in the next room but then, finally, only of Robert. And how good everything would be, by and by.

Now, as she opened her eyes—she was still sitting in front of the mirror—she contemplated herself. She felt, rather than saw, her smile.

Pierre, once long ago, had said to her, "You are safest when you can be amused, darling."

"Laura?" Robert's voice came from the here and now of suburbia.

She turned and shifted into another mood.

"I like your hair when it's damp," she said.

She got up, went to him, and explored his narrow hips. He was wearing a bathrobe of thick toweling but she ignored that.

"Come lie in my bed?" she asked.

"I would like to," he said.

He moved away from her and clicked off the light. The click hung in the air as they lay down together.

She enjoyed the warm dampness of his skin and the odor of the lotion he had used. He made love to her steadily and with precision.

At the end he said, "You are lovely, my Laura," and then, "sleep well, dear," and went to take his second shower.

Tony was hitchhiking home but not because he lacked money. He cared to call his reason "lust for life."

He discussed fishing with the first man who gave him a lift, but since Tony knew nothing about fishing, while the driver did, he soon changed the subject to learning. Tony reasoned that, a man who talks fishing can't have much brains. He skillfully switched over to psychology, although his scanty knowledge of that field was based on three books: a Krafft-Ebing volume, standard equipment in his dormitory, a badly printed paperback and a text filched from the public library.

"No," said Tony's driver, "I've never heard of compulsive dementia."

"Well," explained Tony, "it's a clinical term, rather new, to cover those complexes which have never before been recognized as neurotically determined."

"Hm," grunted the driver. He refrained from saying anything more, although he happened to be a good psychiatrist.

"The condition," Tony went on, "interferes with normal intercourse, you know. It's surprisingly prevalent."

"I see," said the kindly driver. "I've always believed that you can't have a good lay when you have something else on your mind."

Tony, preoccupied, got out farther up the line. He walked into a roadhouse where, to his surprise, he was served hard liquor. This made him feel an obligation to get drunk. He went from the bar to a booth, where he was entertained by a black-haired waitress who called him, "Honey." The name Alice was lettered in red above her left breast. As Tony drank more, she began to resemble Alice in Wonderland eating of the magic mushroom. Alternately Alice kept elongating and then shrinking. Soon Tony found himself repeating a shortened version of her name.

"Al," he said, "All I want, Al, is a little love."

"All right, honey," said the waitress, tall as a tree at that moment. "Al will help you."

She called the bartender whose name, strangely enough, was also Al and he hoisted Tony to the cabins in back of the bar. There he dumped him onto the bed, took three dollars out of his pocket, left a receipt on the dresser, and turned off the light.

Tony did not remember anything when he woke up the next morning. He crawled to the bathroom and then back into bed. The maid woke him an hour later and told him to hit the road or pay for a second day. Tony left.

Grip in hand, he walked out of the cabin. He had decided to return to the last town he had passed and there buy a bus ticket for the remainder of his trip.

"Hey—man!"

He turned around, much too quickly for the kind of head he was carrying.

A fellow Tony's age and two girls were emerging from a cabin. They carried three battered suitcases and were waving at him.

"Going east?" yelled one of the girls.

Tony nodded, a little stiffly.

"We're going to have breakfast first. You want some?" the girl said.

He most certainly did not want any but on this morning, although it was almost noon, anybody could have persuaded him to do anything and he accompanied them into the restaurant. He ordered dry toast and black coffee. A matter of diet, he explained, but felt too sick to tell why.

The other three ate like hogs. Eggs, potatoes, pancakes, sausages, toast and a pitcher of orange juice.

Tony stared at the brown spots on the ceiling. Only sometimes did he look at his benefactors. The boy was a toothy fellow with short blond hair and a completely uninteresting face. The girl with him was healthy, pink and overfed. Tony was not interested. The other, although thin, was fairly sexy. She had mild, brown eyes, jutting breasts and reddish hair piled high.

"You been sleeping alone all night, too?" she asked Tony.

He shook his head no.

"How come we didn't hear anything?" complained the girl. "We were in the cabin right next to yours."

"Maybe they were busy listening to us," the hefty teen giggled.

"I beg your pardon?" asked Tony.

"You English or something?" the hefty one said.

"No," said Tony. "I'm French."

"I knew it," the thin girl said, laughing, and from then on Tony was adopted.

It could not, of course, have happened on a worse day. The sun was too bright, his head too large, his bones too sore. His eyes were swimming in a sour pool of brine. He managed, with a show of lassitude and sullenness—both insulting—to sit alone in the back seat of the car.

The boy drove and the hefty girl cuddled next to him. His one hand was busy and now and again the hefty girl made hoarse sounds. The thin one, kneeling down on the seat, sat facing Tony.

"Aren't they something?" she asked, indicating the two lovers.

"I beg your pardon?"

"They were at it all night and they still want to play around."

"You sound jealous," the driver snapped to the thin girl. "Why don't you—"

"You're damn right," snarled the girl. "Waiting all night for that jerk Dave to show up while you two in the next bed are grabbing off all the fun. I'll never speak to him again."

"That won't bother him none. All he wants—"

"So why didn't he show up? He said he would."

"Maybe his weekend pass was canceled," comforted the boy.

The hefty teen gave a special sigh and said, "Shut up, will you?" Then the redhead, her yellow sweater half unbuttoned, playfully poked Tony. He closed his eyes, stricken by the overwhelming sight. Her breasts, pushed up like giant balloons, were freakish rather than sexy.

Tony's negative reaction suggested weariness from total, prolonged exposure to a thousand and one nights of love-making. This pose only stimulated the large-breasted girl. For one hundred and one miles she tried to seduce Tony with innuendoes and bits of anatomy.

Then the driver pulled the car into a dirt lane and took the hefty girl into the bushes. Tony descended, stretched and struck out for a clump of pines.

The thin girl, May Belle, followed him.

"Wait at the car, would you please?" Tony asked. "I'm going to take care of some business."

"Alone?"

"I have to take a leak."

He stayed in the bushes for a considerable length of time. Then as he approached the gray car once again, he overheard the conversation.

"No. He isn't here." May Belle was fuming. "How come?"

"I think he's impertinent."

"He's what?"

"You know. A queer."

"You mean impotent."

"That's what I said. Let's get out of here."

"Damn right, let's get out of here. Queers give me the creeps."

The driver stepped on the gas.

Somebody threw Tony's grip out of the window and then there was only the grip on the road and dust from the departing car.

Tony knew that he was only about seven miles from his home town. He did not get another lift. He walked for three hours and finally sweated off his hangover.

What a lousy day, he mused. His lust for life had slowly drained out of him and what had he gotten from his adventures? As he rounded a bend, he sighted the town with its tree-shaded streets and graceful campus spires. He did not want to see anyone, least of all his mother and stepfather. Unless it was Tad Howard.

And then he saw the motel and cringed a little, thinking of his last stop; but his desire to speak to Tad, whose father owned the camp, overrode his objections. Tad was really the only friend Tony had in this town, or in any town, were Tony honest.

Tad was his own age but the most willing admirer Tony had ever had. This was partly because Tad seemed to believe everything Tony told him, and partly because Tony did not suffer from all the doubts and sudden sensitivities that constantly threatened and rocked Tad's self-esteem. At least, that was Tony's impression.

Tad was at the far end of the row of cabins, one knee balancing a board of wood which he was sawing. He heard Tony coming up the drive and rose to meet him.

Tad was unobtrusively built. There was nothing special about his appearance. He had thin, brown hair and grave, gray eyes. He was halting, if not shy, in his movements, and his facial expressions varied from wide-eyed surprise to frowning concentration.

He dropped the saw and started to run toward Tony, who clapped him on the shoulder.

They grinned at each other.

"Hi, boy," said Tony.

"Hi," Tad pushed his brown hair back from his thin face. "Been waiting for you," he smiled. "You back for the summer?"

"Sure. Anything new here in town?"

"No. You look kind of beat, Tony. Tired?"

"No. Just worn out. You know."

"Worn out? Hey, come on. Let's sit down in back and talk some. When did I see you last, Christmas?"

"I'm kind of worn out because—" but Tony interrupted himself. Tad just wasn't tuned in, Tony thought. Tad had turned and was leading the way to a big tree whose green shade fell slowly.

They sat down under the tree and both of them stretched. Tony took out cigarettes and offered one to Tad.

"Might as well," said Tad.

They sat and smoked for a while. Tony dragged in a preoccupied manner and Tad puffed slowly so as not to get too much smoke in his eyes.

"How was school?" he asked.

"Lousy. I got thrown out."

"What for?"

"The usual." Tony flipped ashes. "You know."

"You mean you didn't graduate?"

"What's the difference? And you?"

"I did. Week ago."

"And now you're a breadwinner for daddy."

Tad smiled and shrugged.

"Going to college in the fall?" asked Tony.

"No. I would like to, but impossible."

"The old man?"

Tad nodded. He ground out his cigarette and viewed the green meadows.

"He says anybody who doesn't know what he's going to study has no business in school."

Tony laughed. He wasn't really interested. "Tell him you want to go to school to learn everything," said Tony.

"I did."

When Tony laughed this time, it was for real. Tad looked desperately unhappy. He explained to Tony that his father had yelled at him to wake up and look life in the face. "Dad wants me to help out with the motel."

"Anyway," said Tony. "I'm back. What do you say we have a good summer?"

"Let's try," said Tad and smiled at the view stretching out before him.

Then he looked at Tony and Tony smiled back at him and neither of them knew what they really wanted. Nor did they know what they would get.

CHAPTER FOUR

Cher Pierre, she wrote, then hesitated and looked up. She gazed out of the window and listened to the monotonous drumming of Tony's heel. She knew that he was lying on his bed, one leg down on the floor and beating out the rhythm to some melody.

Cher Pierre, cher Pierre, she thought, Tony is not at all like you. I've never really known Antoine, our son …

She picked up her pen and inked out in neat black letters the following:

> Thank you so much for your note, Pierre. I hardly expected an answer. In a way it was as unexpected and brief, as our last meeting. I am tempted to say: And leading nowhere. Just as our last meeting—I don't remember, but didn't I introduce you to Robert that time in Bretagne? You are right, of course, when you say it would not have led anywhere even if Robert had not already arrived. You and I, Pierre, were through six years earlier, or why else the divorce? But I do not intend to dwell on the past. Antoine is well. He has just come back from school, for the summer, and next year, I think, we will spend June and July in Europe. You've never asked, I know, but if you wish, perhaps you might meet him then—

"Writing to Pierre?"

She turned quickly and saw Tony standing in the doorway.

"No clairvoyance," he said as he walked into the room. "I saw the letter from France in the mailbox and looked at the sender, Pierre Le Roux. He is my father, isn't he?"

She winced at the hardness of his remark.

"Or is there more than one Pierre?" he asked as he sank into the couch. The springs sighed and Tony gave an exaggerated grunt. Sprawled in the seat, boredom on his face, he tried to estimate the effect of his insulting remark.

If Tony were Pierre, I'd turn and scream at him, Laura reflected. She abruptly cut off her train of thought.

"Sit up," she said.

"What?"

"Come over here."

"I don't see why—"

"Did you hear me, Antoine?"

Because she had called him Antoine, he responded. She used that name only when feeling tender or when feeling hard. He knew that she meant business.

He got up and walked over to stand in front of her chair. For a moment he was reminded of Captain Barkstow at school but his comparison shocked him. Barkstow was stiff and his mother was not. Barkstow was stuffy and pompous and a bastard with a stone for a heart, whereas his mother ... Tony lowered his eyes.

"There is only one Pierre," she said. She quickly bit her lip. That was not exactly what she had intended to remark.

"Yes, ma'am," said her son.

"And he is your father, even though nothing worked right and we had to separate."

"Yes, ma'am."

"Stop that 'ma'am' business. Robert has been more of a father to you than Pierre since, since the time ..."

"I was six. I remember nothing."

"All right."

Nothing was going as she had planned. Instead of making the present more firm the discussion had made everything vague. And her past frustration had become a hard, present pain.

"Tony," she cajoled. "Let's try and have a good summer." She smiled, as if the remark were a question, rather than a wish. "We'll go to the lake for a week or two and drive into New York now and again—"

"How will I be able to do any of that with the school work Robert's laying out for me?"

He sounded more like a little boy than an accusing adult. She smiled, pleased by the tone of her son.

"It won't be too burdensome. I can help you."

Suddenly his exasperation grew. Help me, he thought. Some things you have got to do alone and nobody can help. The Pythagorean theorem is one example and feeling starved on the inside is another example. Nobody can understand for you and nobody can eat for you, or feel for you—

"What's the matter, *cher?*" asked Laura.

"Mother, you can be so naive."

"But—about what, Antoine?"

"You're so—naive, I can't even explain it to you." He was shouting.

"Please, Antoine," and her patience was heartfelt. "I'm sure there's some way I can, we can—"

"What do you want from me?"

"Why nothing. I love you."

Unexpected though the remark had been it did not surprise her because she had meant it. But it sounded terrible to Tony who was embarrassed, sickened, confused.

"Stop treating me like an idiot," he said. Instead of "idiot" he had nearly blurted "baby." "And you and Robert stop planning my summers for me and my winters and everything."

"But can't I—"

"No, you can't, I have my own ways." And then he ran out of the room and Laura heard him slam the front door.

She sat and was not at all concerned about his lack of respect and his rudeness. She sat and felt terribly weak, recognizing her own helplessness. And her own guilt.

Children did not grow up strong and carefree like weeds. Not without a father around, not with a latter-day husband who was more anthropologist than father. Not with a woman who felt alone—

The slam of the door was a solution for Tony. The more doors I slam, he thought with unusual cynicism, the more I solve. He grinned and felt free of the house and when he saw Miss Lettie Ambru he smiled at her.

She was a woman of round, female proportions who from the rear, at a distance, might have resembled somebody's grandmother. But not from the front and not from close up. From the front could be seen her lightly packed breasts, and from close up her face, with its doll-like unblinking eyes. Her blue-gray hair had been rinsed black and placed under a net.

"Why, Tony dear," she called from her open door.

"How nice to see you."

"Thank you, Miss Ambru, and if I may say so, you're looking every bit as well and hearty as last summer."

She smiled and was about to say, "Oh, you Frenchmen," but restrained herself. After all, Tony was only a boy, a wonderfully young boy.

"That's a lovely compliment." She closed her eyes for effect. She liked Tony's good manners. Miss Ambru fed on falseness. "And you're back for the whole summer, dear?"

"Oh, yes, Miss Ambru. The whole, wonderful summer."

"How nice." She smiled sweetly, staring at the house next door in which, she suspected, that professor and Mrs. Vaughn were closing in an embrace. And this dear, lonely boy, Tony, they've sent him out of the house, she mused.

"Some time you and your nice mother must come over to tea, dear, won't you do that?"

"I'll tell Mother, Miss Ambru. Though she's generally more or less occupied in the afternoons, you know."

"And what about you?" she asked.

"Oh, I can always be torn away, although this particular afternoon ..."

"Tomorrow, dear? It happens I'm baking orange cookies tomorrow morning and if—"

"Delighted, Miss Ambru. I'm sure."

"Oh, you French—" she said with a rapidly dropping voice so that Tony could only guess at what she had said.

He nodded and walked away and thought how easy it had been, talking to old Ambru, the fortress in whalebone. How easy it had been to talk to her, and how difficult to talk with his mother.

He walked swiftly through the small town, trying to kill time before supper. Supper, hell! And walk into that house to apologize? To suffer silence? To bear advice and stupid Robert to boot?

He again felt that disturbing anger, the feeling which he had transformed into politeness for Miss Ambru, and which he now used in another way. With his eyes he attacked a young girl who was crossing the street, hair moving like a fine scarf in a wind, a young bounce to her figure, and a shift and a swing to her buttocks that made Tony shiver. She possessed a simple, country face, but for a moment, to Tony, she was the Mona Lisa.

Once on his side of the street she stopped in front of a hardware store and gave Tony a chance to look closer.

Why do these hicks, he wondered, pack their boobs in tight and high? I bet she has round, ripe fruit shapes ...

He didn't get any further. He had meant to elucidate her belly, rear and thighs, but his dream-girl was suddenly whisked away by Tad.

The brown-haired boy walked without touching her and without looking at her. Hell, thought Tony, if I were walking that close to her ...

The two stopped at the movie house, agreed upon something, then split up. The girl walked inside. Tad glanced at her departing derrière and then walked on again.

"Hey, Tad!" Tony ran after him and Tad stopped.

"Hi," he said. "Walk to the motel with me?"

"Sure. Why aren't you walking to the motel with that oolala I just saw you with?"

"Amy?" asked Tad, keeping his face straight. "She's working. She's cashier there."

"Free movies for you, huh?"

"Yeah," and Tad laughed.

"Free oolala for you, too?"

"Cut it out, Tony. Gosh—"

"Come on, pal, tell me about it."

"Listen. I just met her and—"

"When?"

"Four months ago and—"

"That long?"

"We're going steady," said Tad, as if that explained everything.

"So how is she? Is she good?"

"I said I was going steady with her and that's all I said."

"That isn't saying much, pal."

Tad, his brow puckered, kept still. This gave him a chance to think over what Tony had just said and it struck Tad that there really wasn't much to his going steady, except that the phrase seemed vaguely impressive.

"Yeah," he said suddenly. "There isn't much to it. Yet."

Tony, to his own surprise, felt shocked by his friend's honesty. This took the edge off Tony's assumed superiority. To his credit, he allowed himself to feel admiration for Tad.

"You call a spade a spade. That's why I like you," he said softly.

"We got plans," said Tad who sensed his friend's embarrassment. "We're exploring—" The word shook him up a little. "We're seeing how we like each other and maybe we can make it stick."

"Stick?" Tony's veneer of sophistication had returned and he felt sharp and clever. "Stick what, pal?"

"You know. I mean we haven't talked about it, but maybe we'll get married."

"That's why you go steady?"

That was not why, and Tad suddenly knew it. "I thought so," he said. "I thought that's why I gave her my ring."

"You're going steady," said Tony with slow emphasis, "because that way you don't have to hunt around for anybody else."

"God. What a way to put it, Tony."

"You're afraid to date some chick you really wanna make so you get tied down and that looks to others as if you've got a steady lay."

"God, Tony. There are other things, you know."

"Like what?"

Tad was sure there were other things even though he could not think of a single one at the moment. He could only assume that Tony was right about all the negative reasons for going steady.

"I'll tell you," said Tony and he warmed up to the subject. "Like French kissing and heavy petting."

Tad shook his head. "I can't," he said.

"I bet you think sex is dirty," accused Tony.

"No."

"And because she's a nice girl, you wouldn't approach her. Nice girls, to your way of thinking, don't indulge."

"I didn't say that."

"You didn't have to. You act it. You'd go to a house of prostitution—"

"I never have."

"You want to?"

"No, of course not. I want—"

"I know. I saw her. But she's a nice girl, you say. Therefore you can't ask her. Let me tell you something from my personal experience, Tad, pal. To me the nicest are the ones that do. Get it?"

Tony laughed, so that Tad immediately took him less seriously. In a way that was a shame, Tad felt, because a hell of a lot Tony had said made sense.

"Take for example," said Tony, "my trip home. Just to show you."

"Go ahead," said Tad. "Tell me."

They started to turn in at the motel but then Tad led the way down a path next to the motel where they could not be seen from the office in front.

"Old man looking for you?" asked Tony.

"I don't think so. But why take a chance, hey?"

They both laughed and ran to the last building on the motel property. A group of three cabins stood wall to wall and at the end of those leaned a shed for tools, lumber and pipes.

"Wait till you see what I got in here," said Tad as they ducked into the shed.

It was dim and warm inside and smelled of lumber. Tad reached into a barrel filled with folded burlap sacks and pulled out a bottle.

"Something, hey? Raspberry wine …"

"Raspberry? Man, that's like trying to get loaded on a banana split."

"You're nuts. Raspberry wine is stronger than—"

"Ice cream. Stronger than ice cream, right?"

They argued for a while as if delaying for heightened pleasure. They knew they would soon sit down in the shed, relaxing in the summer warmth among the lumber, like a couple of Huckleberry Finns.

"So tell me what you were going to tell me," said Tad.

"First, open the bottle, man."

"All right."

They sat and grinned at each other, as if the first problem had not yet been invented.

CHAPTER FIVE

"You seen Tad?" asked Mr. Howard of his wife.

"No, I haven't seen Tad," said Mrs. Howard to her husband.

They stared at each other silently in the kitchen behind the motel's office. They had long practice in this sort of thing: the innocuous opening remark, the silence as if they were gathering forces and next the mean and useless battle.

"I only ask," said Howard, "because I have the welfare of my son at heart. Unlike his drunken mother, I care."

He turned away as if finished, but that was also part of the act. When the silence behind him became too long he flipped up his suspenders, rubbed the fat, round, stubbled chin as if he thought he might need a shave, and sniffed noisily. "Cat got your tongue?" he snarled. "Where's Tad?"

Mrs. Howard said, "How can I keep an eye on him? I sit around the house because I'm sick and I'm trying to get well. I'm trying ..."

"Yeah. On that medicine, dearie, you will never get well." He nodded at the cupboard in which the bottle was kept. "Alcoholic wife."

"Run-around husband."

"Stop right there, Nella. I ain't no run-around."

"I was only fooling. One look at that stomach of yours and I know no other woman would want you, but I just thought you'd like to think I thought you were still a young man." She blinked foolishly, not sure she had gotten it right. Then she had an urge to look at the cupboard but she restrained herself.

"Go ahead," said Lambert. "It's there. Unless you've finished it already."

She leaned back on the green couch and closed her eyes. "Oh," she said. This too was part of the game.

But Lambert was tired of it. There was something he wanted to do. He yanked at his pants as if intending to hoist them up over his belly, a gesture that always signaled he was ready to leave.

"Oh," his wife said again. "Oh, oh—" She was trying to switch the topic from her drinking to her suffering.

But Lambert did not play by the rules this time. It was getting dark outside and he had something to do, so he walked out.

When Nella Howard opened her eyes and saw that her husband was gone, she was enraged. She arose, marched to the cupboard and took a long pull from the bottle. Then she shoved the bottle to the rear of the cupboard and shuffled back to her couch. Lambert came in again just as she was sitting down. She closed her eyes.

Lambert picked up the glasses he had left on the table, watched his wife sink back with a sigh, and then—feeling mean—moved to the cupboard and opened it. The liquor inside the bottle was still in motion.

"Now just look at that jiggling booze. Why don't you, seeing as it wants release, let it go, hey?" Lambert said.

Mrs. Howard snapped open her mouth and spewed hate and filth at her husband.

"... and never forget, Lambert Howard, who caused all the pain I suffer. Never forget what my doctor said about Tad's birth."

"Nuts," said Lambert. "That was more than seventeen years ago, sweetheart."

"Seventeen years of agony and—"

"Boozing. And boozing."

"You fat cheapskate, if you had paid for the proper care and not denied me the medical—"

"Nuts," Lambert repeated with a smirk.

"Now you listen here, Mr. Slopgut!" she screeched.

He had never heard her call him that before and he stopped short. "What?"

"You had to have your way night after night," she screeched. "You had to get me pregnant, you careless slop. I dislocated my spine giving life to that brat. I'll never let you forget that, Mr. Slopgut, never, you bastard!"

Medical opinion, of course, had nothing to do with her self-diagnosis, but she had repeated her accusations for many years. Lambert shrugged and walked out of the kitchen. He had something else to do.

It concerned Cabin Number Seventeen. It was a five-day rental and the couple had picked Howard's place, they said, because they loved the view and the walk to the lake nearby. Lambert had never seen the couple take the walk to the lake and knew better why they loved Number Seventeen. He himself loved it ...

"So, like I told you, she was a slob," Tony said. He looked at the all but empty bottle and thought, it has no effect whatsoever, just like a banana split. "And since I was the only eligible guy in the road house, she kept after me. Drink after drink."

"They served you liquor in the roadhouse?"

"Of course. It's easy for me, because I look grown up. What's that you're doing?"

"Putting the lantern on, it's so dark in here."

"All right," said Tony, "so I'm telling you this to show you that you got to decide, so to speak—after taking a look and feeling it out—what your position will be." He stopped and stared at Tad. "What you doing now?"

Tad was leaning forward, staring at the bottle between Tony's knees and pushing the lantern toward it so he could see better.

"God," he said. "It's almost empty. You drunk?"

"I told you. Like a banana split."

Despite his sarcasm, the banana split was giving Tony a splitting headache. He blamed his lack of concentration on that.

"Where was I?" Tony said.

"I don't know."

"Oh, yes. This bag of a waitress trying to pick me up all that time. Followed me to the cabin."

"No," Tad said.

"Yes. Now the point is, you pick, see? Not for convenience, but because you're you. And you deserve a special chick. Dig?"

"I want the bottle," Tad said suddenly, completely ignoring Tony's philosophy.

"Leave me some."

"Just let me have a smell, huh, Tony?"

"You a lush? Listen, I'm just coming to the good part of my story. Not only was this waitress trying to get me into bed, but this cute little chick, a customer, was giving me the high sign ...”

"In other words, you excited her."

"Exactly. She was dying for my kiss."

"Did you hear something?" Tad asked, turning and peering.

"You listening to me or what?"

"Go on, Tony."

"So I give the waitress the slip and signaled to the other to follow me out to the cabin ..."

"What's going on here, anyhow?"

Tony gasped and Tad jumped as Mr. Howard came to the door. Then the motel owner's voice softened.

"Why hello, Tony," he said, sweetly, with a tea-party grin. "Didn't know you was back from private school." Lambert had respect for private schools because they cost money.

Tony got up and shook hands with the man. Lambert turned to his son. The voice went from sweet to sour and from there to pure acid.

"You know I been looking for you? What's that bottle you got there? You been drinking in secret? Don't you know what that will lead to? Have I got to carry a double curse in my house, you bum?"

"I brought the bottle, Mr. Howard," said Tony. "Cherry wine from my grandmother in Vermont."

"Oh?" said Howard.

"No more dangerous than a banana split. You know grandmothers."

Lambert laughed as if he accepted the reasoning.

"And Tad," Tony continued, "I was keeping him company while he was doing some work here. Carpentry."

"What carpentry?" asked Lambert of his son.

Tad, trapped with another's lie, tried to follow it up. "Well, after I fixed the door in Number Five, I—"

"Never mind that," Lambert snapped venomously. "What carpentry were you doing here, in the shed?"

"Why I wanted to fix this board, I—"

"Did I ever tell you to fix that board?"

Neither Tony nor Tad could follow the man's logic. Lambert was yelling and making more fuss than the situation seemed to warrant.

"Did I ever say," Lambert said, "to go into the shed and fix that board in the wall? Did I tell you once or a hundred times to keep your hands off things unless I specifically give you permission to monkey with them?"

"Yes, sir."

"Don't you yessir me, young feller! Now get in the house and stay there. "

Lambert turned to Tony and suddenly grinned. "If Tad was going to a fine military school like you, son, maybe I wouldn't have to put on an act like this, huh? What do you think, Tony?"

Tad was gone by then and Tony wanted to leave too. He disliked Lambert's familiar manner. The man was entirely too gauche for the young aristocrat's taste.

"Undoubtedly, Mr. Howard. And I'm sorry about the wine. But boys will be boys—you know that. Now, if you'll pardon me, I've got to go home."

"Sure, sure, sure. And give my regards to the professor, hey?" He waved the boy goodbye.

Tony stopped in the lane outside in the dark to catch his breath, to let his head calm down. He saw the light go out in the shed. But Lambert Howard didn't emerge. Tony, puzzled, turned to go home. A dead branch under his foot cracked with a sound like a whip and Tony cursed while he stumbled and held out his hand to steady himself against the back of the shed.

Now he heard Howard come out. He could not see him on the other side of the shed but he heard the fast scramble inside, the fast steps through the door, and then he saw Lambert walk away, so casually that Tony stood and thought again.

When Lambert had gone, Tony moved quietly to the dark shed. Then he saw the point of light.

One clapboard was tilted out of line on the wall and next to it was the space made by the studs. There was a hole in the beaverboard on the other side and light issued from it.

"I'll be damned," said Tony.

And for a while he stood there and watched the couple in Number Seventeen excite each other with their hands and their mouths and then he watched them make love.

Lambert Howard was not often lucky enough to get a couple that liked to make love with the bed lamps on. Lambert, reminiscing, chewed his lower lip, increasing its purple sheen.

He saw the light go out in Number Seventeen. He chewed on his lip furiously now, thinking about those two in the dark in Number Seventeen, how they would breathe in the dark now, exhausted.

Had he known that Tony at this very minute was using his, Lambert's, peephole, the motel owner would have reversed his opinion of Tad's friend.

Unsuspecting, however, he moved through the night toward the house.

Inside, Tad was walking into the kitchen. He said, "Hello, Maw," but he could tell by the way his mother looked past him that she was in a twelve a.m. condition and it was only nine o'clock. They must have had a special fight, he thought.

"Stop rattling those pots like that—heavens," she said.

"Okay, Maw."

"What are you up to anyway?" she demanded "You fixing to cook something? You know what those cooking odors do to me in my weakened condition."

"But I haven't eaten yet, Maw."

"Stop calling me Maw as if I was some kind of a peasant, or something."

"Yes, Mother."

"And none of your lip."

It must have been a bad fight, all right, thought Tad. He did not react to his mother in any other way. Most of the time he felt safely dull. It was a matter of many years' training. He had somehow managed to get himself two mothers. One raised me, he would tell himself, and she is the one who does not hurt me and sometimes gives me a touch of love. The other mother was a gray woman who sat eternally on a green couch. That woman was hardly more than a spirit—all the life in that grayness came out of a bottle.

"You better watch out for Paw," she said peevishly. "He's been looking for you. If I wasn't in such a weakened condition I'd give you a thing or two for all—what you doing there? I asked you time and again—"

"I'm fixing a sandwich, Mother."

"I've asked you time and again—"

"Leave that boy alone," said Lambert from the door.

The silence was the usual terrible kind now.

But this has nothing to do with me, Tad told himself. It is something between them. Thus he dissociated himself from parental conflicts. Tad, head hanging, moved toward the door.

"Where you going?" yelled his mother.

"I told you to quit shouting at the boy," said his father.

"All I'm doing is telling him to stay put and take what's coming to him. You were looking for him, weren't you?"

"Come here, boy," said his father.

Tad did not feel like a football being tossed back and forth. His self-image was both less concrete and more profound. He felt like a sailor caught between Scylla and Charybdis.

"What were you doing there in the shack?"

"Just sitting around, Dad. With Tony."

"Just sitting around. Doing what?"

"Nothing. Just talking."

"About what?"

"Oh, school and what's been happening since we last saw each other."

"I bet," said Mrs. Howard. "Sex talk, most likely."

"You been talking about sex?" asked Mr. Howard. "Answer me."

"Well, I think once or—"

"And what brought that up, in that shed of all places?"

"Nothing."

"Don't you lie to me."

"I'm not, Dad."

"Gimme that glass of chocolate milk on the cupboard there, dear," said Mrs. Howard, interrupting the cross-examination.

"Get it yourself," said Mr. Howard.

"In my weakened—"

"Get it yourself!" Howard hated to be interfered with while teaching his son. "I'm not your slave."

There came an imaginative stream of filth from Mrs. Howard, but she got up to make her drink.

"I think I'll go," said Tad. "I have a headache."

"Headache?" yelled Howard. "Can't keep off the booze and then has the nerve to complain he's got a headache! I got a good mind ..."

"You been drinking, you filthy kid?" asked Mrs. Howard.

"No, Mother."

"Liar, I know your kind and how you lie."

"Stands to reason," said Mr. Howard, "that the kid would drink. He sees his own mother doing it."

"I'm going," said Tad. "I don't want to listen to you two and the way you talk to each other."

"Don't want to listen? You listen good! When I tell you a thing, you listen good!"

"You have nothing to say to me. You're talking to my mother."

"Don't you tell me what I'm doing, you stupid, punk kid."

"Leave that boy alone," said Mrs. Howard.

"Shut your drunken mouth." Then Lambert turned to his son. "And you," he said, "I'm going to teach you to make fun of your parents and put on that superior air. I've got a good mind to whop the stuffing out of you for what you done today."

"Don't talk like that," said Tad, reddening.

"You threatening me, kid?"

"All I—I don't know what you're talking about any more. Honest," he said in a pleading voice.

"You don't, huh? A whopping means—"

"I wasn't referring to that."

"You double-talking me, you punk? Come here."

"Don't," said Tad as his father moved toward him.

His father bit his lip once, snapped one suspender. "I'll teach you to remember what a whopping is like. I'll—"

"Don't touch me," said Tad. "I'm warning you."

"Don't be afraid of him," said Mrs. Howard to her husband.

Lambert hauled out at his son, who saw the old man's swing come at him like a knobby branch tumbling awkwardly from a great height. Then he felt the hard clout on the side of his head and swayed. His father's eyes focused, sharp as needles on Tad's face. Then with intent and directness, one fist came straight across and hit Tad's right eye.

Red existed all of itself, hot, sharp, defined.

Tad saw his father's eyes widen, saw him try to step back, and then saw his own hand lash out and cut the old man across his loose face.

"Oh, oh," screamed Mrs. Howard. "You evil boy—"

"Shut up!" yelled Tad.

"My chocolate—"

"Shut up, shut up!" yelled Tad, panicking. He ran out of the room, out of the house and into the dark night.

CHAPTER SIX

Tony was convinced there had been a logical progression in the night's course of events. First, the sheer phantasy of what he had been telling Tad. Next, sex more concrete though still only viewed through a hole in the wall. Third, the real thing. Naturally.

He walked down the dark lane and from there into the brightly lighted town. A country-town odor lingered in the air, field grasses, sweet musk from the mill and the vaguely exciting aroma of wet sheets hanging on a line.

Tony stared at the neon that said BAR, the neon that said HARDWARE, and the marquee lights that spelled out BIJOU. At that point the lights on the marquee went off. Tony started to run toward the theatre.

He felt as if he had never had a girl before, but he was still unconscious of the fact that he would proposition Tad's steady.

As Tony reached his destination, Amy came out of the dark theater lobby. Tony grinned and bowed. The girl looked a bit baffled.

"Amy?" he asked.

"Yes?"

"I'm Tony."

"Tony?"

"My best friend is Tad. Tad and I—"

"Ah!" she said. "I know who you are." Tony noticed the slowness of her delivery and thought of a cow. He stared at her bulging cardigan and became more than a little excited. "He's told me a lot about you," the girl said. "He likes you." She touched her fine, healthy hair before going on. "Where is Tad?" Amy asked, looking through and past Tony.

"Uh, that's why I'm here. He can't come, Amy, and he's terribly sorry. He asked me to tell you that he'd call and explain later. Sore?"

"No, I'm not sore." Her smile was mannered and not for Tony.

"I mean, don't be. You know. He's got enough troubles."

"Yes, I know."

"Which way are you walking? He asked me to walk you home."

"That was very nice of him, but you really don't have to bother."

"No, no. Please let me. For Tad." Tony was lying through his teeth. He was fast becoming interested in the buxom girl, although he realized that no matter how demonstratively she arched her young back and pushed up her too-small brassiere, she would insist on certain conventions.

Tony took her arm. She paid no attention to his hand. Tony, studying her bust, noted that she did not jiggle or bounce in front at all. Must be wearing some kind of armor-plated bra, he mused.

"What is wrong with Tad?" Amy asked.

"The usual trouble with the parents. You know. They made him stay home tonight because of his not having done some chore or other."

"Poor boy," Amy said noncommittally.

"He is so fond of you," said Tony.

"I like Tad, too," said Amy.

That stopped all conversation for a while.

Now the only contact between them was Tony's hand around her arm though Tony doubted that it meant anything to her. In fact, she said, "Would you mind letting go? It's so warm tonight and your palm ..."

"Of course," and he let go.

And then, extending the theme of the heat, she unbuttoned the two upper buttons of her cardigan.

"How come," Tony asked, "I've never seen you around?"

"We just moved into town six months ago."

"And right away you snapped up the nicest boy in town, hey?"

"He is very nice," said Amy.

Tony felt like groaning as she went on platitudinizing. "Tad is considerate, kind, respectful and very intelligent. I admire that in a person."

She said the word person as if this referred to some species far superior to man, woman, child and most certainly to animals and foreigners.

"I am glad you found each other," said Tony with venom.

He felt that she was invulnerable now. Nothing he thought, nothing he said, nothing he did, would mean anything to her. He took this verdict so seriously that he became horribly depressed.

"Tony?" she asked in a small voice.

"Yes," he said.

"I think you're a nice boy, too, or else Tad wouldn't think so much of you."

Unspeakable bitch, he thought, but at that moment she ended her delivery by placing her hand on his arm. Tony felt like melting.

"Thank you. Very nice of you, Amy."

She moved her hand away.

Then suddenly, with nothing solved, nothing decided, they were at the lawn on which sat prettily the dark house where Amy lived.

They looked at each other in the awkwardness of boy and girl saying good night. Then Amy asked, "Would you like to come in and have a glass of iced tea?"

The house was dark except for one window which shone with a ghastly blue shimmer of light. Somebody was sitting there in the dark, watching television. "I, uh, rather not disturb ..."

"We won't. We'll just sit in the kitchen and talk quietly."

Tony could think of nothing more dull than to drink iced tea. "I mean," he said, "I don't want to interrupt your folks' TV program."

"They're not home. My parents work at the mill, the night shift. Come on."

"Yeah," said Tony dully as he followed her through the gate.

He wanted to ask who was watching TV, but he did not. He said nothing all the way across the pretty lawn, on to the porch and through the door with cut-glass panels, and into the dark house which smelled of linoleum wax. Then he saw the gaunt man through the archway, gaunt with age and with the blue glow of the light from the tube.

"That's my stepfather watching the late show," said Amy.

Bluish, gaunt, he did not turn to look at them.

Tony was briefly startled but briefly only, because he followed Amy into the kitchen where she turned on the light and then Tony felt completely bored.

She was efficient in the kitchen. She moved swiftly, getting the pitcher of iced tea from the refrigerator, glasses from the cupboard, sugar from the table, spoons from the drawer, two cookies from the breadbox—two cookies, that was all—and fixing everything on a black, flowered, dime-store tray. Here and again she shot an efficient smile at Tony. He understood her less and less.

"Are we ready?" she asked.

Everything was ready on the tray and Tony thought it appropriate to nod.

"You carry it, then," she said.

She sighed, undid the top button on her cardigan with no emotion whatsoever and walked out of the kitchen door.

What else to do but follow with the tray? What else? So he walked behind her into the room with the blue light and the stepfather in one chair and up to the coffee table where Tony set down the tray.

On the TV a romantic lover was making advances to a sullen-faced, black-lipped woman.

"Come on, come on," said Amy.

Somehow the comment sounded forbiddingly vulgar to Tony. He walked around the coffee table and sat down next to Amy, his back parade-ground straight. Then he noticed something strange.

All the buttons on her cardigan were undone now and her breasts, bra-encased, stood out like two dangerous turrets.

Tony had an impulse to throw himself forward and draw the halves of her cardigan together like a curtain. But he did not move. He only said, "That old man is staring at us."

"He's all right," said Amy. "Don't mind him."

The old man's eyes were riveted on the girl's breasts.

"Open me up," said Amy.

"What?"

"Oh, for God's sake," she said and, arching, rid herself of the lacy material. The bra moved and then her breasts sprang free.

Nevertheless, all Tony could think of was, the stepfather is looking, too.

"Well?" Amy asked. "Or do you prefer iced tea?"

"Gosh," said Tony, a word upon which he had always frowned. "Listen, honey," he coughed, desperately wanting to curtain her breasts. "I—" He felt badly confused.

"Don't mind him," Amy said. She nodded at the stepfather. "You want to see more or no?"

"But, he's staring."

The old man's eyes, giving the impression of marble, were feasting on the girl's globes.

"So let him look," shrugged Amy. "That's all he does." She waited and watched beads of sweat forming on Tony's forehead. "But I expect something more of you."

"I never. I mean—"

"He can't talk or anything," said Amy. "He's paralyzed. Come on," and she put Tony's hand on her breast.

Tony rolled the flesh between his curious fingers.

He wondered whether Tad had ever played with her like this. And then Tony gave a violent start.

The stepfather had made a sound. His mouth had opened and a noise like that of a groaning, subterranean spring had issued forth.

"Amy, let's get out of here. Let's get—"

"I told you he doesn't mind. Come on now, here," and she put Tony's hand on her breast again.

For a moment he desired the smooth, warm skin and her hardening, pushing nipple, but then suspicion swept over him. He could not be sure, but was she watching the old man watching her?

Then Tony's desire lessened and all he could feel was his own sweat.

"Amy—"

"Shut up and hold still. Close your eyes, Tony."

He obeyed. And with his eyes closed, the whole focus of his lust came back to him. His hand on her again came alive and his mouth showered hot kisses on her. Without thought, now, he began to press himself against her ...

"... the zipper," he heard her say and then he awoke to reason.

How could he, Tony Vaughn, Esq., have succumbed to a drab, tasteless girl? A girl to whom love-making meant little more than wrestling with strange boys in the presence of a horrible, old man? Tony struggled up into sitting position.

"What's the matter?" asked Amy. She was very busy with him. "I said, what's the matter. Don't you want to?"

Her breasts resembled blue marble and were just as beautiful and forbidding to the touch. Her skirt was up in a disreputable array, and her legs down on the floor so she could balance herself and not slip off the couch. And that dull single-mindedness was on her face.

"The old man," he said. "How can you take it, him glaring across the room at you with that blue face?"

"I said he doesn't matter. Don't you hear?"

There was no way of communicating with this unusual girl, Tony mused. He tried another approach.

"Does Tad," said Tony, "can Tad, I mean, does Tad—"

"Tad, Tad, Tad." She sat up, her breasts heaving. "I guess I know," she said with some rancor, "why you and Tad are such good friends. Birds of a feather flock together, I always say," and she adjusted her hair, sitting up with total disregard for her nakedness.

"Now listen," and he put his hand on her again.

She pushed him away. "Cut it out. What do you think I am, anyway?"

He had no idea what she was.

"You better go," she said. "I'm going to watch TV."

"Now come here, Amy."

"Let go."

"All I meant was, I want to watch TV too," he said.

The remark was so asinine that Tony winced. None of this made a convincing male, a determined lover, or even a weary Casanova, as once he had been in the back of a car. Amy was all concentrated strength, the strength of the negative at this point, as she placed the cardigan around her shoulders and the dead sheen of ice into her expression.

"Goodbye."

And so, goodbye. Tony left hurriedly, making a wide circle around the blue-faced man, who was still peering at the girl whose head was thrown back, not caring how her breasts showed large and naked and strong as marble. She blinked rapidly as she watched the TV lovers.

She's abnormal, Tony decided. One insane chick.

The verdict made him feel quite all right again.

At twelve o'clock that night Tony still had not returned home and his stepfather, Robert Vaughn, was anxious to take his bath and get to bed.

"I agree with you totally," he said to his wife, "that the boy is unmanageable, has no respect for his elders, and doesn't—"

"I didn't say that he was unmanageable, I said that he is so hard to reach.

I feel, Robert, as if he dislikes me ... his own mother."

"That's your problem."

"Robert, perhaps if he and I took a trip, just he and I perhaps, then we ..."

"I'm teaching summer school and don't see how I can get away to humor the boy."

"I didn't say that, Robert. I suggested ..."

"What? What did you say?"

"Don't shout at me, Robert."

"But you are so exasperating, Laura. Why in the devil's name don't you make yourself clear? I'm going to take a bath," and he set down his book and got up from the couch.

"I'm trying to say as clearly as—"

"I'm going to bathe. We'll discuss it tomorrow."

Robert Vaughn was not autocratic by nature but only by necessity. When he knew no other way out, when he could not rid himself of unpleasantness except by stepping on somebody else, then he became autocratic.

"Robert, I can't reach you, either. I can't ..."

He was already going up the stairs and Laura, in sudden helplessness, wanted to cry and for Robert to see it. But he had gone and she was alone.

In a moment she arose and moved to the front door. There was no point in going upstairs; this was not Wednesday, Robert would sleep in his own bed. He would lie in the dark and go to sleep. She would lie in the dark and brood. Wearily, she thought, I'm alone, body and soul.

To sleep, perchance to dream ...

But she could not go upstairs and hope to sleep.

It wasn't that easy any more. When the day is unnatural, Laura knew, so the night becomes unnatural. And as she felt half dead in the daytime she felt half alive in the night. And if—she took a deep breath to stop everything she was beginning to feel and to think. And then she went outside, to walk, to tire herself.

The walk meant nothing. She strolled as far as the campus and turned back because she did not want to be stopped by a campus guard, on the alert for neckers and petters.

Laura gazed down the length of the campus road at the old trees. A street light spilled a quiet pool of yellow on the grass. The sight reminded her of a small stretch of road near the Loire where she had often walked. But there, everything had been touched by sadness, the cool river, the moist trees and the night. She had felt sad and alone because she had lost Pierre. She had run, then, into a handsome young man who had become her lover.

Maurice? Marcel? She could not now remember his name. But they had spent many happy hours together. And it had been her first affair since breaking off with Pierre. Quiet in the beginning, then full in the growing and complete in the end.

Maurice had been younger by three or four years, something they had discovered later and had laughed about. She, being American, had retained some unspoken idea that the man must be older and the woman younger to build a good relationship. "*Un pert louche, ça,*" she had said laughingly to him. Then he had laughed too, but from lack of comprehension.

"Look at your thigh," he had said. "It says, 'Come here.' It doesn't say anything about '*c'est un peu louche,*' or about 'let me see your birth certificate first.' And your breast," he had said, "doesn't say, 'Wait, let me first count the age bands in your skin.' No, it says, 'Take me.'"

He had smiled, surprised by his own stream of explanations because he usually said only direct things and simple. He had stopped talking and smiled, and then he had taken her, directly and simply ...

And once, much later, he had stood under the trees in a little park in Dijon and watched her walking with somebody else. He had nodded at her and gone away, not wishing to disturb either her present or the memory of their past. She had given a little start and then he had slipped away ...

She gasped now as she saw a young man gazing at her from across the way.

"Mrs. Vaughn?" the young man called as he started toward her. "I'm sorry if I startled you—"

"Tad?" she asked. "Aren't you Tad, Tony's friend?"

"Yes, ma'am. I'm sorry if ..."

She laughed in relief and walked over to him to pat him on the arm.

"I'm just so glad it was you and not what I was thinking," and she laughed again. "I was actually daydreaming in the middle of the night—isn't that funny? You fitted into the whole thing so that I thought for a moment the daydream had become real."

Tad smiled, liking the woman and liking the directness with which she had made her explanation.

"Sorry the dream didn't come true," he said.

"On the contrary, Tad. It's frightening to have a dream come true. Ever think of that?"

"No. No, I haven't, but I'm thinking about it now."

"Don't," she said. "It's too dark for that."

This time, when she stopped, neither of them laughed. They were both amazed at how easily they had struck up a conversation. But then the spell broke and each returned to his separate, unsolved mazes.

Laura's feeling was one of regret. She did not know Tad well, but she realized and the comparison came easily—that Tad lacked Tony's hostility and resentment.

"What were you doing here, Tad, waiting for Tony, perhaps?"

"I was. Yes, I was."

"You don't know where he is?"

"No."

"I don't either," said Laura. "Tad, I was taking a walk. Would you like to join me?"

"Yes," he said, "that would be nice." Then they walked without talking.

To Tad, Mrs. Vaughn was the epitome of womanhood. She was gentle and soft, so unlike his own mother. For the briefest of moments, Tad envied Tony. Then he said, "I wanted to see Tony. He's my only friend."

"A terrible thing must have happened to you, Tad, to look for your only friend."

A great welter of emotions swept over Tad. He hoped that he was not going to cry.

"I had a fight," he said softly.

"That bad?"

"My parents."

She fluffed her hair and looked at the night sky, in order to appear casual. She did not want to frighten him.

"Everybody has fights with their parents," she said.

They had come to the campus crossing, the one on which Laura had not wanted to travel before.

But without protesting, she started down the road with him and never thought about it.

"I hit him," said Tad suddenly. "I punched out my own father."

"Oh Tad—" It was regret not reprimand and she did not know what to say next.

"And worse," said Tad. "I wanted—I felt like—or almost, I mean—doing the same thing to her. My mother."

"You must have felt badly," Laura murmured.

Tad had been convinced almost hopefully that she would now reprimand him, that she would say, "Yes, it's right for you to feel rotten and guilty." She had done nothing of the sort and he was forced to look at her again now, this time to see if she had meant it. She inclined her head toward him and her eyes were quiet and the lips drawn into a half-smile. Obviously she was going to say nothing else.

"Mrs. Vaughn," Tad began, but whatever impulse had struck him was not strong enough to make him go on.

She smiled at him and touched his arm.

"Let's walk more. I'll tell you about Europe. This looks like a park in Europe. Want me to tell you about it?"

He said, "I couldn't concentrate on it. I'm too upset."

His own honesty relieved him. He suddenly thought, what would I like to be doing more than this, more than walking down this lane? And he could not think of anything that he would like doing more. Except imagining that the walk would go on and on, tree after tree, lamp after lamp, and that he and she would walk always in closeness …

The impossibility of the dream made him feel suddenly depressed; and Laura, noting his mood, responded to it.

"Maybe nothing has been worse for you than this evening ..."

"Oh, no. I mean ..."

"Let me finish. I don't mean walking with me. I'm talking about that fight you had—nothing more traumatic has ever happened to you before. Besides, Tad, whatever caused the fight. That source must have been worse."

He thought about it and didn't answer.

"And whatever that was, the cause, or the causes, all of them, they were not entirely your doing, were they?"

It helped him, but in a surprising way. He recalled the years of two indifferent parents, the million and one insults they had showered on him, his inability to defend himself, his hopeless, helpless— Then anguish found a way out. He burst into tears. Pain racked his ribs and throat and he felt as if he might never again be whole. Laura led him to a bench, sat him down and stroked his head and face. He cried until he had used up all his tears.

Then breathing fully and deeply, he sat up. She gave his hand a squeeze and moved away.

"And now, Tad, don't say you're sorry, or you'll spoil your new-found freedom."

She handed a handkerchief to him and he blew his nose.

"Thank you," he said.

"Keep it."

"Thank you," he said again and this time he looked at her. "I mean for everything."

The moment had come so easily. The simple look, face to face, the regard for each other. Not a word. It had come so naturally that neither of them was disturbed.

He took the handkerchief and dabbed a wet spot on her neck and then shoved the handkerchief into his pocket. Neither act had been self-conscious. Laura thought, Tad, if you asked me now what oppresses me I would say it is that Tony is not like you.

"I can leave now," he said softly, staring at the soft puddle of light thrown by a street lamp. "Leave without worrying about going home."

"Where are you heading?"

"Nowhere specific. I just mean that I've changed."

"Why don't you go home, then?"

"Because I don't want to spoil the way I feel."

They might have said more about this and to each other, but they had silently agreed to abide by the conventional code.

"All right, you two." They turned, startled. "Get them I.D. cards out, because I'm reporting these goings-on to the dean."

An old man, silver badge shining, came hobbling out of the bushes. He seemed nervous and eager, almost like a wild dog that hadn't eaten in days.

"I seen the whole thing, and a fine report I'll—" He stopped dead in his tracks and craned his neck. "Mrs. Vaughn—" he began, cringing. "I do beg your pardon."

Now he tiptoed past them, talking all the time, but still resembling a dog. Not a hungry dog, but a terribly anxious hound. The old man had made a natural mistake, he told them. He had been tracking two young varmints through the bushes and had assumed, being weak of eye, that they had stopped to pet on this very bench. But no offense meant, you understand, he fawned.

"And ain't you Tad?" he asked, leaning closer. He really was nearsighted. "Why, how are you, Tad boy?"

"Fine. Thank you, Mr. Bates."

"I just seen your father down at Eddie's Grill where I take my supper. He was there looking for you."

"I don't go to Eddie's," said Tad. "I don't drink."

"Well now, what I meant—"

He stopped while the woman and the boy got up.

"But he was looking for you," said the guard. "Real anxious, too."

"All right," said Tad. "Good night."

They walked away, disregarding the old man's feeble attempts to engage them in conversation. They stopped in front of Laura's house.

"I'm not going home," announced Tad.

"But maybe ..."

"I know my father," said Tad, his anger breaking through. "I know what he's like, my old man, and what that other old man, that creepy campus guard, left out."

"Tad. Perhaps ..."

"It's bad enough that my mother's always drunk," Tad said with sudden hate, "but when my dad gets potted, too—to hell with them. I'm leaving."

"Tad?"

"Yes, Mrs. Vaughn."

"If you could go to the cottage with Tony, by the lake, would you stay there for a while?"

She really wanted him to go there. She did not ask herself why, or whether it was for him or for Tony.

CHAPTER SEVEN

Cher Pierre,

Thank you for sending the present for Tony. He reads French well. At the moment he is out at the cottage with a friend and perhaps I will take him the book this afternoon. I say perhaps because I have the feeling that those two would rather be left alone. Rather a sad thought, isn't it? I won't dwell upon it.

Thank you, I am well. Please don't judge my life barren. After all, I do have my clubs and my gardening ... Forgive me, I probably sound as creaky as an old woman, don't I?

You asked me how Tony is. He is progressing nicely and fortunate indeed to have a young friend of warm qualities. Although he needs a lot of love.

Laura left the sentence as it was, without making it clear to Pierre, or to herself, to whom she had been referring.

At that moment Laura's husband was clearing his desk and preparing to come home. The semester was over. As he passed by the motel, he saw Mrs. Howard sitting at the window. She was thinking about her ungrateful son and took a quick nip from a white-labeled bottle.

Mr. Howard, installing an outside light, waved absently to Robert Vaughn. A card from his son lay in Lambert's pocket. "Dear Dad," it said, "I thought I'd stay away for a week. Then I'll come back. I'm sorry about what happened." But Lambert was not thinking about Tad's card. He was wondering what the hell was wrong with the plug.

The two friends were lying in the grass behind the cottage, two seals playing in the sun. Their feet were sticking into the cool water and their flesh was hot.

"Did you tell them where you were going when you wrote that card?" asked Tony.

"No," said Tad.

"Why not?"

"Because I—I want to be away from them. I want this time all to myself."

"I'm here," said Tony in a bantering vein. He wanted Tad to admit that he, Tony, was needed.

"That's different," remarked Tad.

The nearest cottage, hard by the lake, was surrounded by fragrant pines. A lawn sloped down to the greenish water. On the lawn lay three lovely figures.

"You know any of those chicks?" asked Tad.

Tony finished scratching himself and then he said, "Sure. Which one do you mean?"

"The blonde who keeps looking over here," Tad said.

"Oh, her. Sure, I know her."

"Yeah? How well, I mean?"

"They are the only neighbors we got, man, so naturally I have taken the trouble to make their acquaintance," Tony said.

"Strange they're your only neighbors. The other side of the lake is pretty crowded with cottages. And here there's nothing but wild shoreline."

"That's right. Just wild on this side, man."

"How come?" Tad said.

"Because she and those other two and me...."

"I meant, how come no cottages on this side?"

"Oh. My old man—I mean my stepfather, he owns all this shoreline and a big stretch going landward."

"A lot of fine land," Tad said, stretching and turning toward his friend.

"Valuable property, you mean. If this were mine," said Tony, "I'd bring builders in. But you know professors," he added, "they don't understand how to make money."

There was heat torpor in both of them and they lay silent for a while. Then Tad gave a start. "Look what she's doing," he said.

"What?" Tony did not bother to turn.

"She's taken off her bra and she's lying on her belly."

"Well?" inquired Tony, sounding his weariest.

"Yeah, well," said Tad, and he sank back and stared up at the patch of blue sky.

This will not do, Tony thought. Tad is no longer interested in The Adventures of Antoine Vaughn, Esq. This situation, the boy knew, would have to be corrected.

"I told you I know the blonde. Actually, I am more familiar with the brunette. I dated her first."

"Uh-huh," said Tad.

"The tall redhead. You see her?"

"Yes."

"Well, she's married. She's the oldest and is hitched to some goof from New Jersey. Weirdest thing happened when I took her."

There was no answer from Tad. He just sighed.

"You listening to me?" inquired Tony.

"Yeh. You said 'weirdest'." Tad sat up. He did not look at his friend but across the shiny lake at the dark trees on the other side. "Listen, I meant to ask you something," he said.

"About what?" Tony said.

"Women. You know."

"Of course. Ask." Tony relaxed.

"Well—"

"Wait, I know. You've met a tease and you want to know what to do about it."

That was not quite what Tad had wanted. He was not after a trick of seduction. He desired some extensive knowledge of womankind. Something to answer his every need.

"Not exactly," said Tad. "I have to explain this more."

"Go ahead," aided Tony.

"Have you ever met a girl who looked and acted boy-crazy but who froze whenever you tried to give her a squeeze?"

"Talking sex and then wanting to turn you off when you got hot?"

"Uh, yes."

"Never seen any reason for confusion on that score," said Tony, staring at a fleecy cloud. "I know what they want and I give it to them."

Tad's silence was like satisfying meal to Tony. He watched the changing shape of the cloud.

"I'll give you an example," said Tad.

"I wish you would, man. So I can apply myself in a specific way."

"Remember that girl you saw?"

Tony raised up and squinted at the cottage with the three girls in front. The blonde was still lying on her stomach, her bare breasts flattened against the ground. Tony felt a wonderful ache in his body as he ogled the exciting curve of her back and imagined her fabulous nakedness, touched by the tender grass.

"I don't mean that one," said Tad. "I'm talking about that girl Amy you saw me with."

Tony lay back again. The little white cloud had drifted away, so he focused on a piece of peach-colored fluff. He was bored by his friend's problems.

"My steady," said Tad, surprised by Tony's lack of response, "You remember."

"I do."

"Good. Now here is—you know—a very attractive girl. I mean, she has appeal."

Tony did not answer. He closed his eyes to the flower-shaped cloud.

"All right," said Tad, misunderstanding the silence of his wiser friend. "Maybe you didn't see her close up. But her face is fresh and healthy and she has pretty eyes. And her body," Tad went on, "well, if you had seen her that day, how she's built, you'd—"

"Never mind," said Tony.

"What?"

"Never mind. I've seen enough of them to know they're all alike."

"Well," said Tad. "I don't know about that. All I—"

"Don't tell me I'm wrong," Tony said. The sudden anger inside him made him jerk up. He intended to have his say. "I'm sick and tired of hearing about these bags. You talk, talk, talk about those bitches as if they were so important, as if I couldn't even do without them. You're wrong."

From a distance, where the three girls were sunbathing, came a catcall. The blonde, supported on her elbows now, waved one lovely arm.

Tony, quite unexpectedly, broke out into a sweat. Tad was squinting at the girl and now all three beauties laughed. The blonde placed a hand on one naked breast. She was too far off to be seen distinctly but the knowledge that she was bare-bosomed was in itself exciting to Tony.

"Hey," said Tad. "Look—maybe ..."

There was a stream of profanity from Tony and then he was running up the incline to his father's cottage. When the screen door banged, Tad got up and loped after him.

The pine-paneled room smelled of warm wood and the sun, filtering through a green topped tree, made wonderful patterns on the planked floor. Tony sat slumped in the big chair by the fireplace, his face a mask.

"Tony, what happened?" demanded Tad. He stood, feeling helpless, by the chair. "Didn't you see how that blonde ..."

Tony again wanted to shout but a wave of confusion pushed him down, sucked the strength out of him, so that he could barely reply.

"Please," he managed to say, sitting forward with head down now so that Tad could not examine his face.

"All right, Tony," said Tad. "I won't bother you, if you want to be alone."

Alone. Tony did not really want to be alone. If Tad walked out of the cottage and went across to the cottage with those girls ...

"No," Tony said.

Tad sat down on the floor by the fireplace. "Why are you feeling bad, Tony?"

Impossible question, Tony thought. He spread out his hands, palms upward.

"You've listened to me," said Tad, "when I've had it bad. Every time. You've never talked to me about your troubles."

"I know," mumbled Tony. He was afraid, if he said more, that he would melt.

"And you don't have to tell me, but if it helps ..."

"It wouldn't help."

"Try, why don't you?"

"I can't," said Tony, swallowing hard, although the fact that he now had an appreciative audience pleased him immensely. He could build a story, a vivid tale of woman-trouble and unrequited love. That would really grip Tad.

But as Tony looked at his friend, his taste turned flat and the images took on a grayish tinge. He simply did not want to lie any more. He raised his head and signalled his friend.

"Tad?"

"Yes, Tony."

"If I tell you something, will you swear—"

"You don't have to ask."

And then Tony began to tear himself down.

"I've—I've been exaggerating, Tad. All those stories about women and the rest."

"That's okay," said Tad. Then he grinned. "So might I, if I had any fantasies to embroider, you know?"

"No," shouted Tony. He wanted all the credit for himself, all the glory of confessing how unscrupulously he had manufactured tales.

"Tad, I have only taken—out of all those women...."

"Hey," came from outside.

Tony tensed. His face turned red. Not only because this interruption was destroying his story-line, but because it had come from one of those disgusting sunbathers.

"Send her away," he ordered Tad.

Tad glanced up, past the top of Tony's chair and smiled easily.

"Hi!" he said to someone. "Come in." Then be got up.

Tony's mother entered and the color drained from Tony's face and left him strangely pale.

Laura looked remarkably unlike anyone's mother. With the easy balance of the well-proportioned, she stood in the doorway. Tad noticed how wonderfully unconcerned she was about her appearance. Tony saw only his mother, a woman he hardly knew. Tad saw much more—the beautiful, kind lady who had been so warm to him a few nights earlier. For the first time, he understood what she was.

She stood there in the room, and despite her ease seemed a little shy. Perhaps she is hoping, Tad thought, that she will be made to feel at home. Her mood gave Tad a curious thrill. And he was impressed by her body. She possessed soft curves. Her thighs showed round and firm under her tight-fitting white slacks. And her breasts, while not large, made a prominent thrust beneath the simple, yellow blouse. Her neck line and short sleeves revealed a summer-warm skin. Sun-color everywhere. When she lifted one hand to push her hair away from her neck, Tad looked away.

"What do you want?" Tony asked without ever trying to hide his mood.

"Why, nothing," said Laura. For a moment she seemed vaguely perturbed, but then she smiled, "Brought you a book," she said, pulling a volume from a blue canvas bag. "Didn't bring anything for you, though," she remarked to Tad and smiled at him.

It seemed easier for her to smile at Tad than at her own son.

"That's all right, ma'am," he said. "I wasn't expecting a treat."

Then she walked to Tony's chair, still holding out the book.

"From Pierre," she said. "He hopes you can still read French."

This time her smile didn't work.

"He hopes?" said Tony. "How come?"

Real embarrassment.

"Well," said Laura. "I hope, too, of course."

Tony laughed grimly. Laura dropped the book on to an end table and moved to the window bench, where she sat down. From there, she would be able to observe her sullen son.

"We got some iced tea," Tad said, trying to dispel the growing heaviness. "If anyone likes iced tea, I'll—"

"Stop saying iced tea. You said it twice in a row. I'm neither deaf nor stupid and you know I hate the stuff."

"You do? Since when do you—"

"Never mind, never mind this stupid discussion."

"I'd like some iced tea," said Laura without any special emphasis. Tad bolted for the kitchen.

"Did you have a fight, Tony, you and Tad?"

"Of course not. Why do you walk in here and immediately assume the worst?"

"Because you're in a touchy mood and looking extremely unfriendly, Antoine."

He did not like her use of his real name and he determined to make her sweat.

"Maybe that's just my way of being surprised, having you suddenly walking in here."

"But, Tony. I mean, it's just a casual—"

"Casual?"

"Why ..." She was too startled to know what was best to answer.

Tad, bearing a tray, walked in at the moment and she was glad. But Tony went right on. "There's never anything unplanned about mothers walking in," he said. His tone changed. "Aren't mothers always spying on their teenage children?"

"Thank you, Tad," said Laura, accepting the glass of iced tea. "Now, what do you mean, dear boy?" she asked, turning to her son.

"For example," said Tony as he made himself comfy, "the two Babcock sisters are vacationing at the next cottage, along with one round, sexy blonde. And you walking in here unannounced could mean, Mother, that you are concerned about the state of my virginity."

She laughed. There was surprise and humor in her voice.

"I don't mind if you have a girl," she bubbled.

"Have? Have?" said Tony and smiled artificially. "Having lived abroad—in France, specifically," he interjected, "you may not know the vernacular significance of your remark."

"What a vocabulary you possess, Tony." She did not laugh this time, simply because she refused to offend him. "And if you mean sleeping with a girl, I don't mind you doing that, either."

Tad hastily gulped an ice cube. He could hardly believe his ears. Tony had no reply.

"And as far as advice goes," Laura went on, "I have only one piece to give. When you enjoy a girl, don't look down on her for having fulfilled your wish." Then she sipped at her drink.

Tony was genuinely confused. "I don't follow you at all. First you come in here as if you had scented the remnants of lust and then say it's perfectly all right for us to entertain girls, Boy, I don't follow you."

There wasn't much Laura could do. She tried to explain herself to him.

"Antoine, I'm not an old witch. You talk to me as if you hardly know me."

"I know you well."

"Why don't we understand each other anymore, then?"

"I don't know what you're talking about."

"We used to get along, didn't we?"

"When I was six?"

The ground was not only trembling, but positively quaking now. The mood hung in the air, scaring all of them and Tad stood up quietly and left the room.

The other two waited until he had closed the screen door.

"Are you talking about the time we left Pierre?" asked Laura cautiously.

"I'm talking about the time afterwards," Tony said loudly. "I'm talking about the lousy time afterwards, when you had fun and I had none."

She stiffened, remembering those months. She had felt angry and lost and had sought out lovers. Not many, but each had been a change for the child, a bewildering change.

"Antoine," Laura said bravely, "if I neglected you—"

"If?"

"Please, let's not fight. I'm trying to make it up to you, Antoine."

Tony, to kill his emotion, laughed hard and nervously.

"I'm trying to reach you, Antoine," and she got up.

Her son shrank into his chair and when she saw this, she cringed.

"I don't need you," he said coldly.

"Perhaps I need you," she said helplessly.

She reached out to touch him. Tony sat up straight and stiff in his chair.

"You need me? Why, that sounds filthy! Don't talk filthy to me. Filthy."

As the sun slowly went down, Tad strolled by the lake and in the woods.

Sometimes he could hear their faint voices and then he would walk away, in order not to feel their pain, not to know anything about their quarrel.

He idly chewed a blade of sweet grass, wondered what to say to Tony when his mother had gone, what to do in the evening, where to walk and how far he might be able to skip a stone along the water, how far he might walk without seeing a soul.

He came out by the water again and found himself next to the Babcock cottage. The sun had sunk below the horizon and there was nobody on the lawn. He heard a laugh, but that came from inside the house.

At first he did not listen to the babble. But then he heard the girls' clear voices.

"Maybe they're just a couple of queers," and laughter.

"Because they didn't jump when you took off your bra?"

"No. Because they didn't wave back when we waved," and more laughter.

Suddenly the light jumped in the nearest window and Tad took a hasty step back into the bushes. But not too far. He saw the three girls, one dressed in a bathrobe, hair wet, just out of the shower; the other in shorts and shirt, and the blonde, naked from the waist up. Her high breasts bounced like rubber.

"I'll fix supper," said the brunette, and the half-naked blonde called after her, "Make mine parboiled man. I'll eat that any time."

Tad felt more shock than desire, but he moved closer to the window. The redhead was drying her hair and the blonde had stopped in the middle of the room. Then Tad saw why she was standing so still. There was a long mirror attached to one door and she was examining herself. She ran her hands up her sides, held her breasts.

"Which would you want, if they weren't queers?" she asked.

"They aren't queers."

"Ah," said the blonde and looked in the mirror. "If they aren't queers, what would they be doing there by themselves?" She slowly rolled her breasts, made them tight and high as she squeezed. Tad's throat was dry.

"You know Tony?" asked the blonde.

"A little. Just from town."

"I'd like the other one," said the blonde. "What's his name?"

"That's Tad."

"Gads," said the blonde. "I'd like to have him."

Tad's knees started shaking when he saw what she did next. With one pull on the side-knot of her bikini, she shed the scarf, placed one hand on her belly. But not out of modesty. She stood in front of the mirror and started moving her hips.

"Tad," she said, "you'd love this—"

Tad, in the dark outside the window, blushed furiously. He saw how the girl ground her hips. He thought of leaving. He had already turned away. His excitement was high, but he was ashamed and confused. He shivered.

"You do it," he heard.

Curiosity overcame him. He again moved into position. To look is dirty, he chastised himself. Not the excitement. That isn't dirty. But to look and not to touch, that's what is wrong.

"That—" he heard. "Yes—I'm imagining it's—"

He heard his name and looked again. He could not see much of the blonde because she was obscured by the redhead. The redhead was sitting on the edge of the bed and the blonde was lying behind her. He could see the blonde's legs, one down, and one bent at the knee, and the girl made a low sing-song sound in her throat. Tad could not see her face. One arm was over her eyes and the other was stretched back along the pillow.

The girl was in a rhythm and it caught Tad in the back, in the hips, and he moved without knowing it. He knew only his growing excitement, swelling like a storm.

"Supper ready!" somebody yelled from the kitchen. Tad glanced into the room once more, where the blonde lay naked on the bed.

"Ah," said the blonde. "What service," and she laughed.

She sounded relaxed, even limp.

"That will cost you," said the other, standing up and yawning.

"Okay. I'll let you have Tad next," and both of them laughed.

The evening wind touched Tad's bare skin and he trembled. He was moist all over. The only heat in him now was fury, for their laughter, their ease, and his own isolation. The blonde combed her hair and then wriggled into a sundress shaped like a big, orange sack.

"Coming!" she yelled. "Coming!"

The night came with the wind mounting in the dark. It played among the trees and the black water and the dust on the road. It brought coldness.

Tad felt it in the dampness of his scalp ...

The three girls in the cottage paid it no attention and thought of the wind only when the fire roared. They sat and talked about days of love and laughter as they sipped at cokes ...

Mrs. Howard heard the wind and thought how obscene the howling was, how like Lambert and his salacious grunting. She took an untidy swallow from her glass of spiked chocolate. A vision of her husband, lewdly embracing a young girl, danced through Mrs. Howard's head. That rotten Lambert sure was enjoying himself. Now he was sinking his teeth deep into the little hussy's silken flesh; and she, the sinful witch, was squirming, encouraging him. But as Mrs. Howard dreamed on, the body of the girl became mud-streaked, dirt-caked and odorous. Mrs. Howard, sadistically satisfied, stuck her nose deep into her glass and gulped two large mouthfuls of chocolate cocktail. Then, for the

first time in years, Mrs. Howard began to retch ...

Tad went back to Tony's cottage. He still felt chilled.

The cottage was dark and drafty, too. All warmth of the day had disappeared.

"Tony?" Tad called softly.

There was no answer. Tony, Tad thought, had gone back to town with his mother. He felt unutterably alone.

When he heard the sound, Tad gave a start. Wind sound. Up in the sky, a cloud gave way and the big orange moon emerged. Sound ... The sound of crying.

Tad found the door to the bedroom and tapped lightly. He was barely able to distinguish the huddled form. "Tony. You sleeping?"

Silence.

Tad trod on the patch the moon had made on the floor as he moved toward the bed.

"Hey now, hey," said Tad. He gently patted the prostrate figure. Then he drew back his hand. He had touched soft hair and a round arm.

"Is that you, Tad?"

"Yes," he said. "Yes, Mrs. Vaughn. I'm terribly sorry."

She sighed and rolled over on to her back.

"Don't be upset, Tad," she murmured. "I hadn't meant to startle you."

"You okay, Mrs. Vaughn?" He could now see her hip and thigh and the curve of her breast. "You been crying?"

"A little," she admitted.

"Where's Tony?"

"He ran out."

"Oh."

"We talked," she said carefully. "We talked and we had a most terrible fight."

"I'm sorry. I'm really sorry." He meant it and wished he had the courage to stroke her hair. The wind shifted clouds and inky darkness fell over the room. Tad heard and then felt the woman sit up.

"Tad, please don't mind if I talk. That's better than crying."

"Please do," he said. And then, "You helped me once—"

Unexpected for both, that was the trigger. Laura tried to hold back her tears, but she could not. And when she leaned to cover her face, Tad placed his arms around her. He comforted her with words and touched her back.

"Can't reach Tony," he heard her say through her crying. "My fault."

Tad understood everything and he caressed her softly, naturally.

"You lie down now," he said. "Then you'll feel better."

He lowered her to the pillow, one arm still under her. He did not know how to pull it away without seeming callous or cruel, so he let it remain and with one hand stroked her arm.

A round arm, full and soft to the touch. She turned toward him, her face to his. The tears on her face were warm to his skin.

The moon washed into the room. Cold light, cold comfort. Only the face against Tad's was warm. And against his body he felt the softness of her breasts.

If asked, neither would have been able to explain how their closeness had blossomed. Tad, because she needed him, had grown bold, and Laura had responded to his touch. She kissed his bare chest. Fire-fanned, he tentatively laid his hand on her breast. Their mouths met and Tad thought, I'm kissing the woman, and Laura thought, I'm kissing Tad. They had no choice, then, but to go on kissing.

He felt her arch up against him and he no longer sat crouched, legs together, hiding himself, but suddenly twisted around and stretched out next to her. For one panicky second he felt her push him away, but she had only been trying to help him find her. Her blouse came open and something ripped. The bare breast under his palm belonged there, belonged to him now, and asked for his attention.

"*Mon Dieu*—" she said. "*Mon Dieu*—" He could not understand her words but the sound excited him. And her hand, he could feel her searching hand, and he trembled.

He could feel her move smoothly and then she was sitting up. He grabbed for her.

"Yes," she said. "Yes, darling, but like this ..."

He relaxed, with his heat held in, and watched her pull off the blouse. Her bare shoulders and arms were as he had never imagined. He looked, permissible now, because next he would touch. Then her breasts, lovely golden fruits, and her lush hips were revealed in all their splendor.

"Wait," she said. "You, too."

He felt one twinge of shame, then obeyed.

"You do it," she said softly, as she lay down next to him, her eyes closed.

Tad felt awkward. Full of haste, he trembled. But the sight of the naked woman lying next to him gave him courage. The wanting of her became his wanting, and once he had kicked himself free, he went to her. He clawed at her, pushed himself against her, thrashed without quite knowing how.

"Slowly," she commanded. "I'm here, I'm not leaving."

Very briefly he thought, how fantastic that she should know how afraid he was that she might suddenly disappear.

"I'm here," she said again. "You see?"

She took his hand and moved it along her passion-hardened breast to her thighs. Then she abandoned him.

For a moment he felt lost, but then he knew what to do. There was hunger in his fingers for the heat of her.

"Now," she said. "Take me now—"

Was she the aggressor or was he? Tad no longer cared. She lay beside him, a hot sun in which to bathe. Gratefully he possessed her, made of her body an exquisite plaything ...

CHAPTER EIGHT

It had been a long, tiring walk and Tony was reminded of the time he had been abandoned by the eastward-bound teen-agers.

No sun, however, now brightened his path. The sky was saturated with fast-moving night clouds. And Tony was going not to see Tad but away from him. As far as he, Tony, was concerned, he was completely finished with his mother. That woman knew only her own guilt and nothing of what he, Tony, needed or wanted. Bitch, he thought.

Getting home after midnight would not raise any eyebrows. His stepfather would either be asleep or reading in bed. But he and Tony did not have the sort of relationship which would require one to say good night to the other.

When Tony came to his street, only two lights were visible, one in his father's bedroom, the other in Miss Ambru's kitchen. Tony wondered, briefly, about the result of a coupling of those two. Then he dismissed the question. When he got to his room he undressed quickly and fell onto his bed. He was exhausted.

On wakening, Tony felt a great need to be clean. He showered vigorously, then climbed into clean chinos, summer shirt, white sneakers. He brushed back his black hair and stuck the comb into a pocket.

There was lukewarm coffee in the kitchen, and dry toast. He fried two eggs, all the while watching his stepfather. Robert was sitting under a tree in the garden.

The garden was lengthy and looked as if it had received the loving care of an accomplished landscape architect. There were spaced trees, pruned bushes, harmoniously placed flowers and artfully scattered summer furniture.

The professor, looking very much the country gentleman, lounged in the insipid morning sun. He, too, seemed to have wanted to appear particularly fastidious. His long face was shaved pink and his hair had been neatly parted. He was wearing light-colored slacks, an Egyptian cotton shirt and a Paisley ascot. His pipe drooped from his mouth and he was sipping at a glass of light sherry. A copy of the *National Geographic* lay across his knees.

Tony watched him from the kitchen window, then went out into the garden.

"Hello, son," said Vaughn noncommittally.

"Hi, Robert. How come you're home?"

"To be disturbingly frank," said Robert, "I have only a week before summer school."

"Ah! That's nice."

Tony sat down on a stool at the feet of Robert Vaughn.

"Yes." agreed Robert. "It is nice to sit and contemplate." He puffed heavily and let out a wisp of colored smoke. "Where's your mother?"

"Huh?" Tony regarded his stepfather and cocked his head.

"I asked," said Robert, "where your mother is, since this is my first day off, today being Thursday, yesterday having been Wednesday." He coughed low in his throat. "Laura wanted me to take her shopping this afternoon, I think."

"Oh, she's at the cottage."

"Ah. Really." Robert idly flipped a page of his magazine.

"Came to see me and Tad," said Tony. "But I took a long walk last night and decided to sleep over here. Funny you didn't hear me come in."

"Hm," murmured Robert. "I may have fallen asleep in the tub."

"What are you reading about?"

"How the Eskimos spend the winter. Extremely interesting."

"Anything about their sex life?" asked Tony casually.

"Indeed, yes. Eskimos, in that respect, are practically animals."

"How practical?"

"What?"

"Never mind. Go back to your article."

"Did your mother say when she would return?"

"No."

"Ah. Uh—did you speak at all?"

"We always do, Robert."

"Of course."

"Maybe she'll wait until next Wednesday, Robert. One week may be all she'll be able to take, what with the mosquitoes and the glare on the water. You understand."

"Of course." Robert set down the magazine and stared up into the abundant foliage of the tree. "Perhaps, I ought to go out to the lake myself. For some relaxation."

"Before Wednesday?"

"Why, yes. Swimming would condition my body. I'm getting awfully soft."

"Tell me more about those Eskimos during the long winter months, Robert."

But Robert was saved from further comment by the drifting voice.

"Hello."

At that sound Tony gave a start, but so did Robert Vaughn. There was Miss Ambru peering over the fence, smile beaming at them, glasses glittering.

Robert Vaughn immediately began to heave himself out of the chair.

"You dropped your magazine, professor," smiled Miss Ambru.

"I know. It's nothing."

"Pick it up, professor. It will get moist on the lawn."

Vaughn picked up the magazine, dropping his pipe in the process.

"You dropped your—"

"I know, Miss Ambru. I'm picking it up this very moment."

Vaughn had wished to flee gracefully, but he was making a fool of himself.

"And how is the lovely Mrs. Vaughn?" asked Miss Ambru.

Vaughn, magazine in hand, shoved the long-stemmed pipe back into his mouth.

"Just fine," he said grimly.

"I don't see her around."

"That's because she isn't around," said Tony.

"Ah? She isn't around?"

"She trekked off to the woods, much to Daddy Bob's chagrin."

"Well, I should think so, professor. Imagine a young woman showing such independence. I do hope that you'll soon be able to afford a vacation."

"I am on my vacation. If you'll excuse ..."

"Busy, even on your vacation?"

"He's preparing for summer school."

"My, isn't that interesting? You professors lead the most enriching lives."

"Yes," said Vaughn. "However, teaching does take a certain amount of energy, so if you will excuse me—"

His hasty exit allowed the full force of Miss Ambru's personality to focus on Tony.

He grinned winningly at the old maid. The bizarre had always intrigued Tony, and this baby-faced old woman held his attention.

"Now I recall, young man," said the spinster, "that I spoke to you a while ago about tea and cookies and I've been wondering ..."

"I've been in the woods, too, Miss Ambru" said Tony. "Indeed I have been and now I'm back. And a cup of tea would just hit the spot, particularly with one of your nice orange cookies."

Many years ago Miss Ambru had been told that her voice was singularly bell-like, and she imitated that sound now. Tony, nauseous, decided to forgo a certain amount of physical and mental comfort in order to get his kicks. He wanted to observe this bird in her own nest. Getting up, he impulsively placed his hand on top of Miss Ambru's.

"I think you're wonderful to remember that cookie and the cup of tea. Simply wonderful."

Miss Ambru, unused to receiving affection from young men, pinked prettily.

"Coming now?" she asked.

"Now," said Tony, and then he vaulted over the fence.

Tony waited politely and let his hostess go up the steps ahead of him. Vaguely instructing him to make himself at home, she dashed to the bathroom to check the guest towels. They were all in a line. While there, she gazed into the mirror. Her appearance was also in line, she thought.

Tony had meanwhile picked up a brown postmarked parcel. He noted that the wrapping bore no return address. A smile appeared on his face as he settled down into a couch. When he heard Miss Ambru descending, he hurriedly replaced the package on the lower shelf of an end table. The woman entered, in one hand a tray of musty, store-bought cookies.

"Homemade?" asked Tony.

"Why, this recipe ..."

"Lovely," said Tony. "I can smell them from over here. I'll not touch them till you bring the tea."

"Why, how sweet of you, Tony. I always say ..."

"Some time," said Tony as if his hostess were not talking at all, "some time when you feel experimental, I wish you would try an old Continental custom, something I saw in Europe, you know."

"My!"

"Yes. And that is cookies served not with tea—" the pause was suspenseful—"but with just a spot of sherry."

"Sherry?"

"Sherry. It's a lovely wine, you know."

Miss Ambru darted out of the room.

Tony felt that he was being treated like a suitor. He was by no means wrong. There was something quaint about this situation, he thought. With a suitor's anticipation he awaited Miss Ambru's return.

She came flying into the room with a pink-labeled bottle.

"It just so happens—"

The sherry turned out to be cooking sherry, but Tony pretended not to know the difference. The bottle, he noted, was half-full and the price, stamped there by the supermarket, was low.

She set down the bottle and splashed wine into two glasses.

"I feel as if I'm contributing to the delinquency a minor."

"Oh, don't feel badly, Miss Ambru. I won't tell."

"Why—why you dear boy, you," she beamed.

Then she handed him a glass and tipped up her own. They sipped slowly, savoring the flavor.

"Ah!" bubbled Miss Ambru. "Wherever did you learn of this interesting custom, Tony?"

"From my mother."

"Indeed?"

"She's practiced it for years."

"Is that the truth?" Miss Ambru smiled, showing her dentures. "Well, she did live in France for—how long was it?"

"Not long," said Tony. "She isn't that old."

"Of course, what I meant to say …"

"Forget it. No harm done. Miss Ambru, do you have any hobbies? I mean, do you enjoy reading?"

"Why, yes. As a matter of fact, I subscribe to several magazines. And I often buy books advertised in them."

"Is this one?" Tony reached for the brown parcel and held it up. Miss Ambru twittered, "Oh, my dear. Hand that book over immediately. It came in the mail yesterday and I've hardly had a chance to examine the table of contents. It's a rare and wonderful classic." Then Miss Ambru snatched the package and started out of the room. "Excuse me a few minutes, will you please?"

Tony poured himself another drink and refilled Miss Ambru's glass. The bottle was now almost empty. The wine was warm by the time Miss Ambru had returned.

She offered no excuses for her absence.

Tony lifted up his empty glass, and kept sipping on air until Miss Ambru noticed.

"Why—you've really finished your spot of sherry haven't you?"

"It seems I have," and Tony set down the glass "but I positively won't accept any more unless you promise to drink with me, Miss Ambru."

"All right. And wouldn't you like another cookie, too?"

"That would be nice. Yes."

She again left the room, undoubtedly, Tony thought, for a private perusal of the book.

The room in which he was sitting opened to the hall and across from it was the den. Tony stood up, stretched, and struck out for the den.

A wastebasket was overflowing with brown paper. On the desk lay the book. Tony knew the tome well. It had been standard equipment in the dormitory back at military school. He slammed the door shut.

He pulled out the book and smiled at it like an old friend. Then the door opened.

"Why, you dreadful—"

"Miss Ambru," exclaimed Tony, with the shaky poise of an ancient matinee idol. "Fancy running into this manual here, in your hospitable home!"

Miss Ambru, frozen, looked aghast. Tony went right on.

"I have several times seen this title in small advertisements in the back of certain kinds of magazines. I've never actually seen the book itself. It seems to be a book that appeals to a special readership. I've always wanted to read it, but the advertisements say, 'adults only.' Chronologically, I'm still a child. Do you think I am a child, Miss Ambru?"

Miss Ambru, understandably, said not a word. Tony placed the book back on the desk and walked toward her. He reached out for the bottle she was carrying.

"Let me uncork it. We'll sit in the parlor and while we have another cookie and a spot of sherry, you must tell me what you know about that little volume."

She let him take the bottle and lead the way into the other room. She wanted only to put as much distance as possible between themselves and that book.

They sat down and this time Tony poured. Generously, it might be added.

"Now, Miss Ambru," he said as he leaned back, glass in hand. "Tell me about that wonderful book."

Hate, helplessness, fear, shame and cunning all warred within Miss Ambru's soul and rendered her helpless.

"It was written by a well-known doctor, a—"

"A man trained in the West but with an understanding of the mystery of the East."

"Why—how did you know?"

"I told you," said Tony, grandly. "Advertisements, remember? The good doctor has a message for all of us."

"Oh, certainly."

"To save humanity, isn't that it?"

"Of course, yes."

"Miss Ambru." Tony waited, while Miss Ambru took a good, therapeutic dose of sherry. "After you have worked your way into the volume, have delved into the volume, would you be willing to share some of the extraordinary secrets of which the doctor writes? I mean, after you've absorbed, would you mind sharing your knowledge—"

He let his words hang so that she could compose herself and give an acceptable answer.

"Surely, dear boy."

"I am so glad." To make her feel safe, he stood up, his sherry glass emptied. "May I come again tomorrow, for tea and cookies. Perhaps then you could tell me about it?"

"Why, I would love to," said Miss Ambru.

Diplomatically, Tony made his excuses. As he walked out, he felt like a most clever fellow.

She watched him leave and thought, that poor, innocent boy. I will tell him some time about what that guard has seen with his own eyes while making the rounds of the campus. About his own mother—of course, living abroad all that time. That poor boy's own mother, thrashing around in the grass with that poor boy's own best friend ...

Laura woke up at four in the morning and, seeing Tad beside her, she got up and lit a cigarette. Then sleep finally returned to her again. Later Tad, awakening, became aware first that the bed was warm, next that the body close to him was female, and then that he desired that body. Half asleep, Tad's craving for her was uncomplicated. One answer from her, the slightest touch of an answer, and he was with her smooth, sweet-smelling body ...

When he awakened the second time, he was alone in the bed. He heard Laura singing in the shower and realized what they had done. He could not feign sleep and felt that he could not get up. If he were to arise, she might come into the room ...

He closed his eyes as the drumming water slackened. Laura stepped out of the shower stall and walked into the bedroom.

"Tad?"

He smiled weakly.

"Good morning, Tad."

"Hello, Mrs. Vaughn."

She sat down on the edge of the bed. He stiffened, as not to roll against her, and she smiled at him.

The ends of her brown hair were damp and there as a soft glow to her skin. With one hand she fingered the buttons of her white bathrobe.

"I brought you some coffee," she said, setting down a green cup on the night table. "And I think it's time you called me by my first name." She smiled sadly.

He wanted to place his arms around her, to comfort her, but restrained himself.

"We have to talk about this situation, Tad. Tad? Look at me."

"I want to say," he began, but his voice broke. "I'm sorry for—"

Laura placed a warning finger to his lips. She said, "Look into the future and imagine yourself as you will be a year from this day. I want you to tell me how you will remember what happened between us."

Tad, lying under the mound of blankets, blushed to the roots of his hair.

"Take a deep breath, Tad, and then tell me what you would think."

He closed his eyes. And then he said, "I would think, how wonderful—" He ended in a whisper that made Laura feel like saying thank you. She touched his arm lightly and then stroked his forehead. "Would you now still say to me you're sorry?"

He looked at her. "No," he said.

She smiled at him, got up, and left the room. He relaxed now, full of thanks not only for her having left the room so that he could be alone, but for the night and for the waking. Because he was young and unprepared for love, he did not recognize a dawning emotion.

Mrs. Howard, at this very moment, was silently bemoaning her fate. She had recently been cursed with an affliction which she found hard to bear, a violent urge to vomit whenever she drank.

Lambert Howard reached into the cupboard and pulled out a box of bran flakes. Mrs. Howard's brow furrowed.

"Lambert."

"What's the matter?"

"The sight of those flakes makes me sick."

"Go on. Get away with you. If you'd eat some, you might regain your health."

She waited until he had arranged a bowl and spoon on the kitchen table.

"You going to eat that gook right here?"

"Where else? On the road, maybe, instead of in my own kitchen?"

"Why don't you have your breakfast where you spend your nights? She too lazy to feed you?"

"I've been sleeping next to you for twenty-five lousy years and last night was no exception. If you had been sober, maybe you would have realized it."

"That's your story."

"Listen, I was right there and—ah, to hell with you." He gave up the argument and bit into the mushy bran.

"Ugh—"

"What's the matter now?" he bellowed.

"Those sounds," she said, eyes rolling.

"This cereal is soft and makes no crackles whatsoever!"

"That's not what I'm talking about. You eat like a pig. Those terrible noises, you make with your lips are absolutely disgusting."

Mrs. Howard was enjoying the fact that her husband was disturbed by her comments. She thought of her next approach.

"And incidentally," she added, "just why do you need health food?"

"For my health, you old bag. I'm an active man, always working. Nobody can say that Lambert Howard is a lazy bum. You should eat some bran, yourself. Might pep you up."

"Ever since you manhandled me on our wedding night, I've been unfit for a normal life. But you, you Lambert, with all that health food you're gobbling, should possess the strength of ten."

"I'm fit all right, don't you worry."

"Then maybe you should give that son of yours a good lambasting."

"Why?" he asked, baffled.

"Tad, like his father, is a lecher. I got proof that he's been playing around."

"All right, tell me about it."

"I've been talking to Mrs. Botskins ..."

"Her? I know you're stupid, but you can't be dumb enough to believe what that old witch says."

"Well, she happens to know. I spoke to her on the phone right after she heard it from Carl."

"Who in hell is Carl?"

"Her boarder."

"Hah—boarder."

"He's a respectable old man or else he wouldn't have such a good job—campus cop."

"Carl," said Lambert, "is an old lush."

"You're an impossible liar. Tad and this woman were sitting together on a park bench one night after midnight."

"That's rich. Carl is as blind as a bat, even when he's sober. Now how could anyone like that see two people sitting in the dark?"

"You just don't want to hear the truth. Right there in the dark Tad sat with that woman!"

"Doing what?"

"You tell me. They jumped apart when Carl came along ..."

"That's rich. What woman?"

"That professor's wife."

"Huh?"

"The mother of that boy friend he's got, that Tony kid."

Lambert was disappointed. Why shouldn't Tad be seen with Tony's mother? Tad and Tony were best friends. He pushed his cereal away with distaste and prepared to leave.

"That's how I know what you've been up to!" said his wife.

"Huh?" he asked.

"Tad's your son and an apple never falls far from the tree."

Lambert grunted because, as far as he was concerned, no part of the story was worth arguing about. He went out and sat in front of his office until an elderly customer happened by. The old man wished a quiet cabin far back from the road. But the only free cabin, quiet and far back from the road, was Number Seventeen. Lambert, who rented that cabin only to couples, sent the man away.

CHAPTER NINE

Lambert Howard went to town to purchase nails and a bagful of fuses. He wished that, upon his return, there would be something to do. But there were no lights to install at the motel, no partitions to make, and no holes to bore. If I only owned more land, he dreamed, as he passed a real-estate office, I could build plenty of cabins. They would stretch all the way down to the lake and across the long meadow. Perhaps someday even a marina and a roller-skating rink will bear my name.

He stopped on the tree-lined square and sat down on a bench. After a time a girl walked by and Lambert Howard watched how she bounced. Just so much, nothing obvious. Lambert Howard was good at spotting a bounce. Wasn't she the girl Tad was going with? Amy?

The girl walked into the grocery, her rump swinging prettily. Lambert licked his lips. Now if that one, some dark evening, were to come to the motel with a good-looking boy, Lambert would surely give them number seventeen. He would love to see that chick in action.

Then Miss Ambru emerged from the store. She was toting a bag of greens which, Lambert figured, concealed a bottle. Cooking sherry, most likely, he mused as he spat out tobacco. As Lambert silently laughed, Carl, the old campus guard, moved into view. His bones were soft from old age; and his brain, from too much booze. Carl, now as always, was going from hangover to clarity. How in the world could that old bird have seen his, Lambert's son, with that woman? Impossible, Lambert muttered.

Despite himself, Lambert had an impulse to follow Carl into the bar but then common sense reigned. He would feel like a fool, he thought, consulting a drunk about his own son. If only Tad had turned out as well as Tony. There was a fine fellow.

At that moment Tony came walking across Lambert's field of vision. Lambert, an approving smile on his lips, did not call out, simply because the boy seemed absorbed in his thoughts.

Tony stopped to speak with Miss Ambru. To Lambert it looked as if a quarrel were developing over Miss Ambru's big bag of groceries. The boy—polite little bastard that he was—insisted on carrying the bundle. But the little gentleman, Lambert noted, was not getting anywhere at all. Miss Ambru clutched the groceries to her bosom and waved goodbye.

Turning, Tony bumped Amy, who fell. Lambert wished he were years younger. The boy picked up the girl and helped her to brush herself off. After a curt "Thank you," the girl headed in the opposite direction.

"Hey, Tony," Lambert called.

The boy, when he saw Lambert, frowned. Oh my God, he thought. What a bore. But having nothing more exciting to do, Tony crossed the street and came up to Lambert's bench.

"Sit a spell, boy. Sit a spell, won't you?"

"Thank you, Mr. Howard. How is Mrs. Howard?" and Tony sat down.

"She's a sick woman, as you might well know, boy, and she's often full of crazy talk." Lambert sighed. Then he said, "Tad used to help, but with him gone, all of the burden falls on me."

"How do you carry on in the face of adversity, Mr. Howard?"

"I just plow my way through, Tony."

"Well, you certainly set a fine example to youth, Mr. Howard."

"One must do what one must."

"Good that you have the motor court to take your mind off your troubles."

"Oh, yeah," said Lambert. "I'd be lost without it!"

Tony let him laugh. Then he said, "Does your work keep you up late at night, Mr. Howard?"

"Huh?"

"Do you have to stay up very late to watch—"

"Oh, yeah. Sometimes, yeah," and then Lambert burped, the sound of which interrupted the conversation. When he had recovered, Lambert changed the subject.

"Well, Tony, how you been getting along since coming back from school?"

"Fine, sir."

"Good. I'm glad my Tad has you for—"

"I haven't seen Tad lately."

"Haven't seen him lately, hey?" repeated Lambert. He was turning things over in his mind.

"Have you?" asked Tony.

"Have I what?" Lambert said.

"Seen Tad."

"Why, no. Not recently. What I meant to ask—"

"I didn't think you had. Unless he's come into town," Tony said.

"Huh?"

"Come into town."

"No, no, he hasn't."

"That's what I figured."

"Huh?"

Tony, playing with Lambert as he might with an idiot, said, "I haven't seen either him or my mother."

"He wrote me," said Lambert. "He posted a card."

"I know. I watched him pen it."

"Watched him pen it," repeated Lambert.

"Yes. At the cottage."

"Huh?"

"At the cottage," Tony said.

"You don't seem to know what I'm talking about, Mr. Howard." Tony smiled cruelly. "I am talking about my father's cottage—not one of yours. Tad and I have been staying out at the lake."

"Aah—" said Lambert helplessly.

Tony had no idea why he had told this to Mr. Howard. But for some un-known reason he nurtured a small, hard knot of resentment against his one friend. Tony thought of his comments as subtle, legitimate moves in an amus-ing game with dumb Mr. Howard.

"He's at your cabin at the lake?" said Mr. Howard.

"Yes. I told you that."

"And you—I mean, he's still there, alone?"

"Not alone. My mother's there too."

"Aah," said Mr. Howard. "Tad's not alone."

"That's what I said," Tony felt an unreasonable resentment against—whom? Lambert was nearest and so it was Lambert on whom Tony concentrated. And then Tony saw Amy again, walking from the drugstore to the other end of the square, and his attention was momentarily diverted.

Then Lambert said, "I'm kind of anxious to have Tad come back to the house. I know—and maybe you know—that he left in a huff, but I do wish he'd forgive and forget. After all, he does have a home and a father that wants him. So maybe—"

"What did you want to ask me, Mr. Howard?"

"Well, seeing that Tad is at your cabin and—"

"You want me to ask him to come back."

"Well, now, I don't want to force you, but I'd kind of like seeing my son, Tony. And if Tad isn't involved in—"

"I beg your pardon?"

"If he isn't terribly busy, maybe … maybe he would come back to help his father out of a jam."

Tony said, "Perhaps I might, in return for a small favor."

"What's that, Tony?"

"I was wondering, Mr. Howard, if you'd allow me, sometime, the use of one of your cabins."

"Just you?"

"As a matter of fact, what I had in mind—"

"I don't want to hear anything about that, son. Of course I'll rent you a place."

"Thank you, Mr. Howard."

"But no trouble, you hear?"

"Oh no, Mr. Howard. No, no."

"When?"

"Tonight?"

"Hm," said Lambert thoughtfully.

"Something out of the way, Mr. Howard. Do you own a cabin to the rear of the court?"

"Why to the rear?"

"I want to be discreet, for all our sakes."

"Tell you what, son. Pay me now."

"Now?"

"Right here."

Tony sneaked his hand into his pocket and then handed the bills to Lambert.

"Very good, son. Now listen." Lambert bent close, his breath sour-smelling. "Instead of driving into the court, go down the lane next to it and when you come to the last cabin—"

"The one with the shed attached?"

"Yeah. It's numbered seventeen."

"Got you."

Lambert, as Tony crossed the street, wondered for a moment who the girl might be. Minutes later he knew.

"I'll be damned," he mumbled. "Fooling around with his own best friend's steady ..."

They returned, silent still, from their walk along the shore. Once Tad had reached for her hand but Laura had pulled away. Back at the cottage they sat down on the porch.

"Move your chair closer?" she asked.

He got up, pushed his chair closer and sat down again. Her hand was hanging over the side of the lounge and he imitated her pose, wishing he could touch her and not feel so constrained.

If he had looked at her more critically, he would have seen her subtle smile. She closed her eyes. Then he felt her hand searching for his.

"I want to hold your hand," Laura said.

Their fingers interlocked.

"How did you know I wanted you to say that?" Tad asked.

"Intuition."

He rubbed her fingers and glanced at her legs.

"You're nervous," she said.

"Huh? How can you tell?"

"Because I'm nervous, too."

"Each time I feel something, you feel it?"

"When people are close, that can happen."

"Yes," he said. "Yes, Laura."

And when he had said the yes and the Laura, he knew why he had kept silent during their walk. He was afraid to show her how much he desired to possess her.

"It's hot here," he said lamely.

"I know. Your palm is sweaty."

Tad immediately tried to jerk away his hand but she held on. Laura laughed softly.

"When two people are close—" she started.

"I don't feel good," said Tad. "I want to get up."

"What's the matter, Tad?"

"I don't know."

"Look at me," she said.

He had the distinct impression that she knew.

"Something's wrong," he said.

"What, Tad. You?"

"Yes."

He relaxed, no longer wanting to hide. He squeezed her hand. "I'll tell you, but please don't laugh. I think there's something wrong with me because I want you again. I want you for all time," he said quickly, as if afraid.

"Wrong?" she asked.

"Yes, wrong. I mean—"

"What do you mean?"

Suddenly he no longer knew what he meant. Her hand stirred in his. "Laura, am I wrong?"

"Come," she said. "I want to show you something."

Without letting go of his hand, she got up and went into the bedroom. The blinds were drawn against the sun, "Turn on the fan," said Laura. While he turned on the fan she lay down on the bed. "Come sit here," she said, and she patted the space beside her.

He sat down next to her but did not know what to say.

"If I hurt you, that would be wrong," she said, "or, if you hurt me. But wanting someone, Tad, that can't be wrong. Touch me, Tad."

He put his hand on her.

She stretched and smiled up at him. "It doesn't hurt at all, Tad."

His hand rested on her bare thigh just below the edge of her shorts.

"You want me?" she asked.

His touch answered her.

"And I want you, too," she said. "Kiss me, Tad, but don't hurt me, please. When you make love to me, you must give me the privilege of loving you, Tad."

The thought was new to him. "What do you mean?"

"You feel my hand?" she asked.

"Yes." Her hand stroked his arm.

"I can't give myself completely unless you're tender. That's what makes a woman respond most readily to a man. A lover," she went on, "doesn't rape. To rape is to steal something which has not been given."

"But I didn't mean—"

"Don't sound so shocked, Tad. You can rape a woman even though she holds still for you. Even, as a matter of fact, because she holds so still."

He moved his arm over her back. He felt the strap of her bra and wished there were nothing, nothing to interrupt the smooth curve of her flesh.

"You feel me now, don't you?" she asked.

"Yes. More than before."

"Now you are tasting me," she said. "Before you just gulped."

"I wanted you that much."

"This way, you'll want me more—"

She reached to her back and unsnapped the bra.

"Undress me," she said. "Slowly, Tad."

When he had taken off her blouse and her bra and she lay naked beside him, he began to tremble.

"Slowly," she ordered. "You're still clothed. Slowly, Tad—"

He had begun to tear at his clothes but she put her hands over his and held them.

"No," she said. "Like this."

Then she ran her hands along his body, touching him lightly—like a moth, he thought, like a moth circling the fire ...

"Slowly, Tad. Step by step. Respond to my every answer." She moved. "You feel me answer?"

He nodded mutely and at that moment the need to rush left him and he felt capable, he felt sure.

"Now," she said, "I want you, all of you—"

And that is how Tad learned that to have a woman is to have her answer. And love-making was changed from an act whose strength was frustration to a beautiful, enriching experience.

It was darker now, almost the dark of night, and he felt her next to him and knew she was as quiet inside now as he.

"Laura?"

"Yes," she said and touched his cheek and left her hand there.

"Laura," he said again. "The words are so simple and common but I tell them to you now as if I had invented them."

She lay still, not moving.

"I love you," he said to her. "I want you never to stop."

She had known he would say it before the words had come out; the feel of it had been in the air and inside each of them. She heard him and she felt it and lay still.

Now it's here, she thought, and everything inside her stopped. This is the crossroads and I must choose which route to travel.

I must turn away, Laura reflected, I must turn him away, too. Tad doesn't know that "I love you" can sometimes be true for only a moment.

The greed of the young, she thought, to think of forever. She wanted to cry and Tad, sensing her mood, held her close. Laura wished that Tad knew that this embrace would end.

Tad, of course, knew nothing of the sort. He and Laura arose after a while and dressed. As she prepared their evening meal, he walked on to the porch, stood there and looked out over the lake.

Now, Tad thought, now ... He did not know quite how to finish the sentence, but it did not seem to matter. He stretched and smiled at the dark lake and thought now again. And then he stood easily by the railing, hands on his hips and finished the sentence. Now I'm grown and a man, he reflected. I've changed.

Then Laura called to him and he went into the kitchen where she had set out the meal. The yellow lamp made a warm light on the table.

"Like a picture," he said, admiring the multicolored vegetables and the golden chops.

"Sit down and eat," she said.

"It looks too good."

"Hurry now, before it gets cold."

Tad ate with so much gusto that he brought smiles to Laura's face.

When he had finished, he sat back and said, "Something else you gave me. That wonderful meal."

"What?" she asked. Laura did not want to know what he meant.

"What else?" he said. "You mean what else did you give me?"

"What I meant—"

"You gave me the way I feel now," he said. "I can't tell you in clever words how I feel now, but I've never felt this way before and you gave it to me."

She wanted to take all he had said and feel happy with it but knew that she could not. If she allowed him to go on like this, she would make it harder for him in the end.

"Thank you, Tad," she said, permitting herself only that. And then she switched to the next topic.

"Tad?"

"You want me to wash the dishes?"

"No. I'll do them. What I—"

"I'll dry them."

"All right," she said and stood up.

She said nothing else until the dishpan was filled with hot water. Then she said this straight out.

"I want us to go back to town tonight, Tad."

"Tonight?"

"Yes. To stay is just to delay and to delay means only that we aren't facing ..."

"Listen," he said as he turned to grab her by the arm. "Laura."

"I know, Tad," and she moved a little so she could face him. "You and I are not alone in the world. We ..."

"But that's what it felt like to me," he said.

"Yes. And to me, for a while," Laura said.

"And you're saying that now it's finished?"

She knew she had wanted to say that but she also knew that she did not want this interlude to end.

She looked at Tad and wanted to seize for him that instant. He had been good for her. Her body was more alive now than it had been in years. It was awake and she did not want it to go back to sleep.

"Not finished," she said. "I don't mean that Tad."

He kept holding her arm, more possessively now.

"But, but we have to make some sense," she said helplessly.

"So the neighbors don't talk?"

"Precisely, Tad."

"And why else, Laura?"

The quiet in the room was oppressive, because each knew how wide the gulf between them was growing.

Not only was Laura's existence foreign to Tad's, but she had a son who was still Tad's friend. And because he now possessed so much less of her than ever before, he might destroy them.

"We'll drive back to town the long way," she said, "and I'll drop you off first."

"But I'll see you."

"Yes."

"Tonight, Laura. I want to be with you tonight."

"Yes," she said, absently. "Yes, we'll think of a way."

CHAPTER TEN

It had not been easy for Tony, in spite of all his glibness, to persuade Amy to let him pick her up that evening after the movie. But he had managed it.

Her vagueness had not bothered him one bit. If she really had not wanted to go with him, she would have said no and that would have been the end.

He had spent part of the afternoon with Miss Ambru. They had feasted on cookies and sherry and, when Tony had decided to go, Miss Ambru had expressed her sorrow.

"It isn't often," she had said, "that anyone your age shows such respect for the thoughts of his elders."

"But Miss Ambru, no one but you could have explained that book in such lofty terms."

"Well, the attitudes of love is a lofty subject."

"And I had thought, before speaking to you, that that book was a manual for sex fiends."

"Oh, dear."

"But now I know that it explains Yogi postures for the Christian practitioner," Tony had said.

"Of course."

"Some time, Miss Ambru, you must do me the honor of demonstrating those Christian-Yogi positions."

"Well—"

"I would be honored."

"Well—" and then she had giggled all the way to the door.

Tony would have enjoyed the subtleties of this conversation more if he had not been so preoccupied with his plans for the evening. He had had hours to kill before Amy would be free. He had taken a shower and changed his clothes, then he had wandered into town. At ten p.m. he had seen Amy walk off with some other guy.

Minutes later, she reappeared.

"Oh, hi," Amy said. "Where have you been?"

"Waiting for you."

"Who was that young man you walked out with?" he asked.

"Him? Nobody."

"What do you mean, nobody? I saw somebody."

"He's an usher here, sometimes. What do you want to do tonight?"

The question baffled him. When he had set up the date, he had made it perfectly clear that he did not want to go to her house but had instead, at great expense, arranged for a motel cabin.

"Would you like a coke or something, first?" he inquired.

"A coke?" she said.

"You don't like coke."

"Not especially," she said.

He took Amy's arm now and walked her away from the marquee lights.

"I'll give you something nice," he said, nudging the side of her hard-packed breast.

She stiffened perceptibly. "Are you talking dirty to me?"

"Why, no."

"All right. Don't you talk dirty to me."

She did nothing about his pressing fingers.

"I won't, Amy dear," Tony said.

"Where you taking me?"

The street down which he was heading led to the motel.

"Out there," he said.

"So quick?"

"Amy," he said, "I want to be with you, where we can be alone."

"Is there television in that place?"

"The motel?"

"Yeah, where you're taking me, where else?"

"I don't think so. But—"

"What do you mean, you don't think so? Yes or no?" Amy said.

"As a matter of fact, I asked specifically, knowing how much you like television. I was told no."

She made a sullen sound but kept walking. Perhaps, Tony thought, she doesn't feel my fingers at all. He dug into her breast a little more.

"You cut that out, Tony," she said. "We're walking right under a light."

He cut it out. When they were past the light, he dug again and she said nothing.

By the time they had reached the cabin, they had stopped a few times and whispered into each other's ears and their tongues had met.

"Let go of me," she said. "That light is shining right on us."

He let go of her. He was getting the hang of her particular kind of morality.

"Don't you have to go and get the key?" Amy asked.

"No. It's all arranged," he said, "to keep this discreet."

And in fact, as per arrangement, the key was in the lock of the cabin door and they entered the cabin without any delay.

Tony flicked the switch next to the door and two lamps made a lovely, yellow light on the double bed. He kicked the door shut with one foot and took the girl straight to the bed.

"You were right," she said. "No television at all."

"That's okay, dear. We'll talk instead."

"What?"

He sat her down on the bed and began to unbutton the front of her dress.

"Hey," she protested.

"Hold still."

"Hey. The lights are on. You can't—"

"I can't see you without the lights, dear. And—" with a low, heated rumble—"I must see you—"

"Hey."

She was startled by the change in him. Unprotesting, she watched him unbutton her and unhook her bra. When she was naked to the waist, he caressed her and kissed her on the mouth. She allowed him to push her back on the bed and she sighed when he squeezed one breast a little too roughly.

"Hey," she said. "Tony?"

"Yes?"

"Turn some," she said.

"No," he said.

"What?" Amy said.

She looked up at him, not understanding his complaint. So far this evening, she had done everything he wanted. Now that she had made one simple request, he had refused.

"I forgot to make a phone call," the boy said.

"Phone call?"

His hand was still on her breast but his skin was clammy.

"I'll be back in a jiffy," he said. "You can bet on that."

Tony shut the door behind him and took a deep breath of the night air. There were moths going around and around the light overhead and cricket sounds coming from the meadow, but he knew nothing of that.

A nervousness was in him as he looked at the shed next to Number Seventeen. Soon a hole the size of a quarter would be punched through the wall and a bloodshot eyeball would stare at a half-naked girl with big, round breasts ...

In the cabin the girl sat up. She scratched her bare arm and once she absently rubbed her left breast. She was waiting for Tony.

Where the motor court ended, Tony ducked into the phone booth by the side of the road and dialed.

Mrs. Howard, nipping her chocolate concoction, shuddered when the phone rang.

"Yeah?" she crowed.

"Is Mr. Howard there?" asked Tony.

"No, he isn't and if you—"

"Would it interest you to know where Mr. Howard spends his long evenings away from home?"

"What's that?"

"Do you want to know where he is, I asked."

"Who?" And she coughed.

Tony, as if he were touching a toad, grimaced. He felt as if he had been touching toads and worms and crawling beasts all day and evening.

"I'm talking about your bum of a husband, woman. While you sit there like a drunk sow with your brains coming apart, he's out."

"He's out? Why you tell that bastard to come straight home, because I'm sick."

"You tell him."

"What?"

"Why don't you tell him, Mrs. Howard?"

"But you said he was out."

"I can tell you where to find him."

"You run right over there, hear me, and tell that filth to get on home."

"No, I won't."

"But I'm sick."

"I'm getting sick too, you drunk," and Tony meant every word of it. Mrs. Howard was now fully aroused.

"Don't hang up! Where is—where is my husband?"

"You know cabin Number Seventeen?"

"Where's that?"

"Oh my God."

"Don't you take the name of the Lord in vain in front of a God-fearing woman."

"Amen. Now, Mrs. Howard, next to cabin Number Seventeen is a shed and your husband is in there and the girl he is looking at is naked."

"Don't you talk filthy to me."

"Amen," said Tony.

He hung up, not because he was convinced that he had said enough but because he could not take any more of this call. The drunk woman at the other end of the line disgusted him and he hated himself for having made the call. He left the booth and walked out to the highway where it was dark and he breathed deeply again. He thought of Amy in the cabin, the way she might be sitting there now, but the thought gave him no pleasure. This evening was to have been a joke not only on dirty old Howard but on the girl herself. The joke had turned sour.

Tony walked away from the motel and wondered if Mrs. Howard had understood anything about the call he had made.

She had understood, all right. Too soaked in sick fogs to do anything at the moment but continue to drink, she had decided to act later …

Lambert Howard stood by the hole in the wall until his eyeball ran with tears and his feet, which were flat anyway, ached like crazy. He would not have minded the aches and the pains if there had been something to see. He had, of course, enjoyed watching Tony tossing all over the bed with that big-breasted girl. Tony had gone, however, and now all Lambert could see was the young one sitting on the bed all alone. She was stripped to the hips, of course, but all in all the show was extremely boring. How long can any man stand with one eye to a hole in a wall and look at two big breasts and nothing else?

Tony would return, Lambert was sure of that. But the waiting was ghastly. And now, much of the time, Lambert could not see the half-naked girl. She had begun to wander around the empty room. Once Lambert's peephole was suddenly obscured with a threatening mass of flesh but he was unable to decide upon which portion of the girl's anatomy he had feasted. And then she went to the john. As he waited for her to emerge, Lambert suddenly jerked erect with pain. For an agony of time he was not even sure why he had stiffened. But gradually one horrible sound, that hateful whining, magnified, and he knew.

"Lambert, you bastard …" From a distance, but sharp and clear now, came the voice.

He dashed out of the dark shed and into the open where, as soon as he had turned the length of the court, he saw his wife. Obviously not accustomed to being outside, she was standing in one spot, her attention devoted to keeping her balance. Like an ugly, wounded bird, she flapped the air with her arms. And she kept hawking and yammering and cursing.

If the customers should hear her, see him with her, they would pack up and leave. He ran past all the cabins, his skin drenched, his face a mottled purple. As soon as he had reached the drunken woman, he shot out one arm and caught her on the side of the head. She fell down immediately. Lambert dragged her into the kitchen of their home, where he threw her to the couch. There was blood on the side of her face and dirt in her nostrils. She lay there, panting, as if she had run the mile in four minutes. Then Lambert, his own breath coming in short gasps, sat down by the kitchen table, the better to watch her. Suddenly his wife reared up, shifted around and sent him a scathing glance.

"You bastard."

He wanted to clout her again but he was too winded. "If I ever catch you out there again in the middle of the night, I'll—"

"I'm sick."

"Don't give me any of your excuses."

"Hand me my chocolate, Herman," she said, an odd glitter in her eye.

"Herman? Who's Herman around here?"

"Please don't yell so loud, Herman. Or Mama will hear."

"Mama?" he said.

"Shush, now. Or I won't let you do that again."

"Do what, for God's sake?" Now he thought he knew her drunkenness was a delirium. But he was wrong. His wife was in the process of going insane.

"Don't you take the Lord's name in vain in front of me. I'm a God-fearing woman." She was once more temporarily in touch with reality.

Lambert, anxious to get back to his post, stood up.

"Where you off to, Herman?" Again, she had lapsed.

"I'm going to attend to a customer. And you," he said, bending over her, "are going to stay put."

"I know what you're up to," she said and looked past him. "I know what goes on."

"Drunk talk," he said and walked out.

"All I got to do," she said again, "is look at the phone to see the whole thing."

And she did indeed see something there. The round dial contained a moving picture. Arms, legs and heads, some belonging to Lambert and some belonging to a large, naked woman, first merged then grew apart. Lambert was crawling like a louse along the woman's white belly until the woman gave herself a slap with the flat of her hand. This made a big, dark stain on her white belly. No, not a stain. A hole from which all her guts fell out. They fell out of the belly, out of the picture and on to the kitchen floor. They flopped and writhed there like shiny, fat worms and Mrs. Howard immediately looked away. The worms, moving along, climbed up into the bowl of the lamp that hung from the ceiling. From the bowl hung some of the worminess down into the room.

Mrs. Howard bent over and threw up.

Lambert Howard stood in the gloom of the motor court and cursed himself for having left his post in the shed. He kept thinking that Tony had returned, finished the job, and gone. Right this minute Tony and the girl with the heavy breasts were probably walking slowly down the highway, back into town. But hoping against hope, Lambert struck out in the direction of the cabin. Perhaps, he thought, they are so tired from love-making that they are resting.

Lambert went as fast as his aching feet could carry him. Now and then he rubbed one watering eye.

And then he saw the darkened cabin. Had they left, he thought? His heart pounded with anger. Or had they merely succumbed to modesty?

Tony, stopping in the lane, wondered whether he should go back. If he should return to Amy, would she attempt to make him go the limit? Perhaps, he thought, he might peep at her; providing, of course, that Lambert had disappeared. Tony approached the shed from the rear.

Lambert, hearing a noise, the sound of Tony's feet, called out, "Who's there?"

Tony, frightened, melted into the darkness.

For a moment neither could decide what to do. Later, only one of them decided to go into the shed. The other made his way to another cabin in which two people, love-sated, found each other again and moaned in pleasurable agony.

The intruder, hearing them purely by accident, straining to see them, shrank when he heard their muffled conversation.

"Yes," she said. "Yes, Tad, yes ..." And the boy answered, "Laura, my darling."

The peeper, because he could not stand to watch anymore, ran off.

CHAPTER ELEVEN

The following afternoon found Laura alone in her living room. She was wondering what to do about her affair with Tad. There was really no one to whom she could talk, with whom she could sort it out. Not with Robert, not with Tony and, sadly enough, not with Tad, either. He was too much in love with her, she knew, to think clearly. And she could not force herself to bring their affair to a quick, cold end.

She walked from the window and went to her desk. Taking paper and pen, she sat for a while. She closed her eyes and folded her arms and then, with each hand, she held her breasts for a moment. When she opened her eyes, all she could see was herself and Tad. I must not want him that much, Laura thought. She began to write:

> Pierre, mon cher, perhaps I am telling you this only because you
> are not here. If you were, I would probably restrain myself. I want
> to tell you, Pierre, that I have taken a teen-age lover. He is Antoine's

age. I have had better lovers but this boy slays me. He takes me, I give; and I wonder, is this a child? I know that I should end this. But then I remember all … Yes, everything, in my life, which should not have been allowed to end. Please do not answer this, Pierre.

She mailed the letter immediately. Then, wishing that Tony were with her, she went back into the house. They had not talked since their cottage quarrel. I must do something for Tony, she mused. Then she heard him banging into the house. When he saw her, his face went immediately stiff and shut.

"I see you're back," he said.

"Last night," she said. "How are you, Tony?"

"Here's a letter for you," and he held it out to her.

"Oh? From France?"

"No, not from France."

She took the letter and checked the envelope. Local postmark.

"Don't leave, Tony," she said, while opening the envelope. "I was going to make some tea. Will you have some with me?"

"Iced tea?"

"If you like."

"I detest iced tea," he said.

"And there are some cookies," she said absently, as she opened the sheet of paper she had pulled from the envelope.

When she said "cookies," Tony gave a short laugh but she had not heard at all. She started reading and walked slowly to the nearest chair and sat down, almost missing it.

"You don't look well," said Tony. "Maybe you spent too much time in the a.m.?"

She did not answer and he kept watching her. "Too much exertion," he said. "Spend more time in bed, maybe."

The sheet of paper fell out of her hand and Tony bent to pick it up.

"No," she said.

He gave a start, jerked back and watched her fumble for the paper. Her face, he thought, was ugly with terror. Why does she dislike me so much? She must be getting old.

Laura balled up the paper and when she spoke, her voice seemed like that of a stranger. "Tony. You brought me this letter. Where did you get it?"

"The postman gave it to me."

"He doesn't come till three. It's not three yet."

"So, he did you a favor and skipped the whole street to rush down here and give you the good news. Whatever it is."

"Antoine, *je t'en pris* …"

He hated it when she spoke French to him. He froze up and it showed in his voice.

"Don't horse with me," he said. "I've had enough."

"Antoine—"

He saw tears shining in her eyes. He was thinking, all I need is more of the kind of crap she was shooting at the cottage. Then Tony turned and left the house.

She let him go. She could do nothing but sit and watch him leave. The worst, to her, was that strange phrase he had used, "Don't horse with me." It made terrible sense.

The letter she was holding started: "Take this serious, madam, and don't horse with me."

It went on to say in affected, bad English, how she had been seen with Tad. Stark naked and making love to the boy. No one, stated the author, was going to interfere with them, providing, of course, that Laura paid and paid dearly. Sin was going to cost her a certain amount of money. She had better prepare herself the author said, for the next letter which would tell her how much. When she doled out the money, the author would forget what he had seen. She could then keep right on going with her little-boy lover.

Antoine, she thought, I didn't know I've been that wrong, and that bad to you ...

Tony, satisfied that he had not allowed his mother to gain the upper hand, wandered down the street. He felt strong and calm. So calm.

Passing Miss Ambru's house, Tony saw the spinster looking at him from a window and he waved at her. Easiest thing in the world, he mused, to wave and to smile with aplomb and to bow in the Continental manner. But I'm wasting my talent in this town, he thought.

Tad, standing in front of the motor court office, was watering the lawn. Tony nodded. "Long time no see."

"Hi, how you been?" was all Tad said, with the briefest of smiles. He kept right on sprinkling the lawn.

"Okay. When did you get back?" Tony asked.

"Last night. I thought you'd return to the cottage."

"What for?"

"Just to check. It is your mother's summer house."

"You're in a strange mood," said Tony, noting the boy's uneasiness. "Have any trouble with your old man?"

"Not really. He hardly talked to me. I don't think he cared about my running away."

"And your old lady?"

"The same."

Tony watched his friend turn off the hose, coil it up and wipe his hands on his pants.

"How's your mother?" asked Tad out of the blue.

"My mother?"

"Yes. She was so tired last night."

"She's all right," said Tony. He picked a blade of grass and chewed on it. Then he squinted into the distance. "We had another fight a few minutes ago."

"What?"

"We had a fight, I said. Ever hear of a fight? What's the matter with you, anyway? Nerves?"

"Let's not stand here," said Tad and looked away. "I got something to do in the rear."

He turned and walked the length of the court. Tony followed slowly. By the shed stood a lawnmower and Tad dropped to one knee.

"This needs fixing," he explained.

"You're hand is trembling, Tad. What's wrong?"

"Problems," said Tad hopelessly.

Tony stood up and stretched. "Stop fiddling with that gizmo," he said. "There's nothing to repair there and you know it."

"You're right," said Tad, climbing to his feet. And then he talked quickly, avoiding Tony's eyes. "I don't know what to do. I didn't know it would be this way. I feel terrible, Tony, terrible."

Tony nodded. "Kiddo," he said, "we used to be friends, remember?"

"I remember."

Tad's despondency, thought Tony, is comical. "So talk, man. Talk," he said.

"You want to go into the shed?" asked Tad.

"Sure."

What a great place for a confessional, thought Tony, as they sat down amid the crates and boxes.

"So? Out with it, kiddo," commanded Tony.

"I'm in love," said Tad.

A laugh broke from Tony. Tad waited, saying nothing, feeling less. He could not sit and listen to the laugh and allow himself to feel anything. When Tony had finished chortling, he said, "Congratulations, kiddo. Don't mind the way I laughed, you know? That was just surprise, mostly, and nervousness. A simple kick like being in love really bowled you over, hey? So much so that you completely flipped out."

Tad nodded in agreement. "I guess I did. But—"

"Well, boy," said Tony, "I think she's swell."

"What?"

"Swell, you know? She's built like something out of a hot dream, she's intelligent, and she's got a lot to offer a man. What else, huh?"

"You mean—"

"Do I know her? Look, kiddo, try and be a little Continental about this. You've known her, I've known her, she's known some others. But so help me,

I wish you the best. I mean—we're friends. No secrets, no harm. Tell me, how did you get her into bed?"

"My God," said Tad, feeling weak with confusion.

"You've had her, haven't you?"

"Yes," said Tad.

"So? Is she something or isn't she something?"

"Beautiful," said Tad.

"Of course. One look at good old Amy walking down the street and you know she …"

"Amy? Amy?" said Tad and slowly got up from the floor.

"Isn't that the party we're talking about, huh?" asked Tony.

"Hasn't your mother told you about the two of us?" yelled Tad suddenly. "Answer me. What was that fight you and she had after she and I returned home?"

"My mother?" Tony asked dully. "Tad, what—"

"Your mother, Tony, yes! I'm in love with her... And she loves me, too. Forget Amy."

"You, you slept with my mother?"

"Why, yes."

Tad thought that Tony was going to faint. Tad watched his friend stand up, the face gray now. And then Tony swayed. His face was old and gray and his eyes had the glitter of fever.

"I hate you," Tony said. Then, tears blinding his eyes, Tony ran out of the shed into the yellow light of afternoon.

Clack, clack, clack. Each sound was a hammer driving a nail into Mrs. Howard's skull. She could visualize the nail, but the booze she had tanked up on blocked out the pain.

"How much longer you going to continue that racket?" she asked her husband.

Without bothering to look up, Lambert moved slowly along the keyboard of an old typewriter.

"You studying to be some kind of a secretary or something? You don't make enough money with your sleazy court?" she said.

"Shut up." He kept pecking at the machine.

"Don't you use the Lord's name in vain."

"I didn't. All I said was, shut up."

For a moment, she hesitated. Had he said something filthy or not? Of course he had.

"You're a liar," she said with finality.

"Shut up or I'll have you thrown into an institution."

The remark was not a new one, but her fear was. Only the previous night she had risen, light as an athlete, from her couch of pain, to walk down a pink-colored corridor of an institution. Extremely ugly people, one in each room, had taunted her. Glop had been running from their hideous wounds but she, pure as an angel, had not been harmed by their mocking eyes. At the end of the corridor, she had passed by the room marked Atomic Anglification. Hands had reached out to pull her in, but she had been guided to safety.

"Ha," she said. "Not for me. Purification by fire is not for me, a reader of the Good Word."

"They got a chapter on you in that book?" Lambert said.

"And you're mentioned too, lump-gut."

"Under what name?"

"Tempter of Virgins," she said promptly.

"Dry up," he said and typed again.

An unsatisfactory conversation. She could not rouse him. "Husband," she said. "You haven't got enough dough to stash me away."

Lambert stared at her, grinned and then roared with laughter. "That's what you think, dearest, that's what you think."

"Let me see it," she said. "I always say, seeing is believing."

"I will, dearest, by and by."

Had she been stronger, she would have killed him. First, purification by fire; then, the grave.

"You—you Tempter," she said ineffectually.

Lambert only laughed. And typed again.

"I saw you," she said.

"Hm?"

"With that woman."

No answer at all this time. This made her imagination leap. And then she heard the jangling of a bell and a small voice.

"You're writing her a letter right now," she said.

He gave a start. "What? You're bugs, woman."

"You can't fool me. The telephone knows everything."

"Just shut up, will you?"

Gazing out the window, she saw Tad and then she knew her next approach. She marveled at the brilliance of her own mind.

"Carl was wrong about your son."

"Stop talking," he said. "I'm busy."

"Wasn't Tad he saw with that woman. It was you."

Lambert, really annoyed now, growled deep in his throat. "Go to hell."

"You," she said again, fired by righteousness. "You were with that Vaughn woman." And then the telephone in her hand jangled again. "The both of you were making love in Number Seventeen."

She saw how angry he looked and was convinced that she had been right. Standing up, she went to the cupboard and found her bottle. After having taken a swallow, she sat down again.

Lambert, not trusting himself to speak, folded the letter and shoved it into an envelope. Then he thought of an idea for a diverting maneuver.

"Guess what I've done," he said and jiggled the letter. "Just typed up an application to your institution."

Congratulating himself on his cleverness, Lambert walked out. Had someone told him what a stupid mistake he had just made, Lambert would not have believed it ...

I must find Tad, Laura thought. She had torn up and then burned the blackmailing letter. Why had Tony sent it? He was a monster. Tad must be warned. Perhaps even now, Tony was searching for Tad.

Laura climbed into her car and drove into town. There was a red light at the corner and she squealed to a stop. Then she heard the voice.

"Mrs. Vaughn."

As she turned, shock hit her again. The postman was hurrying toward her. He leaned into the window.

"I've got another letter for you. Just wait up a sec," and he was gone again.

She wanted to scream after him that she didn't want the letter, and her desire to step on the gas and to crash through the red light was strong. She did neither of these things, of course. Instead she sat through a change of light, sweat beading her forehead. And then the postman, waving the letter, emerged from the yellow-brick building. She thanked him and drove off. The letter, happily, had been mailed not locally but from France.

Before she had reached the motel, Laura pulled over to the side of the road and contemplated her letter.

She remembered her years with Pierre, what fun they had had despite the arguments toward the end, senseless arguments. Young and inexperienced, she had not been able to cope with Pierre's idiosyncrasies ... disappearing all evening without telling her ahead of time ... forgetting a birthday or running out of money just before they had planned a week at the beach ... insisting on fastidiousness yet not lifting a finger to help around the house. She had insisted upon the divorce, even though still madly in love with him. At the end he had said, sadly, "If we had been older, perhaps we would have known how to preserve our happiness ..."

Sighing now, Laura opened the faultlessly penned letter.

> *Chere* Laura, perhaps—and I am judging by the tenor of your notes, not by the look in your eyes nor by the sound of your voice—perhaps you are worse off than you admit. You speak of your husband with apparent lack of interest and of our son with detached politeness. The only person to whom you seem devoted is your young friend. You ask, perhaps next summer we might

meet? But you sound, *cherie*, as if you need me now. I said once, "If we had been older ..." We are, Laura. Remember that.

He had signed off abruptly. Laura rested her head on the steering wheel and cried with a force beyond stopping. Images flooded her mind: a son with two heads, a little-boy lover, a fussy, old-maidish professor.

Pierre had written his note with a touch of concern, yes, with love, but he had written it before he had gotten the last epistle, in which she had told him about her affair.

Too late.

Then she dried her eyes. She felt empty and she went to see Tad because there was nothing else to do.

CHAPTER TWELVE

When Tad saw Laura drive into the court, his face lit up with happiness. The sight of her was a thrill to him. Now she would comfort him for having mishandled Tony.

Mrs. Howard, peering from a window, watched them. But somehow, the image of her son fused with that of Lambert's. And Mrs. Howard was drunk enough not to be able to tell the difference.

Let those sinners play, she thought. I'll soon purify them. She took up her bottle and swigged burning liquid.

"You look so happy," Laura was saying to Tad, "it's going to be hard to talk to you, Tad."

"I have something to say to you, too. Come back with me?"

They walked to the rear. Mrs. Howard, curious, lurched out of her couch and went to stand by the door. From there she could see the length of the court. Of course, she brooded. The shameless slut and the shameless Tempter were disappearing into Number Seventeen. Then she trudged back to her couch. How to punish the malefactors? She would proceed cautiously. Justice was on her side and the wheel of justice, as the Lord had said, grinds slowly.

Laura, as soon as they had entered Number Seventeen, began to talk.

"First, Tad, if you see Tony you must send him to me immediately. Something ugly has happened."

"He was here, Laura."

"You don't know where he went?"

"He ran out. He was so upset that he ran out and I ran after him. It was awful," said Tad.

"You're not making much sense," and she frowned at him.

"I'll tell you." He swallowed and then took courage. "I wanted to tell him that I loved you. I had to, Laura."

"But—"

"Let me finish. I told him, but very badly. I misunderstood something he had said and thought that he had heard about our affair from you. When I blurted it out, he turned gray. I'm sure he wanted to faint but he ran away."

She sank down to a chair and held her face. "Tad," she said. "You mean he hadn't known?"

"No. He almost died from the shock."

To Tad's surprise Laura gave a great sigh of relief. "Thank God," she repeated again and again, "thank God—"

"I goofed," he said. "Why are you so glad?"

"Sit down, Tad."

He sat down and stared at her.

"I received a blackmail letter today. Someone knows about you and me. I thought Tony had written the note."

"But he wouldn't."

"Thank you, Tad, for being loyal."

"Wonder who—"

"I don't know." Gazing into Tad's eyes, she said, "And I don't care, Tad. But before rottenness starts, our affair must end."

He knew that she was right. But he clutched at a straw.

"Laura. I can't just ..."

"Yes, you can. You will keep the good and you will learn from the bad. As I will."

"And never see you—"

"Perhaps you will go to school soon," she said. "And there you will learn to love another."

He had to smile with her, and when he did, it forced the tears out of his eyes.

"Maybe," he said. He wiped his eyes and was not really crying. "I'll take you with me, anyway," he said.

"The good."

"Yes. Thank you."

They got up and walked toward each other. Their mouths met in a parting kiss.

Lambert Howard had seen Laura drive by and, like a true amateur thief, patted the pocket in which lay the letter. He had wondered why she had pulled off on to the side of the road. Perhaps she had been waiting for Tad. My son must be good, Lambert thought, to rate a dish like that.

Lambert had decided to let her have one more fling with Tad before he put the screws on her.

Now, as he waited in the square for Laura to return from Number Seventeen where, he suspected, she was making love to Tad, Lambert grinned. How ashamed she would be when he told her to her face that her game was up …

Then he saw her car. Jumping to his feet, he signailed her to stop. As meek as a lamb, she came over to his bench.

He gave her an easy, country-boy smile. "Use Number Seventeen?" he asked. "Or were you out at your cabin again?"

"I thought it might have been you," she said. "Spy."

"Clever." Then he became stern. "So let's keep right on being clever, Mrs. Vaughn."

"What do you want?"

"Money."

"How much?"

He grinned and spat out tobacco. "Well, let me see, now."

"How much?"

"To begin, I'll content myself with one thousand dollars."

As she reached for a checkbook, he gaped in astonishment. "Don't make it out to me," he said.

"As you like. How about to Tad? His full name is Tadsworth?"

"Sure, make it out to Tad."

"For his educational fund," and she filled out the check.

"Well now," he said and examined the check, "maybe if there's enough coming in as time goes by, I will send him to college."

"Do." She closed her handbag and seemed ready to go.

"And now a little more business, Mrs. Vaughn."

"More?"

"Why, sure. You keep using the boy, you keep paying some. Don't that seem fair? You see, Mrs. Vaughn, I'm honest. I won't tell you that this is the last payment. It ain't. I want more."

"Oh?"

He sucked his teeth and stared at the sky. "Your husband owns a real fine piece of property. It runs down to the lake behind my motel. Going to waste, right now."

"And you want it?"

"Why, sure."

"And what do I get, Mr. Howard?"

"Well, peace of mind, let's call it." He leaned closer, nudged her arm with his. "Looky." He produced a key. "I'll let you have Number Seventeen for as long as you want. I ain't no piker. Take the key."

She pocketed the key. "Mr. Howard, what if I refuse to pay you more black-mail money and refuse to prevail upon my husband to sell you that property at some ridiculous price?"

"Why, you'd be sorry."

"No, I wouldn't."

"I'd break it up between you and my boy."

"You can't. It's finished."

"Huh?"

"Let's say that Tad and I have parted ways."

"But you took the key."

"That doesn't mean a thing, Mr. Howard. Now, tell me what else you would do."

"Why, speaking frankly, I'd go to your husband. That's what."

"With what?"

"With what?" said Lambert and his mouth hung open.

"You see, Mr. Howard, to convince my husband that I have been unfaithful to him, you would require more than the filthy tongue of a lying worm."

She walked away and left him to dope out the riddle.

Was it possible that two people could be different from what his imagining had contrived?

Two days had passed and still Tony had not come home. Robert Vaughn was becoming angry.

"Be patient," Laura said. "I gave him a bad shock, Robert."

"What shock?"

"I will tell you when he returns. Everything."

Vaughn grumbled and opened a book on the evolution of man.

Tony, during the first night had, in fact, come back. He had stood in the dark on the other side of the street and stared up at the blind windows. He had had an urge to enter, to tell his mother what he knew. Her answer?

He had shivered. She would not lie, he had told himself. She will hurt me with the truth but she will not insult me with a lie. He had almost gone in.

But strength had ebbed and he had hitchhiked out to the cottage.

The day after he had spoken to Laura, Lambert Howard awoke with an awful headache. In the kitchen he found his wife sucking a bottle.

"You've been with your lady friend again, haven't you?" she accused.

"The institution," he reminded her.

She shrank into herself.

As he left the kitchen, she imagined him heading for the red room in which, God willing, he would be cleansed of sin. And if he were not, if he managed to break away, she would do the job herself. The good Lord wills it, she thought. My mission in life.

Lambert, standing in the next room, studied Laura's check. Why hadn't she and Tad used Number Seventeen last night? he wondered. He had waited in the dark for three, long hours. Perhaps they had had too much during the day. Of course, he smiled. They will return tonight.

The thought cheered him and some of his headache seemed to disappear. He went to the shed and then into Number Seventeen. He measured with his eyes and figured lumber costs and the price of photographic equipment. Before the day was out, he would have selected and installed the best infrared devices. Then he would have proof for Robert Vaughn.

After checking, Lambert hopped into his pickup truck and drove into town.

Going to meet his girl friend, Mrs. Howard thought. Although preoccupied by her general ill health, she was determined to carry her heavy cross of responsibility. Trembling, she arose. A divine power gave her courage and a holy vision pushed away all her doubts. The Lord had chosen her to clean up this valley of filth. Only she could carry out His will. Her mission was to destroy sin.

Filling her lungs with air, she yelled for Tad. He came running, surprised to see his mother leaning in the doorway. She told him to run down to the pharmacy to buy a tube of liniment for her burdened back. A benign smile on her lips, Mrs. Howard watched him walk off to town. Now she could begin. Alone, without any assistance, she would do the work of the Lord.

When Lambert returned—frustrated because he had been unable to make his purchases—he found his wife in her seat on the couch. A green-labeled tube of liniment lay by her side. That, thought Lambert, is a good sign.

"I hear a noise in Cabin Number Seventeen," Mrs. Howard said.

"Huh?" Then he caught himself. "From here?"

"Listen."

Lambert strained to catch a sound. "You've got bats in the belfry."

"Earlier this afternoon I went outside to sun-bathe. And not only did I hear a noise but I saw somebody go into Seventeen."

"Baloney," said Howard and left the kitchen.

Mrs. Howard smiled.

She watched him go to the end of the court but, instead of entering Seventeen, he disappeared behind the shed.

Because the sun had gone down, Lambert could hardly see the figure emerging from the woods.

"Why, Tony boy," he said.

Tony, cursing himself for not having waited until midnight to return to town, stared at the man.

"You been hanging around back here for a while, hey?" asked Howard.

"No," said Tony. "Just coming up from the cottage."

"Ah, the cottage," said Howard. "Yeah, yeah."

Lambert's words sickened Tony. Don't talk of the cottage to me, he thought. That's where your son took my mother.

"I just asked, Tony boy, because my wife has been hearing things. You seen any prowlers back here?"

"No," said the boy. "I got to go, Mr. Howard." Tony, without bothering to explain why, turned and plunged through the woods.

Instead of going home he angled toward a farmhouse he knew and bought there for a dollar a pint of rotgut. Then he sat in the woods and drank until late that night.

Mrs. Howard was terribly nervous. Why hadn't her husband checked Cabin Seventeen? He had returned to the house without having gone inside, the damn fool, she thought.

Lambert, as he puttered around, glanced at Seventeen now and again. Only he and Mrs. Vaughn possessed its key.

"There's somebody in the bathroom of that cabin," his wife said. "When I first went outside, the window was open but then someone closed it from the inside."

As Lambert left her to go to his desk, he wondered if Mrs. Vaughn and Tad had shacked up already. When Lambert had finished his paper work, he arose to look in on his wife. She had disappeared. He cursed foully and long and walked outside but did not see Mrs. Howard. This time he decided to check Number Seventeen.

Seen from the shed, nothing. Bed made and bare. No clothes or shoes anywhere. Safe to go in and check what the old witch had been yammering about.

When Lambert opened the cabin door he smelled kerosene. The floor was sopping with oil. Frantic, losing his wits entirely, thinking only of a property that could go up in smoke, Lambert raced to the bathroom to rummage for a dry mop.

Then he heard the loud puff behind him.

As he peered through the doorway of the bathroom, he too, had a vision.

A one-gallon gas can was spewing flame. The fire was spreading in a solid sheet behind him and in front of him.

Then he saw the witch through the flames, the drunken bitch waving at him a few feet back from the cabin doorway. She was singing a hymn.

Mrs. Howard, after having thrown the kitchen match into the oil, had watched her husband go the way of all flesh. The Tempter of Virgins was paying heavily for his sins …

Mrs. Howard's eyes, two atomic liniment lamps now, smiled as she watched Lambert go up in flames.

Tony saw the lights go out in the house of his parents but one light stayed on in the house of Miss Ambru.

Having cookies and tea, of course, he thought. Should I tell her I'm homeless and beg for shelter?

"Tony?"

He gave a start.

"Over here, child," Miss Ambru's voice softly called.

Then he saw Miss Ambru at the window. Tony approached slowly, his head still aching from the liquor he had drunk, and stared up at her.

"Well," she said, "am I glad it's you. I've been hoping and praying that it wasn't a prowler. Is something wrong?"

He breathed carefully. "No, Miss Ambru. But thank you for asking."

"Something is wrong. Why else would you be standing there in the dark? I bet you've had a terrible argument with your family ..."

"Yes," he said and hung his head for the theatrical effect.

"You poor, poor dear."

You poor, poor bitch, he thought and when he looked up again she was gone. Then the door opened.

If she says "poor, poor dear" again, he thought, I'll go in and punish her. I will absolutely—

"You poor, poor dear, do come in," she said.

That settled that.

She took him upstairs. He suggested that she allow him to spend the night. And she agreed. Then he suggested that she pour a drop of sherry. And she agreed to that, too, but when she returned, she was carrying a bottle of cherry liqueur. A cure-all for stomach cramps, she said. Then she suggested that they sit a while and talk as they had done before. And it was Tony, this time, who agreed.

She sat on a chair in the guest room and he sat on the bed opposite her. She was wearing a padded, pink wrapper and resembled a cherub-faced madame. He was wearing ghastly white.

"And have you been studying your manual on love, Miss Ambru?"

"Why, yes. Religiously. The attitudes of love make up a kind of religion, you know."

"I wish I were better acquainted with the priests."

Miss Ambru lifted her empty glass to her mouth. Like me, Tony thought, she's been sopping up booze for hours.

She refilled her glass, sipped and smiled.

"I could show you a few of the positions of love which the book describes," she offered. "They are relaxing, you know."

"I can imagine."

Tony set down his glass and, with the act, his depression vanished. Sadism returned. He hated the woman for trying to sucker him.

"The book contains instructions on how to massage certain muscles for the express purpose of relieving tension. Why don't you lie down, dear, on your back and I'll work your shoulders a little?"

And now she's conning me, Tony thought bitterly.

He lay down on his back, an expression of contentment on his face. Closing his eyes, he waited for Miss Ambru's weight to distort the mattress, but when nothing happened, Tony realized that she had temporarily lost her nerve. He opened his eyes to see her punching the bottle.

"And how is your dear mother?" Miss Ambru asked, avoiding his gaze. "I forgot to inquire."

Tony could hardly believe his ears. How phony could this dame get? Only the phrase "I love you" would have infuriated him more. His stomach was tied in a black knot and his eyes saw red. For one hateful moment, two individuals—his mother and Miss Ambru—merged into one mass of protoplasm.

Then, as Miss Ambru spoke, Tony's head cleared and he coughed.

"Relax, dear," she was saying as she sat down next to him.

"Thank you," he said. "You are wonderful." And with that lie he found his focus.

He let her rub his shoulders, which involved her leaning down on him, ever so lightly, as she finished a stroke. He guided the talk.

"So much goodness in your hands," he said drowsily.

Because his eyes were closed he could not see her smile. He smelled warm powder and female heat.

"A woman like you, so alone," Tony said. "Why?"

"Relax, dear," she hiccupped as she unbuttoned his shirt. "Better directly on the skin, you know."

"Are you getting tired, Miss Ambru?" Tony asked.

"Oh, no, dear. I'm quite all right."

"I'll support you a little, so you don't tire."

He put his hands on her sides. The corset was absent. She felt large and soft and when her fingers moved along his shoulders, he sighed contentedly.

"How warm you are, Miss Ambru," Tony said.

"Yes, terribly hot."

She undid the top button of her housecoat and fanned herself.

Now, Tony decided, I'll go into my Sleeping Beauty act. Just to find out more of her plans.

"So relaxing," he mumbled and lolled his head. "I'm dozing off."

That was the last he said for a long time.

As soon as she had been convinced that he was really sleeping, she stopped rubbing him. He felt her breath—odor of synthetic cherry—and then she kissed him on the forehead, the cheek, the mouth.

What next? he wondered. Should I pretend that this is a legitimate part of her routine? At that point a fire siren came to his rescue.

Howling, the engine raced to the far end of town. Then another and one more.

They both jumped. And they used the interruption as an excuse, each for their own purpose. If the embrace had not been so grim it could have been horribly funny.

"I'm afraid of that sound," she cried.

"Me, too. Hold me, Miss Ambru."

They clung, rolled over and dug at each other, and Miss Ambru's wrapper fell open in front and Tony was exposed to a great deal of pinkness.

Tony had constructed his plan. He would go so far, then cut the woman dead. A word, a laugh and then his exit.

None of that happened. He found no words. He found her small mouth. He could not laugh because he was biting her. He could not walk out because her big softness was pressing into him. He dug at her with his hands and slowly mad redness spread over him and his lust rose to a hard, hungry point.

He felt her give and thought of warm pudding. She made a sound and called his name.

"Robert."

"What?"

"Did you hear that woman scream?" The scream had issued from the Ambru residence.

Laura jumped out of bed and opened a window. The stream of invective flowing from her neighbor's house shocked her.

"Fiend, foreigner, murderer, lunatic ..."

"She must be out of her mind," said Robert, crawling out of bed.

"We'd better check," and Laura wrapped a robe around herself.

"Don't meddle."

"But listen to her."

The yelling stopped suddenly and a man said something hateful.

"That was—"

"Don't meddle, I say."

"That was Tony."

"I said—"

Laura ran out of the room and the house. By the time she had covered the distance to the Ambru house. Tony, pale and tired, had emerged. He seemed beyond surprise.

"Antoine, what happened?" Laura said.

"Forget it," he said. "I'm as bad as you."

Miss Ambru had not heard Laura and Tony Vaughn's voices. She was on the phone. Damn the police, she thought. Why doesn't someone answer? I'll call the fire department instead. She dialed and the man listened to her tale of woe.

"A fiend in your bedroom? Who is this? Oh, Miss Ambru." The man lost interest and told her to try the police again. "You might not be able to contact anyone immediately, however," the man explained. "I understand most of the force is checking out a real fiend, someone who murdered her motel-owner husband ...”

Miss Ambru hung up. Other fiends did not interest her. Then Tony and his mother stepped inside.

“I accuse that boy of rape,” Miss Ambru snarled.

“Tony has told me everything. You seduced him and he seduced you,” Laura said.

Then Robert Vaughn walked in. “What’s going on here? Rape? Seduction?”

“Just that,” said Tony, sounding tired. “Miss Ambru and I became involved sexually tonight. She claims I raped her. But, actually—”

“Ugly, ugly boy.” Robert’s hand shot out and slammed against Tony’s face.

“Again!” screeched Miss Ambru. “The fiend—”

Then Laura was pushing Robert. “Stop it, she’s done as much as he.”

“Are you defending him?” Robert yelled.

“Yes, I’m defending him.”

“You must be out of your mind. He’s disgraced—”

“I don’t see it that way.”

Tony only listened. He could not remember ever having seen his mother that angry before, or that strong.

“I’m calling the police,” said Miss Ambru.

“Certainly,” said Robert Vaughn.

“Wait.” Laura, hands on hips, faced her antagonists. “Miss Ambru, the scandal will hurt you. Consider that point.”

“Oh, no, dear. Oh, no. I was the victim.”

“You damn liar,” said Tony.

“Shut up,” Vaughn snapped.

“You won’t defend him?” Laura asked her husband. “You’re taking her side?”

“Tony was wrong. I’ll see to it that he doesn’t misuse my name again. I’ll see to it—”

“How can you stand there and say that?” Laura was livid. “Robert, if you don’t stand up for our own son, I’ll destroy your happiness.”

“My dear, I am totally immune to you. How could you possibly hurt me?”

“I’ll tell you how.”

“Yes, do, slut,” Miss Ambru said.

“What?” Robert said. “Slut?”

“Robert,” said Laura, “I’ve had an affair. I’ve had an affair with a teen-age boy. And if you don’t show faith in our son, I’ll spread rumors of my indiscretion and guilt. Would your precious school board approve of a teacher whose wife is a whore?”

Then Laura opened the door and she and Tony went out together.

Professor Robert Vaughn did not return to his own house until a number of hours later. Drawn and tired, he looked as if Miss Ambru had driven a hard bargain. Tony was asleep on the couch and his mother was waiting.

"Well?" Laura asked her husband.

"I've arranged everything," he said.

"Ah?"

"She'll say nothing, absolutely nothing," said Robert. "On two under-standable conditions."

"Understandable?"

"Yes. First, that that boy—" and Vaughn nodded at the figure on the couch—"must leave town."

"I will go with him."

"As a matter of fact, that is the second condition."

"You traded adroitly."

"Now see here, Laura. I am not interested in the details of your sordid—"

"It was not sordid."

"I am naturally alienated from you because of your conduct."

"I will leave," she said.

Tony was sitting up, listening. "I'll go with you," he informed his mother.

"I will," said Vaughn, "after a time, consent to reconsider all sides."

Laura shrugged and stood up. "Don't bother," she said. "I never want to see you, or this town again."

"Where will you go?" asked Vaughn.

"I don't know."

She did not know until a few hours later when the telegram came. "I want you," it said. "You must come quickly. Pierre."

THE END

Craft Ebbing
By Barry N. Malzberg

By 1963 when this pseudonymous novel was published by Softcover Library, the author was pretty well burnt out, close to stone dry, approaching as he must have been aware the essential end of a career which must for him have begun to feel like an affliction. The paperback original mystery and suspense novel remained a viable category for some writers but television was inexorably reducing the audience and for many in the audience criminous reading was becoming a marginal activity. (The digest magazines, the remaining refuge for the mystery short story had been further devastated by the 1958 forced dismembering of the American News Service, the monopolistic magazine distributor, and its division into weaker component parts.) Rabe, never a cheerful or forward-looking man, had to have been approaching at least creative exhaustion and Softcover Library, a subdivision of the bottom-of-the-market Beacon Books might have been viewed as some kind of signature of shame. Seven years later, Rabe, with his Ph.D. in Clinical Psychology found a faculty position teaching undergraduates at Case Western University and although he lived close to another two decades he virtually abandoned fiction, going grey by the early part of the 1970's.

It is difficult (or perhaps the word is "arrogant") to infer the motives of the dead, let alone those of a personality as conflicted and complicated as Rabe's, but it can be inferred that these novels, written as these two Beacon novels, written in obvious haste and in the case of *Her High-School Lover*, giving every suggestion of a single draft written at desperate speed, were an admission of defeat for Rabe. Defeat, compounded by desperation, seems to be the central engine of all the characters, likewise ambivalence, a kind of push-pull in relation to sex itself, and as the novel speeds to its abrupt conclusion it seems to use simple reversal as the means of resolution. The two teenage boys are afraid of sex—and indeed part of that might come from an unacknowledged, repressed homosexuality—the marriages are disasters, the motel owner peeping through a keyhole into customers' rooms is a poisonous voyeur...what is scariest about the novel, however, is a kind of existential disgust which uses sex as the surrogate for the awfulness of midcentury American life and finds little rescue in either.

The state of the nation at the period of this novel, of course, has been well limned in the then contemporary novels of Cheever, Updike, Swados and

Roth. Even Malamud who in *A New Life* was blaming not Judaism but isolation, disconnection and repressed fury as the central fact of national life. It was both a provoking and provocative time which however nostalgically viewed now was tormenting for those conscious or coming to consciousness. The year these novels were published was the year of the Cuban confrontation and the specter of nuclear destruction; that imminence was avoided but a year later a different kind of disaster seemed to signal the end of the supporting American myths and right on after the JFK assassination came the Gulf of Tonkin, the undoing of George Lincoln Rockwell, the Harlem riots and then the full-blown epic disaster of Vietnam.

All of this is foreshadowed, by luck or psychic apprehension in *Her High-School Lover*; one would not accuse Rabe of being a visionary in way of Pynchon, Cheever or the major contributions to *Galaxy Science Fiction*, but he was sensitive and intelligent enough to, at the least, spot refraction and the angst, the detachment of the emotion of these characters from the grubby, sad and the barely described suburban enclave in which they struggle...all of this was the pre-apocalyptic 50's and 60's for an audience more than half a century down the road. There is barely background in these novels, particularly in *Her High-School Lover*, the stage sets are rickety, spare, hammered absently in place; they are barely representation of a representation...it is the inner lives alone which exist and the sad, somber, almost accidental dances in which the three teenagers, the four tormented engage are described in terms little beyond internal anguish and irrelevant background. The sex is formulaic in the tradition of softcover porno ("no pubic hair, no blood" an editor at Midwood books once explained to me as iron rules) but for at least the first two-thirds of the novel it is perfunctory, and when heat begins as a kind of obligatory function it comes as a reaction against the subtext of the novel. That subtext includes impotence, sexual panic, barely repressed homosexuality and a hatred which for this cast curdles into lust mostly as a condition of the market.

Yet, for all of Rabe's evident weariness and at the best ambivalence to the text, there is much to be inferred from this novel; it is in the heated last third a kind of road trip to hell and the casual pairings, appearing as a condition of the scrappy plotting become not only central to the work but the nature of its resolution. Mother leaves her stale and sterile marriage, elects to take her son back to Paris where his father, 18 years later, is presumed to welcome them; the father, a discarded lover who she has not seen in almost two decades is more than willing to take her...his son, the consequence of their casual affair is eager to go. At home, in the spiritless suburb of the geography of nowhere, the son's high school friend (who has had an affair with his mother) seems content to find a girlfriend who he had previously ignored. The voyeur whose only passion seems to be his telescope is discarded; the characters execute (the wordage limit for a Beacon double novel has been reached even if the plot will not cooperate) a grave and hasty exit and the curtain of this scrappy drama of the dead 50's comes to a conclusion no less scattershot and perfunctory as Rabe found in *New Man In The House*.

A few years ago I wrote in a semi-public form of a 1950's Gil Brewer novel, one of his many minor works all but one of them (*The Red Scarf*, published by Bouregy) paperback originals, "If this novel were any better it would be no good at all"...Brewer's hasty plotting, slam-bang exits, desperate, truncated scenes of confrontation and violence had a pell-mell, make-it-up-as-you-go-along aspect which fit the marginality, desperation, destructive improvisation of his characters' lives and it was this reflected lack of control which gave the novel the urgency and desperation of not only the lives of the characters but of the disastrous inner life of the nation. There would be no attempt to rationalize, to foreshadow, to explain the reversals; they simply *happened* in the way that 11/22 or 9/11 happened, and what this meant was that Brewer was finding at the center of his construction some fundamental terror at the heart of the nation. Rabe was no Brewer, although they were working nominally for the same markets at the same time; Rabe had the formal education and profession which the hanging loose Brewer had perhaps never sought; Rabe because of his training could make his characters a casebook from Krafft-Ebing or the diagnostic handbook. Brewer simply plunged ahead. But the characters of both were plunging ahead, reacting to forces they could not comprehend, mixing and matching and unmatching, mating and unmating in the crazed uncertainty of the dead mid-century and ultimately through Rabe's rickety set the light was coming through. "Light comes through the broken spaces," Leonard Cohen wrote for his summing up.

So what is the ultimate judgment of this wracked soul, Peter Rabe who could slug with the welterweights, dance with the lightweights, back the heavyweights at least into the corners? That is beyond my grasp, Rabe is another country to me or at least another part of the forest; I wrote for this market, I was in a twisted way a contemporary of Rabe, but it is hard for me to judge him. Rabe was no Dennis Lehane, let alone Raymond Chandler, but he bespoke the same darkness and I can judge only the darkness in reference. Rabe might not have been able to judge the beasts who rule today. For his time, his beasts, he did the best he could.

It should be noted as a coda to my own summing up that the first of Rabe's three wives, Claire Rabe, was one of six writers whose novels in 1969 were published as the vaunted opening of the Olympia Press America hardcover line. *Flesh and Blood* was the successor novel to her early 60's Paris-published *Sicily Enough*; both novels (originally published as by "Anna Winter") are passionate, powerfully expressed chronicles of female suffering, sexuality and anger, beautifully written and unknown today. She was probably the most talented of that inaugural group of writers of whom only Clarence Major and I are alive today. Her husband, who had by that time quit, would have fit better into that line than the Softcover Library but Maurice Girodias was as doomed in a different way as Peter Rabe and even less known today. It is a mystery and a injustice, as the Irishman said to his bartender at midnight. It is a outrage Patrick, and not only the law but life itself is a ass.

New Jersey: April 2019